PECOS VALLEY RAINBOW

PECOS VALLEY RAINBOW

ALICE DUNCAN

FIVE STAR

A part of Gale, Cengage Learning

GALE
CENGAGE Learning·

Detroit • New York • San Francisco • New Haven, Conn • Waterville, Maine • London

LIBRARY OF CONGRESS CATALOGING-IN-PUBLICATION DATA

Duncan, Alice, 1945–
  Pecos Valley rainbow / Alice Duncan. – First edition.
    p. cm.
  ISBN-13: 978-1-4328-2690-1 (hardcover)
  ISBN-10: 1-4328-2690-5 (hardcover)
  1. Young women—Fiction. 2. Murder—Investigation—Fiction.
3. New Mexico—Fiction. I. Title.
PS3554.U463394P42 2013
813'.54—dc23   2012043425

First Edition. First Printing: March 2013
Find us on Facebook– https://www.facebook.com/FiveStarCengage
Visit our website– http://www.gale.cengage.com/fivestar/
Contact Five Star™ Publishing at FiveStar@cengage.com

Printed in Mexico
1 2 3 4 5 6 7 17 16 15 14 13

For Phylana Bridges. Thanks, Phylana!

CHAPTER ONE

It was a dark and stormy night. No, really. It was.

Well . . . truth to tell, while it was stormy as all get-out, the sky wasn't dark even though it was really late, mainly because the lightning streaking it in sheets, streaks, forks and stabs kept things pretty bright. I knew the electricity, which had only come to town a couple of years earlier, had bitten the dust because I'd had to read by the light of a kerosene lantern for an hour or more.

I tried not to let the booms of thunder affect me, although they shook the house, and I could imagine canned goods falling from the shelves of my parents' grocery and dry-goods store situated in another building in front of our house. That, of course, meant my obnoxious twelve-year-old brother Jack and I would have a lot of cleaning up to do on the morrow.

I only hoped I wouldn't have to row the whole family to the store from the house. All the houses and businesses in Rosedale, New Mexico, had been built up from the streets because, while we lived on a desert, every darned time we had a storm like the one currently in process, the rivers flooded and all the streets turned into raging waterways. We lived close to the Spring River, and I could envision water bucketing over its banks and heading toward our house. Then there were the Hondo and the Pecos rivers, both of which were probably overflowing even as I sat propped up in my bed and wishing the thunder weren't *quite* so loud.

That's probably because I'd been reading a creepy magazine called *Weird Tales* I'd checked out of the Carnegie Library earlier that very day. At least I wasn't holed up in the attic of a Gothic mansion when the torrential storm broke.

"Annabelle." My mother's voice preceded her knock by only a second. I know it was stupid, but my heart gave a big lurch, and I nearly jumped out of my skin. Danged magazine. I laid it aside.

"Yes?"

"Are you awake?"

"Can't sleep," I said. "So I've been reading. Too much noise to sleep."

Ma sighed. "Me too, although I haven't been reading. I'm going to make a cup of cocoa and have a piece of Miss Libby's pound cake. Want to join me?"

Would I? "You bet. I'll be right there." I loved anything cooked by Libby Powell, my aunt Minnie's friend and companion, as long as I didn't have to eat it in Libby's presence. Libby Powell was a frightful, beastly old woman. She complemented Aunt Minnie, who was intense, plump, sweet, vague, liked to commune with the spirits via séances, and looked kind of like an ambulatory barrel when in motion. Miss Libby was just big. Big and mean as a rattlesnake. But boy, could she cook.

Slipping out of bed, I donned my robe and stuffed my feet into my slippers, first checking for scorpions as usual even though it was November and technically past true scorpion season. However, when it rained like this, even the insects of the field wanted to get away from it and were likely to come indoors to do so. The southeastern part of New Mexico, while confirmed in statehood more than a dozen years before, was still a pretty rugged part of the world even in the enlightened date of 1923.

I joined Ma in the kitchen just as she was pouring steaming cocoa into two mugs. Good. That meant Jack wasn't awake—or, if he was, that he didn't plan to join us. Giving him the benefit of the doubt, which was difficult to do most of the time, I presumed he'd turn human one of these days. At the moment, however, I'd just as soon my parents rent him out to some lonely couple who'd always longed for children and couldn't have them. Jack would cure them of any lingering misery in that regard in no time flat.

As for me, Annabelle Blue, I was nineteen years old and an adult by anyone's reasoning. Well, except Libby Powell's, but as already mentioned, she was nasty and mean and hated everyone except Aunt Minnie and a few other people her age. Anyhow, my birthday was coming right up, and then I'd be twenty! My goodness, but that seemed old to me.

Ma sat heavily in one of the kitchen chairs and sighed. She'd already cut two pieces of pound cake and laid them on a napkin next to yet another kerosene lantern. No formality was expected at this time of night and in this weather. Kerosene lamps were useful in cases like this, but I hated having to clean the blasted things after they'd served their purpose.

"I suppose Second Street will be running like a river in the morning. I only hope the water doesn't slosh over the boardwalk. Your father and I don't need to be mopping up floodwaters from the front of the store."

"I hope not," I said. "Rotten floods. Are they ever going to build a dam or anything to hold the water back when it rains like this?"

Ma shrugged. "I don't know. You'd think they'd have done it by this time if they were going to do it at all."

"I don't know, Ma. Rosedale, New Mexico, doesn't seem awfully advanced in the engineering department. Instead of building that grand courthouse with government money, maybe the city fathers should have lobbied for a dam instead."

Ma chuckled. "Maybe so."

We had a great courthouse, with a dome and everything. It was built in 1911, right before New Mexico gained statehood in 1912, and the people who'd planned and built it spared no expense, primarily because they knew the federal government would pay for it as soon as we were admitted to the Union. Smart thinking, I guess, although I think a dam would have served the citizens of the town better than a fancy courthouse.

I had to admit, though, that the courthouse was useful. Lots of the old men in town liked to walk to Fourth and Main, sit on benches placed here and there on what passed for the courthouse lawn, and gab about the good old days, which didn't sound all that good to me, but who was I to quibble? Still and all, fighting Indians and cattle rustlers, droughts, floods, and people like Billy the Kid, a miserable outlaw my idiot brother idolized, didn't appeal to me one little bit. In fact, I wished I could visit a big city somewhere. Anywhere. Heck, I didn't want to spend the rest of my life in this tiny little hole of a town in the middle of nowhere.

"We don't generally get thunderstorms like this in November," Ma observed after she'd taken a sip of cocoa.

This was true. Our "rainy" season, summer, was long gone. And summertime in Rosedale wasn't so rainy that the town turned green and pretty or anything like that. It mainly just flooded more and left mud so slippery, you might as well have tried walking on wet ice. Clay soil. Doesn't absorb water, so it floods. And people slip and fall and break bones.

In fact, although I wouldn't say so to Ma, whose family was among the first to settle in Rosedale, there wasn't a whole lot to recommend our town. Basically, we were built by and for cattlemen. We sat right smack in the middle of cattle country, and served as a hub for ranchers within a two-hundred-mile radius in any direction you cared to mention. That's what we were in the good old days, and that's what we remained. During the spring and autumn cattle drives, cowboys from all over the place drove their herds down Second Street to the railroad yard, and the rodeos that followed were the highlight of the entire year. We watched the cattle drives, not to mention the dust and mayhem caused thereby, through the front window of Blue's Dry Goods and Mercantile Emporium, which Grandpa Blue had established in 1892. Ma's family had ranched and farmed, but when she married Pa, she gave up the wide open spaces to help him in the family store.

That was all right with me. Personally, I was happy to live in town, even such a town as Rosedale, because ranches in these parts are even more in the middle of nowhere than the town itself. I liked being able to chat with my friends and neighbors when they came into the store, where I worked daily behind the counter. Jack was supposed to work, too, but . . . oh, never mind. He did his chores when compelled to do them by our father's firm voice or, when that failed, by a hand strategically applied to his hind end.

My older brother George was a great guy, but he no longer lived in Rosedale. Smart fellow, George. He'd been an aeroplane pilot in the Great War, had recently left the Army Air Corps and was now married and living in Alhambra, California, with his wife and their baby son. I hoped to visit him there one day, even if only to play nanny for a week or so. I read lots of magazine articles about California, and it sounded like a great place. My two older sisters, Zilpha and Hannah, were married and out of the house, too, although they remained in Rosedale.

Zilpha's husband is named Mayberry Zink, and he's a very nice fellow, although I kind of wished he'd change his last name. Zilpha Zink? Personally, I'd rather die an old maid than have a name like that, not that I'd ever tell Zilpha so. Anyhow, he owns a feed and saddlery store in Rosedale, and can equip you for anything you need in the way of horses or cows, fences or barns, sheep or pigs. There's going to be another little Zink coming along in about six months, and Zilpha and Ma are terribly excited about it. Ma really wants to get her hands on a grandchild, and George's little boy is too far away.

Hannah is married as well, to a banker named Richard MacDougall. Richard is an okay guy for a banker, but I prefer Mayberry, who isn't so stuffy. Richard suits Hannah, however. She's more interested in material things than anyone else in the family.

As for my own personal love life . . . well, I didn't have one. Mind you, I had a gentleman friend, and it was assumed by one and all, including me, that Phil Gunderson and I would marry one day. However, that wasn't going to happen any time soon. Darned if I'd get married at my tender age without having had an adventure or two first. If Phil didn't like that, too bad.

Not that I didn't like and admire Phil, and I certainly didn't want to lose him to some other woman. Still . . . I couldn't help but feel that there was more to life than Rosedale, New Mexico, and I aimed to see at least a piece of it before I married and faded into the woodwork. And if I could do so in the company of Allan Quatermain or Rudolf Rassendyll, so much the better. If you know what I mean.

"Well, no matter what time of year it is, floods are always a pain in the neck," said I after swallowing a bite of pound cake and wishing Miss Libby could be as sweet as her cooking.

Ma only sighed, and we both jumped in our chairs when a gigantic blast of thunder shook the house and rattled the windows. "Good Lord," muttered Ma, pressing a hand to her heart. I couldn't have said it any better.

I don't know about Ma, but after we polished off the pound cake and cocoa and went back to bed, I didn't get much sleep, thanks to the constant booming and crashing of the thunder. I swear it nearly knocked me out of bed a couple of times.

We were both right about the mess that met us the following morning. It was difficult even getting from our house in back of the store to the store itself. School was definitely closed for the day, even though no one had proclaimed an official holiday. However, one had to use one's common sense in situations like these, and it was clear no kids would be able to get to school without swimming, which was flat ridiculous.

Pa grumbled the whole way from the house to the store, muttering to himself about how he was going to build a consarned bridge so we wouldn't have to wade through miles of water and mud the next time it rained. He'd said as much before but, like a dam for the rivers, a bridge from the house to the store remained a fond dream.

When I glanced around the store after removing my rubber boots and letting down my skirt, which I'd kilted under my waistband so as not to get it muddy, I was more relieved than not. The windows were a filthy mess, and a few tins of things had fallen from shelves, but for the most part the store remained undamaged. No floodwaters had encroached, at least.

"I'm going up to see if the roof blew away anywhere," Pa said after he'd made sure the inside of the place was secure and fetched a ladder.

This wasn't as silly a comment as it might appear to those unfamiliar with Rosedale weather. Along with the thunder, lightning and rain, the winds had howled like a chorus of tormented souls during the storm. We got horrible winds in Rosedale, generally in the springtime, although no season was immune, and they'd been known to rip roofs off houses, flatten fences and topple windmills. They'd probably have flattened trees, too, if we'd had any, but except for a few cottonwoods beside the Spring River and a few other places, so far trees were a luxury and Rosedale didn't have many of them.

"I'm going to see what it's like outside," said I, boldly open-

13

ing the front door and looking. Boy, what a jumble! At least water hadn't reached as high as the boardwalk, but Second Street might as well have been another major waterway. If anyone aimed to go anywhere that day, they were going to have to do it via rowboat. "It's going to take at least a day, and possibly two, for the water to recede," I announced to all and sundry.

Jack had joined me on the boardwalk. "Keen!" said he. He would.

Pa climbed down the ladder from the roof to join us, looking unhappy. "Damned rain," he muttered. Pa wasn't much of a one for swearing, so I knew the wind had done some damage to the roof.

"What's the matter, Pa?" I asked. Jack just stood there, frowning, as if he knew he was going to be told to do something he didn't want to do.

"Shingles are gone in several spots," said Pa. "Annabelle, will you row to Gunderson's Hardware and fetch a bundle of shingles and some roofing nails? I should fix the roof today in case we get another storm tonight."

"Hey," said Jack. "I want to row to the store!"

"You, young man, are going into the store and begin picking up canned goods. Then you're going to wash those windows. I can trust Annabelle to do what I ask and not waste time. You've proven yourself to be untrustworthy too many times in the recent past."

"Aw, Pa," grumbled Jack.

"That's enough of that," Pa growled back.

Jack had been in hot water for several months by that time because of his lousy attitude and occasionally unruly behavior. You'd think he'd mend his ways, but he was a boy. What more is there to say?

"Will do, Pa," said I, obedient daughter that I was. Anyhow, even though floods annoyed me, I enjoyed rowing the boat down Second Street. How many other towns in those progressive days of the twentieth century could boast a roaring river as a main street, do you suppose? Well, besides Venice, Italy, I reckon, but their primary mode of transport is water all the time, so Venice doesn't count.

"And get some tar, too. I'll have to tar over a couple of spots."

"Will do."

Jack whined and grumbled as he retreated from the front boardwalk to do his chores while I went to the back room and fetched the rowboat and oars. "Do you want them to put the stuff on your account?"

"No. Let me get some money." Pa didn't approve of credit, although he gave generous credit to many of the ranchers in the area. As he'd said more than once, ranching is a tough business, and he was always willing to give a good man a break when he needed one.

So he handed me some cash, I stuck it in my pocket, put on my sweater, and I set out in the boat to row myself to Gunderson's Hardware about a block east of Blue's on Second Street. I hoped Phil would be there.

He was, and it looked as if he and his brother Pete were being run ragged even before I tied the boat to the horse rail and carefully maneuvered my way out of it, because so many other boats had already been rowed to Gunderson's and were similarly tied to the railing. When I entered the store, I wasn't surprised to see the place packed with people, purchasing everything from shingles to chicken wire to lumber, rope, window glass, tacks and nails.

"Blasted chicken coop blew apart," snarled John O'Dell, who dealt in real estate and was one of our wealthier citizens. "Got my chickens all over the whole damned town." He spied me and said, "Sorry, Miss Annabelle."

I waved his apology away. "I'm sorry about the chicken coop, Mr. O'Dell. Hope you can round up the flock."

He shook his head. "Not a prayer of that, but Mrs. O'Dell is out in her rubber boots trying to find as many of them as she can."

I always treated Mr. O'Dell with special politeness, mainly because I'd suspected him of murder not too long ago and was heartily ashamed of myself for it. Not that he knew of my suspicions, but I have a tender conscience. Sometimes.

"I'll take a shovel, Pete," said Mr. Lovelady. "I only have the one, and there's nobody else I can borrow from since they're all using theirs to shovel out their sheds and barns. My kid's home now working on the stable, and I aim to help as soon as I row myself home. Dad-blasted storm."

By the way, while Rosedale boasted a few automobiles, including our own Model T Ford, lots of folks still got around via mule or horse and wagon. Those of us who owned automobiles kept them in what used to be our stables.

I heard other folks call for nails, hammers, roofing shingles, window glass, paint, plaster, handsaws, and all sorts of materials required to make repairs after last night's disastrous downpour. I waited patiently for my turn to come, listening to all the comments. It seemed to me that we Blues didn't suffer as much damage as a lot of folks in town, and I decided I'd tell Pa so. Might make him feel a little better about the roof.

"What can I help you with, Annabelle?" said Phil, smiling shyly at me. He was such a sweetheart.

"I need a bundle of shingles, some roofing nails and some tar. Do you have tar?"

"For the roof? Storm blew it away, did it?"

"Parts of it."

"Sure. I can sell you some tar. You'll have to heat it up."

"Damned flood," muttered Mr. O'Dell as he stomped to the

door with wood, wire and nails for rebuilding his chicken coop.

"We do seem to have wicked weather in these parts sometimes," I said to Phil.

"Yeah." He sighed. "I tried calling the ranch to see how Ma and Pa made out, but the phone lines are down."

"So's the electric," I said. "Wonder when everything will be back up again."

"Don't have a clue. Probably not for a few hours for the telephone, at least. We're not exactly the center of the universe."

"No. We sure aren't. It's funny in a way, though," I said. "I mean, five years ago we didn't have electricity, and telephones were scarce as hens' teeth. Now we can't live without them."

"True. I guess they call that progress."

Phil had been rummaging around behind the counter of his brother's store. He plunked a banded bundle of roofing shingles on the counter along with a box of nails. I peered at them suspiciously. "Are you sure those are the right kind?"

With a sigh, Phil said, "Yes, Annabelle. Those are roofing nails. Jeez, don't you think I know what I'm doing in my own brother's store? I've been working here for years, you know."

"Sorry, Phil. Of course you know what you're doing. I was just asking, was all."

"Huh." He took off through a door behind the counter and came back a moment later with a bucket of tar. "Want me to put this on your father's account?"

"No, thanks. He gave me the money."

Phil added everything up, gave me the total, and I handed over the loot. He was kind enough to carry my purchases out to the boat for me. Well, I carried the nails. He carried the heavy stuff.

"Thanks, Phil," I said after he'd held the boat steady for me to climb back into.

"You're welcome. Say, Annabelle, want to go to the pictures

with me on Friday?" He blushed a little, which I thought was sweet. Phil was a bashful fellow.

"Sure. If the waters have gone down by then." This was Wednesday, and you never knew about these things.

"Good. I'll come by to get you at six. That all right? We can get some ice cream afterwards at Pruitt's." Pruitt's Drug Store sat right next door to Blue's, and my best friend Myrtle Howell worked there at the cosmetics counter. The soda fountain remained open after six o'clock on Friday nights, unlike the rest of the store, because going to a movie and having an ice-cream soda was about the only amusement available to us young people.

"Sure. Do you know what's playing?"

"I think there's a Harold Lloyd picture there now."

"Oh, yes. I read about it in the paper. I think it's called *Grandma's Boy*. Should be fun."

"Good."

Phil had a satisfied smile on his face when he turned to go back into the store.

As for me, I smiled at his back and reached to untie the boat from its makeshift mooring.

Then I screamed bloody murder.

CHAPTER TWO

Phil came running back to me, his expression a combination of anxiety and exasperation. "Cripes, Annabelle, what's wrong?"

Others who'd heard my shriek had come running, too. I was so horrified, I could only gesture at the muddy water, where I'd just seen the face of the president of the Rosedale Farmer's and Rancher's Bank bobbing in the muck.

"It's . . . it's . . . it's Mr. Calhoun," I stammered, pointing, praying I was wrong and knowing I was right.

"What?" Phil, sounding more annoyed than worried, leaned over the horse rail. I saw his eyes go round as saucers. "Cripes, it *is* Mr. Calhoun!"

Several other people now leaned over the rail, too, and I heard exclamations of alarm and distress from all and sundry.

Pete, Phil's brother, hotfooted it out of the store and looked, too. "Shoot. We'd better fish him out of there," said the ever-practical Pete. "Can you go in and get a grappling hook, Phil? He's probably full of mud and bogged down."

"*Dios mio*, I wonder what happened," said Armando Contreras, proprietor of Rosedale's only gas station and of what was going to be Rosedale's very first automobile dealership come January. He, too, leaned over the railing to get a good gander at the dead banker.

Feeling shaken and shaky, I said, "I don't know. Maybe he stumbled over something and fell in and couldn't swim? It was raining cats and dogs last night."

"But what was he doing here?" asked Armando, a question I couldn't answer.

I glanced at the businesses surrounding Gunderson's Hardware. The local plumber's shop. Mr. O'Dell's real-estate office. Miss Petty's Fancy Dresses. The office of the *Rosedale Daily Record*. Armando's dealership was nowhere near here, so what was *he* doing here, for that matter? Then I noticed the Cowboy Café. Of course. Lots and lots of folks ate breakfast, lunch and sometimes even supper at the Cowboy Café. But would he be doing that after a torrential rain? Oh, who knew?

So as not to think about the head of Mr. Calhoun, which kept bumping against the boat, I said, "Must have taken supper at the Cowboy Café."

Armando looked at me oddly for a moment and said, "Yeah. That's probably it."

What did that odd look mean?

I didn't have time to think about it because Phil came back with the grappling hook just then. "Annabelle, I'm going to untie your boat so we can get at Mr. Calhoun more easily."

"Right," I said, happy to be getting away from the corpse, although, of course, I aimed to stick around nearby until they got him out of the drink. Not for Annabelle Blue to run away from an interesting event, even if it was the death of a prominent citizen. My mother would probably say *especially* if it concerned a death, but that's only because she thinks it's unladylike to watch icky stuff. But, heck, this was Rosedale, New Mexico, where nothing interesting ever happened except every now and then; like today, for instance.

I rowed the boat a few feet away from the action, but stayed where I could see Pete and Phil lower the grappling hook into the muddy water and try to snag a piece of Mr. Calhoun with it. The job wasn't an easy one, especially from up on the boardwalk. After watching them fumble around for a few minutes, I said, "Want me to hook him for you?" Gee, that looks kind of bloodthirsty when written down, but I didn't mean it to be.

"Oh, Annabelle, you don't want to . . ." Phil let the sentence die out, since I'd lectured him before on the equality of womankind. Actually, I think I'd lectured him on the superiority of females versus males, but I don't really remember.

"You can't do it from up there," I pointed out. "And I'm sure you don't want to go swimming in all your clothes. I'm right here, and I can put the hook where it can snag his clothes or something."

I saw Phil and Pete exchange a glance. Then Pete shrugged. He said, "All right. If you're sure you don't mind."

"I don't mind." Truth to tell, I did mind, but not as much as I'd have minded not doing anything at all under the circumstances.

So I rowed back over to the body, tried to determine if he was snagged on anything, decided he'd just come to rest between two pillars holding up the boardwalk, and took the heavy grappling hook in my hands. By that time, of course, it was all muddy and slimy, but I persevered.

"Maybe you can hook him under the legs or something," Phil suggested from the peanut gallery.

"I think I'll hook his belt," I said, picturing the tines of the hook piercing Mr. Calhoun's flesh and shuddering inwardly.

"Well, all right, I guess, though the belt might break."

"I doubt it. Mr. Calhoun always wears . . . wore the sturdiest of duds," said I, sounding perhaps a trifle snide.

It was true, though. Mr. Calhoun the banker was not universally liked in town, mainly because he was hard and mean and was reputed to practice dirty tactics when he could get away with them. He was definitely the richest man in town, and he always looked as though he'd just stepped out from the pages of a Sears and Roebuck catalog—although I'm sure he bought all his clothes in Chicago or New York, where he went on frequent business trips. And I couldn't even get to Alhambra, California.

Anyhow, it was no fun maneuvering Mr. Calhoun's body so that I could get at his belt, but I finally managed and stuck two of the hook's tines underneath it.

"Okay," I said. "Haul away."

I think I heard Phil mutter, "Criminy, Annabelle," but I'm not sure. Phil didn't share my daring spirit. Which only points out one more reason I aimed to have an adventure or two before I married him. When we were well and truly knotted together, we'd never have any adventures at all if he could help it.

The body was heavy from having absorbed a whole lot of water and probably pounds and pounds of mud for however long it had been in the water, and it took a good deal of effort and several grunts and swearwords before Pete, Phil, Armando and a couple of other men succeeded in getting it up on the boardwalk where it fell with a sloppy *whump* that made me shudder. I rowed closer to the boardwalk in order to view the corpse more clearly. I know that was unladylike, but how often does one get to see the body of a drowned man in one's lifetime?

Bracing myself on the boardwalk so I wouldn't flip the boat over and land in the drink myself, I took a good gander at Mr. Calhoun, who now lay faceup on the soaked boards. He looked awful. I guess that's shouldn't have surprised me any, but jeepers, the man was my brother-in-law Richard's boss, and I'd never seen him looking anything but dapper and . . . well, rich. Not any longer. Now he looked like a lump of muddy meat.

"Are you going to stand there in that boat and gawk all day, Annabelle, or will you maybe do something useful and get Chief Vickers from the police department?" Phil again, unappreciative of my natural curiosity.

However, he was right. "I'll go there right now," said I, and shoved the boat away from the boardwalk. It only took a few minutes to row myself to the police station, where I hit a snag. Literally. Fortunately for me, Deputy Sheriff Earl Wilcox happened to be walking into the police department—don't ask me why because the sheriff's office was in another location—and helped me out.

"Thanks, Earl," said I when he'd maneuvered the huge clump of vegetation away from the boat.

"What are you doing here, Annabelle? Anything wrong at Blue's?"

"Oh, no, but there's something wrong at Gunderson's. They just fished Mr. Calhoun's body out of the floodwaters in front of Pete Gunderson's hardware store."

Earl's eyes, which were generally half-closed—I don't think he was a very energetic fellow at the best of times—opened wide at that news. "Holy cow. The banker Calhoun? That one? Really?"

"I wouldn't fib about something like that, Earl. Pete and Phil just hauled his body up onto the boardwalk, and they asked me to fetch Chief Vickers."

"I'll do that for you, Annabelle. Wonder what happened to the man that he got drowneded?"

"I don't know," I said. "Thanks, Earl." Then I turned the boat around. I knew I should have gone directly home, but I didn't. I was sure Pa would understand. I was also sure he'd be mad as fire, because he wanted to get the roof repairs done pronto, but I wanted to see what the police chief had to say about Mr. Calhoun's demise, if anything.

Therefore, I rowed myself back to Gunderson's, where the crowd had grown substantially.

"Is Chief Vickers coming?" asked Phil as he helped me tie the boat to the railing.

"Yes. I ran into Earl . . . well, I didn't actually run into him, but—"

"For God's sake, Annabelle, I know what you mean. Is the chief coming?"

Touchy, touchy. "Yes. He's coming. Have you determined how Mr. Calhoun could have ended up in the floodwaters?"

Phil's face set hard. "Yes."

Yes? Just yes? Darn Phil anyhow! He was always trying to "protect" me from stuff I didn't need to be protected from. "Well?" I demanded. "What happened?"

"Annabelle, you don't need to—"

"Somebody shot him in the back," said Armando Contreras, bless him. He had a tremendous temper himself and a similarly feisty wife, Josephine, and I guess she'd taught him some important lessons about not excluding the fair sex from the significant details of life.

"Oh, my!" I cried, surprised, yet . . . well, not all that surprised, if you know what I mean. As I mentioned earlier, Mr. Calhoun wasn't a popular man. But, really. Shooting people in the back wasn't very nice, even if the person you're shooting is a crummy, cheating banker. It occurred to me to wonder what this would mean for Richard. "Who could have done such a thing?" I said, more to myself than to any one person in particular.

"Just about anybody," grumbled a voice. I looked up to see Micah Tindall, a local rancher. I'd heard he'd been having financial troubles in recent months. "The man was a son of a bitch and a crook." He glanced quickly at me. "Sorry, Miss Annabelle."

"Think nothing of it," I said politely.

"Snake in the grass took my ranch," muttered Mr. Tindall. "Dirty rotten bas—uh, crook."

"He took your ranch?" I said, shocked.

"Tricked me into a loan I couldn't repay." Mr. Tindall glared down at the body of the murdered banker as if he wished he could kick it. "And I'm not the only one, either."

"How'd he do that?" I asked, honestly curious.

Mr. Tindall, still glaring, shuffled his feet. "Probably my own damned—uh, darned fault. I didn't read the fine print, I reckon, and when Calhoun came to me demanding I repay the loan in full, I couldn't do it, and he took my ranch."

"That's terrible!"

"Yeah. I think so, too."

"I wonder if my brother-in-law Richard could do anything for you. Have you talked to him?"

"Naw. Probably won't make no difference now."

"But . . . if this happened recently, perhaps Richard can help you."

"I doubt it. But I'll tell you this. It'd be easier to find folks with a motive to kill Calhoun than folks without one. The fellow was a low-down crook. Ask anybody."

"You really should talk to Richard, Mr. Tindall," I pleaded, shocked at his bald statement and pondering its merit. Was Mr. Tindall only bitter because he'd made a bad business decision, or had Mr. Calhoun truly cheated him out of his ranch? And were there, as Mr. Tindall intimated, others in the same boat as he? So to speak.

Mr. Tindall only shrugged and stumped off down the soggy boardwalk as if he carried the weight of the world on his shoulders—which I guess he did. It was his personal world, but it would be a heavy burden, laden as it was with a wife and four children. Poor man. I resolved to talk to Richard about Mr. Tindall's problem, even if Mr. Tindall wouldn't do it. Couldn't hurt. Might help.

"He's not the only one," said Armando Contreras, who had been listening avidly to our conversation. "Calhoun was a filthy, rotten snake."

"Really? Did he cheat you, too?"

"He cheated everybody," Armando said, sounding grumpy. "I'm glad he's dead, the son of a bitch."

Goodness. That was a bald statement if I'd ever heard one.

"All right, all right!" a booming voice I recognized as that of Chief of Police Willard Vickers called out.

I turned in my boat to see him and one of his policemen, a fellow named Raymond Packard, rowing up to the scene.

"Let's everybody who's not a Gunderson clear out," hollered Chief Vickers. He eyed me in particular. "That includes you, Miss Annabelle."

"But I fished him out of the water. I discovered the body," I said, defending my right to be there and watch what went on.

"You discovered the body, you say?" Chief Vickers's voice had softened now that he was closer to the action.

"Yes, sir. I did. His head bumped against my boat." I shuddered, remembering.

"Well, I think you'd best get along home now anyway, Miss Annabelle. I'll come by and talk to you and take a statement later."

Darn it. I wanted to see whatever action was to take place now. But as a law-abiding citizen, I couldn't very well argue with the chief of police, so I bowed to forces greater than I and said, "All right. See you soon."

Pa was boiling mad when I finally got back home with the supplies he'd sent me off to get. His temper cooled when I explained what had delayed my return.

"Calhoun? The president of the Farmer's and Rancher's Bank?" Both my mother and father—and Jack, the wretch—had gathered around, at first to scold or scoff, but now with varying degrees of shock, horror and fascination. Jack was really peeved because it had been I and not he who'd found the body.

"I don't know why you always get all the fun," he muttered.

Pa whapped him on the back of the head, although not too hard. It probably wouldn't have mattered if he'd slugged him, since Jack must have developed a callus back there from being whapped so many times in recent weeks. "That's enough of that, Jack Blue. A man is dead."

Shaking her head, Ma said, "And you say he was shot in the back?"

"That's what Armando Contreras said."

"What was Contreras doing there?" asked Pa. Sensible question.

"I don't know. Maybe he sustained some damage at his gas station during the storm. Or maybe he was having breakfast at the Cowboy Café."

"Could be," said Pa, musing.

"Anyhow, that's all I know. Phil asked me to row to the police station and fetch Chief Vickers, and I did that. When the chief got there, he told everyone to disperse so that he and Mr. Packard could conduct their investigation."

"Investigation. Huh." It didn't sound to me as if Pa considered the chief and his deputy particularly able men, but I don't think he meant it that way. I think he meant that "investigation" sounded like too highfalutin a word to use in so backwater a place as Rosedale, New Mexico. Couldn't say as I blamed him.

"I understand the man wasn't well liked," said Ma in a hesitating sort of voice, as if she didn't think she should be speaking ill of the dead. "But to shoot him . . . well, that's just terrible. Poor Hortense. And don't they have children?"

"Gladys and Herschel," I said, nodding. "They're grown up now, but they still live at home."

"Still, it must be a terrible blow. I wonder if they know." Ma was always thinking of other people.

So was I, but not because I was nice like she was. What I wanted to do was talk to the grieving family and find out if they knew who could have done the wicked deed. "Maybe you should take them a covered dish or something, Ma. I'll row you over to their place."

I got a look from my mother that told me she knew my motives weren't pure, but she only said, "That's a thoughtful suggestion, Annabelle."

Jack stuck his tongue out at me. Figures. Lucky for him Pa didn't notice, or he'd have received another wallop for his effort.

It was a rotten shame the telephone lines were down, because I'd have loved to spread the news. But the town was kind of in chaos, what with the streets being flooded and all, and there was no telling when the electricity or the telephones would be operable again. The men who handled the telephone wires were also firemen. In a town the size of Rosedale, people had to do lots of things; for instance, our coroner was also a dentist, even though the town was virtually bursting at the seams with doctors. Anyhow, regretting the lost telephone, I just sighed and asked my father, "Would you like me to do anything else in the boat, Pa? Are we going to open the store today?"

"Yes, we're going to open. I expect folks will need all sorts of things, especially if their spring houses flooded or their barns got wrecked. And no, you don't need to do anything else that requires the boat."

"Will you see to the counter, Annabelle? I think you had a good idea about the covered dish. I'll go back to the house and put something together. Although without electric, God alone knows how they'll keep it cool until they can bake it."

"Maybe the electric will come on soon," I said, hoping the floodwaters would still be so deep by the time she'd finished cooking as to render it impossible for Ma to get her covered dish to the Calhouns' house, which was several blocks away, without me rowing her there.

But there was no hope for instant satisfaction. I had to settle in with more stories from *Weird Tales Magazine* while I sat behind the counter waiting for customers. Jack still washed windows, grumbling all the time, and Pa was up on the roof, hammering shingles back into place and, I presume, tarring over them. I'm not quite sure how roofs are put together, not being very good with a hammer and nail. I'm better in a garden. I'm best in a library, but I didn't live in one, more's the pity.

However, I had thought to prepare myself for a dull day, figuring, in spite of Pa, that not many people would be frequenting Blue's after that terrible storm. Therefore, I'd armed myself with *Powder and Patch*, by an English lady named Georgette Heyer. I was partial to murder mysteries, but I'd read another one of her books, *The Black Moth*, and become fascinated with Regency England. Naturally, I'd had to use the library's encyclopedia to find out what Regency England was, but still, her books were smashing—if you don't mind if I drop a Britishism into this journal set in what might as well be the Old West.

It turned out that the day wasn't as dull as I'd feared it would be. Before too long, after I'd set aside *Weird Tales* and picked up *Powder and Patch*, my best friend in the world, Myrtle Howell, hove into view through the front door of Blue's. As I've already mentioned, Myrtle worked at the cosmetics counter at Joyce Pruitt's Drug Store right next door to Blue's, which worked out well for the two of us, being best friends and all.

"Hey, Myrtle, did you hear about Mr. Calhoun?"

"The banker? No. What about him?" Myrtle, who looked a little the worse for wear this morning, stamped mud from her shoes and scraped them on the scraper outside the door before setting foot in the store. Wretched floods. Maybe one day the town fathers would at least pave the streets. We citizens deserved some consideration, after all.

"How'd you get your shoes muddy?" I asked, since Pruitt's was right next door.

"Had to go down the stairs and pick up some stuff from Mr. Pruitt's boat. Lousy steps are all muddy."

I tutted about the mud, but was happy about everything else; she hadn't heard about Mr. Calhoun. Putting *Powder and Patch* down on the counter with a thump it didn't deserve, I said, "He's dead. I found the body when I rowed to Gunderson's Hardware to get some roofing shingles."

"Good heavens!"

Myrtle, suitably startled, astonished and aghast, slapped a hand to her cheek and hurried over to the counter to hear more. "Tell me about it, Annabelle! You found the body? How dreadful for you!"

"It was pretty awful, all right," I told her with unwarranted relish. "His head bumped against the boat when I was untying it from the horse railing."

With a grimace, Myrtle put her elbows on the counter and said, "Tell me about all of it, Annabelle! Mr. Pruitt said I could leave work for about a half hour while he and Frank"—Frank was Mr. Pruitt's second in command at the drug store—"got things organized. That storm knocked everything around."

"Nice of him to let you have some time off."

"Well, my cosmetics weren't jostled, but lots of the pill and powder bottles in the pharmacy rolled around or got smashed when they fell off the shelves, and only Mr. Pruitt and Frank know how to sort them out. I wouldn't be of any help to them."

"That makes sense."

"But you said Mr. Calhoun's head bumped against your boat? Oh, Annabelle, how horrid!" She shuddered, I think with more fascination than dismay. Which I understood completely. Life could be *so* dull in Rosedale.

"Yes. I'd gone inside and bought the roofing shingles and nails and tar, and had just reached to untie the boat, when I looked down and saw his face kind of staring up at me. Only he wasn't staring at anything, if you know what I mean. I mean, he was dead. I could tell. His face was all waxy and covered in mud, and he looked . . . lifeless. It was . . . well, it wasn't a whole lot of fun at the time."

"I should say not. Does anyone know how it happened? How in the world did he end up in the water in the first place?"

Aha. Now came the really interesting part. "At first I thought maybe he'd taken supper at the Cowboy Café the night before and slipped and fallen, but after Phil and Pete came out with the grappling hook—"

"The *grappling* hook?"

"Well, there wasn't any other way to get him out, really. You know how high the water is, and it's all muddy and full of trash and leaves and stuff. But they had a hard time fishing him out from where they stood on the boardwalk, so I offered to take the hook and snag his belt with it."

Myrtle's nose wrinkled. "Oh, Annabelle, how . . . how . . . oh, Annabelle."

"Yeah. It wasn't a lot of fun." That was the truth. I remembered that grappling hook and trying to decide where to hook Mr. Calhoun with it and not wanting to pierce his flesh. "But I got two tines of the hook under his belt, and the men on the boardwalk hauled him out. He was heavy because of all the water and mud and stuff."

"Ew."

"There's worse," I told Myrtle.

"What could be worse than that?"

"He was shot in the back."

"He *what?*" Myrtle screeched.

I nodded solemnly. "Phil sent me rowing to the police station, and when Chief Vickers and Deputy Packard arrived, Armando Contreras told me Mr. Calhoun had been shot in the back. I guess whoever shot him shoved him into the water afterward."

"Good Lord."

For Myrtle, who had been "saved" a month or so prior by a detestable tent revivalist, the mention of the Lord in this context could be chalked up to shock.

"So he was murdered," I said solemnly. "And from a couple of grumbles from the men gathered around Gunderson's, there might be more than one person who could have done it."

"Oh, Annabelle, no!"

"Mr. Tindall said Mr. Calhoun cheated him out of his ranch."

"No!"

"Well, that's what he said. He called him a snake in the grass." And a few other things, but I didn't want to sully Myrtle's tender ears with Mr. Tindall's blasphemies. Anyhow, he'd apologized for them.

Myrtle and I were leaning over the counter, one of us on each side, ready to settle in for a good, solid gossip-fest, when we were interrupted by the entry of Chief Vickers and Deputy Packard, who had come, as promised, to take my statement. Nuts. I'd wanted to grill—I think that's the appropriate word—Myrtle about anything she might know regarding Mr. Calhoun and his family and business practices. Not that Myrtle knew any more about banking than I did. Still . . .

Well, there was always Richard, my brother-in-law and second in command at the bank. Maybe I could grill him instead.

CHAPTER THREE

We'd gone over my finding of the body and fishing Calhoun out of the water and so forth, when Chief Vickers said in his most policemanly voice, "I understand that your brother-in-law, Richard MacDougall, and Mr. Calhoun, his employer, had been having problems on the job. Do you know anything about that, Miss Annabelle?"

My mouth dropped open. "What? I never heard that. Anyway, so what? According to what I heard this morning, lots of people had trouble with Mr. Calhoun," said I in staunch defense of my stuffy brother-in-law. Still, if the chief was implying Richard might have murdered Mr. Calhoun, he was an idiot. Richard would no more shoot anyone in the back than I would. And I wouldn't.

"That's the word I've heard from reliable sources," said the chief.

"Nonsense. Richard has never said one bad thing about Mr. Calhoun. At least not in front of me."

"The employees at the Farmer's and Rancher's Bank claim to have heard them arguing hot and heavy several times recently." Chief Vickers didn't look at me as he spoke, but kept fingering the crease in his trousers. Embarrassed to be asking me about a relative-by-marriage as a possible murder suspect, no doubt. Good thing, too.

"If they were arguing, it was probably because Richard didn't appreciate Mr. Calhoun's dirty business tactics any more than anyone else in town did."

Shaking his head, Chief Vickers finally glanced at me. "Well, as you can imagine, we have to look at everyone who might have had trouble with Mr. Calhoun, Annabelle."

"Then talk to the whole town! According to Micah Tindall and Armando Contreras, everybody hated Mr. Calhoun, because he was a cheat and a liar."

Chief Vickers sat back in his chair, evidently taken aback by my vehemence. Which made me wonder if Pa really did think he was incompetent, and if so, if he didn't have good reason. "If you don't believe me, ask anyone," I said with some heat. "Only this morning, I heard two men say they hated Mr. Calhoun."

"We will," the chief said stiffly, "question all people who might have had a problem with Mr. Calhoun."

I sniffed meaningfully.

"And," added Vickers, also meaningfully, "that includes your brother-in-law."

Nuts to that. "Richard is a fine, upstanding fellow, and everybody in town knows it, Chief Vickers. There are tons of people in town who hated Mr. Calhoun's guts. Why, Mr. Tindall called him a snake in the grass and a son of a . . . well, he hated the man. Said he stole his ranch. Told me so to my face."

"Is that right?" The chief appeared mildly interested. "Well, these are early days yet. We'll do a thorough job of investigating the crime, and speak to anyone who might have information."

"Does that include Richard?" I asked bitterly.

"We have to look at everyone with a possible motive, Miss Annabelle. You know that. But we'll find the murderer. You can count on that."

Could I? When the chief of police honestly believed Richard MacDougall, perhaps the most boring man in all of Rosedale, might be capable of a vile murder? Recalling a few incidents in the recent past, it occurred to me that I, Annabelle Blue, had been better at nabbing the true criminals in various cases than the chief of police and his minions. I resolved then and there to enlist my friends to help me solve this crime before it could be pinned on poor, humdrum Richard.

And poor Hannah! How awful for her to have her husband suspected of such a dire act! No, sir. I wasn't going to sit on my duff and allow such a miscarriage of justice to transpire. Not that Chief Vickers had pinned anything on Richard. Yet. And not that I knew what I could do about finding the real culprit, but I was sure I'd think of something. I was resourceful that way.

"I'm certain if you investigate thoroughly, you'll find others in town who had grievances against Mr. Calhoun and who had much better reasons to kill him than Richard," I told the chief. "People other than Mr. Tindall have told me he practiced low-down banking methods." That was a flat lie, but I did recall Mr. Tindall's bitter statement that it would be easier to find people who hated Mr. Calhoun than those who didn't. "Mr. Tindall was firm in his belief that Mr. Calhoun had cheated him out of his ranch, and he'd said there were lots of others like him whom Mr. Calhoun had bilked. If there were arguments between Mr. Calhoun and Richard, I'm sure that's the reason."

"Huh. Well, we'll check out all leads," said the chief in a flat voice that made me wonder about his sincerity.

The chief's indifference clinched it. I was going to hie myself back to Gunderson's Hardware and get Phil to assist me in uncovering the truth about Mr. Calhoun's demise. Phil, who was a man in a man's world, would have better luck questioning folks at the bank than I would, being female and only nineteen years old. The world was *so* unfair! At least women had finally been given the vote. Of course, Turkey, a nation I'd always believed to practice repressive methods as regards women, had allowed its female population to vote in 1918, but I'm not here to carp. I'm just saying, is all.

Unfortunately, I couldn't leave the store at that moment. I had to wait until Pa came down from hammering shingles in place before I could desert the counter. Fortunately for me, the day didn't prove to be as tedious as I'd feared it would be. Many people seemed to be in need of provisions Blue's Dry Goods and Mercantile Emporium could provide, thanks to the ghastly rainstorm. Naturally, most of them had to row their boats to the store. We Rosedale-ites were hardy folk.

By mid-morning our electricity was restored, which made things a little easier on me, who had a hard time squinting into the shadowy notions corner when fetching Mrs. Dabney a spool of thread the exact color as the one she was almost out of. Mrs. Dabney was one of Rosedale's few well-off folks who could afford a servant to row her around until the floodwaters subsided. Luckily for me, the servant in this instance was a girl I used to go to school with, Virginia Feather.

As Mrs. Dabney proceeded to look over bolts of fabric my mother had selected from the finest warehouses in the eastern parts of the United States where civilization reigned, Virginia and I had quite the gabfest about the demise of Mr. Calhoun. Virginia, like Myrtle, was both horrified and titillated when I told her about the morning's premier event.

"Goodness sakes, Annabelle, I wish I could telephone home. My father was having a huge fight with Mr. Calhoun. He'll probably be glad the man got what he deserved." Then, as the good Christian girl she was, Virginia clapped a hand over her mouth.

Interesting. Very interesting. I said, "Your father's not the only one who had problems with Mr. Calhoun from what I hear." Which hadn't been enough, darn it. I *wished* Pa would finish with the roof so I could go back to Gunderson's! "What happened with your father?"

"Mr. Calhoun cheated him out of a piece of property he was

going to buy. Turned out Mr. Calhoun didn't even own the property in question. And Pa had made a deposit and everything. Then Calhoun wouldn't give the deposit back. Pa went to the bank several times. The last time he went, I understand he really let Mr. Calhoun have it. At the top of his lungs." It didn't look to me as though Virginia had yet decided whether to applaud her father's hollering at the dirty banker or be embarrassed by his behavior. The things we children have to suffer for the sake of our parents.

"Mr. Calhoun sounds like a true villain. I hope your father manages to get his money back. Mr. Calhoun's behavior doesn't sound right to me. In fact, it sounds downright criminal."

"It's criminal, all right. The problem is what to do about it. Pa went to Mr. O'Dell and talked to him about how he might get satisfaction out of Calhoun, but after Mr. O'Dell looked at the paperwork, he said it would take a herd of lawyers to straighten it all out, and the only men in town who could afford to hire a lawyer were—"

"Mr. Calhoun and a couple of others," I finished for her. Boy, it was beginning to look as though Mr. Calhoun truly was a dirty snake in the grass and a son of a buck.

"I'll take five yards of this, Annabelle," Mrs. Dabney said from the fabric aisles.

"Yes, ma'am." Tipping Virginia a wink, I lifted the counter panel and walked over to Mrs. Dabney. Ma was generally the person who handled the fabrics, but I knew how to measure and cut as well as she did.

Which reminded me of the covered dish Ma was preparing for the grieving widow. It seemed to be taking her an awfully long time.

The fabric Mrs. Dabney had chosen was pretty, in an old-ladyish sort of way. It was dark green with lighter green stripes. Mrs. Dabney wasn't known for her flashy duds, so I suspected the fabric was meant for her. "Will you be having Mrs. Wilson stitch up something for you, Mrs. Dabney?" I asked politely as I measured out fabric on our cutting board.

Mrs. Wilson was the local seamstress. Well, Miss Petty was also a seamstress, but according to everyone I talked to, Mrs. Wilson was the better of the two. Besides that, most of Miss Petty's wares were ready-made dresses she probably ordered from the Sears-Roebuck catalog. Anyhow, poor Mrs. Wilson was a widow, her husband having died two days after their last child was born, and she supported herself and her five children as a seamstress. I think lots of the women in town went to her because she not only did a good job, but she desperately needed the work. A noble soul, Mrs. Wilson, and a good, solid Methodist, according to my mother. As we Blues, too, were Methodists, this was meant as a compliment. I thought if God were truly appreciative of Mrs. Wilson's goodness, He'd toss some money her way and make her kids behave. A month or so ago my idiot brother Jack and one of Mrs. Wilson's kids had decided it would be fun to play baseball when they were supposed to be attending a tent revival service. The consequences of that rash act had been terrible.

"Yes. I need a good frock for church, and I ordered a cunning hat from Sears and Roebuck that will go perfectly with it."

"I told Ma we should carry some hats, but so far we only stock work hats for farmers and ranchers."

"Does your mother have an interest in millinery, dear?"

"To tell the truth, I'm not sure. But she's really good with her Singer sewing machine, and she's got the nimblest fingers in town."

"It might be worth her while to try her hand at hat making," said Mrs. Dabney.

Virginia, who had been twitching beside us as we carried on this conversation, finally interrupted. "Oh, Mrs. Dabney, did

Annabelle tell you what happened to Mr. Calhoun?"

Mrs. Dabney stiffened. "Mr. Calhoun? Whatever happened to the man?"

Virginia lowered her voice to a dramatic whisper. "Somebody shot him in the back. Annabelle found him floating in the floodwaters right outside of Gunderson's Hardware this morning."

Pressing a hand to her heart, Mrs. Dabney said, "Merciful heaven! Whatever next? I tell you, this town is going to rack and ruin!"

Hmm. Maybe. There wasn't so much to Rosedale that you could tell what was happening to it if you asked me, not that anybody ever did.

"Do they know who did it?" Mrs. Dabney wasn't so shocked about Mr. Calhoun's ghastly death that she wasn't as interested as anyone else.

"No. All they know so far—at least, as far as I know after talking to Chief Vickers—is that he was shot in the back and shoved off the boardwalk into the water on Second Street. I . . ." I gulped, remembering. "I found him this morning when I had to row to Gunderson's for some shingles."

"Good heavens. Whatever next?"

"I don't know," I answered honestly. "Although I've heard that quite a few people in town weren't all that fond of Mr. Calhoun. Mr. Tindall told me he'd cheated him out of his ranch." I decided that if Virginia wanted to tell her employer about her father's run-in with the banker, she could do it herself. I didn't want to butt in or anything.

"Hmm."

Whatever did that mean? I carried the folded fabric to the counter, ducked under the counter flap and made my way to our beautiful old-fashioned Nelson cash register, which had been bought by my own Grandpa Blue late in the last century.

It was a golden color, had swirly designs on it and you had to crank it to get it open. I really liked the way it chinked. Placing the fabric on the counter and the spool of thread on top of it, I asked, "Will there be anything else, Mrs. Dabney?"

"Hmm? Oh. No, I don't believe so, dear. Thank you." She lifted her handbag onto the counter while I wrapped her purchases in brown paper and tied them with string. As she shuffled through her bag, looking, I suppose, for her change purse, she muttered, "Mr. Calhoun murdered. Imagine that. Reminds me of that line from *A Christmas Carol*."

I looked up from the string I'd just tied in a neat bow. "Which line is that, ma'am?"

" 'So, old Scratch has got his own at last.' But it's unkind to speak ill of the dead, so just forget I said that, Annabelle. Thank you for your help, dear."

"You're welcome."

Virginia and I exchanged a significant couple of glances as Mrs. Dabney bustled off and Virginia followed after her.

So. That made Mr. Tindall, Mr. Feather, maybe Mr. Contreras and perhaps even Mr. O'Dell who'd disliked Mr. Calhoun. And I'd give anything to know what made Mrs. Dabney think of Mr. Calhoun as the devil himself. But if I asked a question like that of a customer, my mother would have my hide.

Speaking of my mother . . .

"Annabelle, thank God the electric's on again. Is Jack through cleaning the windows? He can watch the counter while you row me to the Calhouns' house. I want to get there while the covered dish is still hot."

More to the point, was Jack still anywhere around, or had he done a bunk? It would be just like him to take off when there was work to be done. But no. For once I'd wronged my rotten brother. Mind you, he wasn't doing anything useful, having finished with the windows, but I spotted him in a far corner of the store reading the latest Zane Grey novel he'd checked out of the library. I well remember the day he told me that when he grew up, he wanted to move west. Where the heck did he think we lived, anyway? Valhalla? But it was no good reasoning with Jack. Maybe in a year or two when and if he turned human, although I had my doubts.

At any rate, I let Ma order him around. If I told him to do something, he for sure wouldn't do it.

"Jack, come and mind the counter for your sister. She needs to row me to Mrs. Calhoun's house."

"Aw, Ma," said Jack. But he shut his book, using a finger as a bookmark, and shuffled his way to the counter. "Do I have to?"

"Yes, you have to," came our father's stern voice from the front door. I guess he'd finished fixing the roof. "And don't ever question your mother again when she tells you to do a chore, young man."

"Yes, sir." Jack, who knew when to give up an argument, looked less than pleased about it.

Being the big sister and knowing I should set an example for him, I said, "Thanks, Jack. We'll be back soon, I'm sure."

"Huh."

Which goes to show how much twelve-year-old boys can learn by example. My mother had told me once that it might take years for the lessons of childhood to penetrate a thick skull, and if there was a thicker skull than the one belonging to Jack Blue anywhere near Rosedale, I didn't know whose it was.

I held the hot covered dish, which Ma had wrapped in a towel, while she got herself into the rowboat. The dish smelled wonderful, and I got the feeling our chicken coop had lost a member of its flock. At least Pa had built our coop more sturdily than Mr. O'Dell had built his. Ma wasn't as experienced as I when it came to boats, so she was kind of shaky at first, but she finally got settled and I handed her the dish. Then I made my own careful way into the boat, again wishing we either had paved roads or, better, dams to keep the town from flooding every blasted time it rained hard.

I took the oars in my two sturdy hands and set off rowing east on Second Street to Lee Avenue, where the Calhouns lived in a big white house that was the envy of many a Rosedale resident. Except me. I liked our little house and our little store, and I thought the Calhouns' place was kind of pretentious, given the overall state of the town, which was . . . well, ugly. Mind you, the sky was magnificent, but if you glanced at the earth under your feet, you'd find dusty clay soil (except on days like that one), prickly plants, scorpions, huge red millipedes, centipedes, vinegaroons, tarantulas, spiders, rattlesnakes and, in the summertime when the *real* rains came, toads. Oh, and coyotes every now and then, and the occasional antelope. Wild burros. What else? Heck, I don't know. It seemed to me that every plant had prickles and every animal was dangerous, however.

Lots of other people must have thought about food for the grieving family, because when I rowed the boat up to the Calhouns' place, there were several other rowboats tethered to the front porch railing. I got out of the boat, took the covered dish from Ma, set it on the porch and then helped Ma out of the rowboat.

"You're a lot braver than I am, Annabelle," said Ma, straightening her skirt.

My mother was still a pretty woman, even though she'd had five children and must have been middle-aged, whatever that is. She had light-brown hair she'd passed down to me, and blue eyes, which I'd also inherited. I'm not sure, but I think Ma and Pa were still fond of each other, even though they'd been married for donkeys' years. I thought that was sweet, although I never said so, it not being my place to comment on my parents' marriage. Pa himself was a fine-looking man. Tall, trim, strong and fit, I could almost understand what Ma must have seen in him when they'd married so long ago.

At any rate, I handed Ma the covered dish, and she held it while I marched to the door and twisted the bell. Although the walls of the home were thick, I could hear voices inside. I guess everyone who could get out and row had come to offer condolences and, if I surmised correctly, try to dig up gossip from the remaining Calhouns. I was only slightly surprised that the news had spread so fast. Rosedale's a small town, and interesting information gets around kind of like last night's lightning.

Another friend of mine, Betty Lou Jarvis, worked for the Calhouns as their maid. She stayed there all week, sleeping in a room on the top story of the house. It was Betty Lou who opened the door to Ma and me.

"Oh, hey, Annabelle. How-do, Mrs. Blue."

"Good day to you, Betty Lou," said Ma with a smile.

"Hey, Betty Lou. I guess it's kind of a zoo inside today, isn't it?"

"Annabelle," said my mother in her shame-on-you voice. Maybe I'd sounded a trifle callous. "How is poor Mrs. Calhoun today, Betty Lou?"

"She's doing all right, Mrs. Blue. Thank you." Ma thrust the covered dish at her, and Betty Lou said, "Thank you for this, too. I'm sure the family will appreciate it. Everyone's been very kind so far."

Boy, I'd like to get Betty Lou alone so I could ask her about the Calhouns and how they got along and that sort of thing.

"We won't stay long, Betty Lou. I only wanted to come by with my dish and offer my condolences to the family."

"Go right on in to the parlor, Mrs. Blue and Annabelle. I'll take this to the kitchen."

"Mind if I follow Betty Lou, Ma? I'll be right back again."

"Very well, Annabelle." Ma looked at me as though she knew I aimed to dig into affairs not my own, but at least she didn't argue or prevent me from accompanying Betty Lou to the kitchen.

And wouldn't you know it? When we got to the kitchen, which was at the back of the house down a hall from the parlor, it was full of people! So much for my grand scheme. Nevertheless, I did manage to get one question asked.

"Are Mrs. Calhoun and Herschel and Gladys awfully cut up about Mr. Calhoun's passing? It must have come as a terrible shock. The way he died, and everything."

To my surprise, Betty Lou rolled her eyes. "Lordy, Annabelle, I've never met such a family. You'd think they were all glad the old man got plugged."

I blinked in astonishment. "Really?"

"Really. But I can't talk right now."

She was right about that. To my horror, Libby Powell bore down upon us. How in the name of Glory had she got from Aunt Minnie's old ranch house twelve miles west of town to Mrs. Calhoun's house in the middle of Rosedale?

"Is that you, Annabelle Blue?" snapped Miss Libby. "Snooping again, I'll warrant. Some folks have no decency whatever."

"That's not true!" cried I in my own defense. "Ma and I brought the Calhouns a covered dish, for your information."

"Huh. I hear it was you found the body," snarled Miss Libby.

"Oh, Annabelle, did you really?" Betty Lou stared at me in shocked fascination.

With another snort, Miss Libby said, "Like as not she shot the man herself, just so she could find him and create another stir in town."

"Of all the . . ." But it was no use trying to defend oneself against Libby Powell. Such tactics never worked, and she remained as mean as a rabid dog. "Never mind. I'll talk to you later, Betty Lou. Take care."

"Thanks, Annabelle."

I lammed it out of the kitchen as fast as I could, fearful lest one of Miss Libby's powerful paws land on my shoulder to stop me. I still couldn't figure out how she'd managed to get herself into town, what with everything flooded and all.

Then I saw Aunt Minnie conferring with Ma in the parlor. Oh, goody gumdrops.

Minnie Blue is about five feet tall, approximately half the height of Miss Libby, and used to have bright red hair. Her hair had turned white when she was quite young, but she still had vivid hazel eyes and was shaped kind of like a pumpkin. Also, there's no getting around the fact that she was . . . well, perhaps the least little bit fey. I've always liked that word. For instance, she keeps in constant touch with my uncle Joe, even though Uncle Joe passed beyond this mortal coil years ago. Uncle Joe was my father's oldest brother and a perfectly normal individual save for his unaccountable affection for Minnie, who's always been odd, and I don't care who hears me say it—although I'd prefer it not be my mother or father, who'd scold me for telling the truth. That doesn't seem fair somehow, but there you go. Anyhow, Pa once said he thought Joe died to get shut of Minnie, but Ma told him to hush his mouth.

I'd had to spend several weeks with Aunt Minnie and Miss Libby the prior summer, and those few weeks had been hell for me. Not only had Miss Libby made me peel about seven bushels of onions so that she could pickle them, thereby rendering my eyes red and swollen for days and days, but there had been a murder right smack next to Minnie's chicken coop—and I, Annabelle Blue, who seem to discover corpses a lot, dang it, had found the body when I went out to gather eggs.

Minnie also wore clothes that had been fashionable in her

youth, which means they were about forty years out of date by 1923. She looked like an old-time settler—which I guess she and Uncle Joe had been. Still and all, how many people do you know who claim to keep up with their relations who've been dead for decades? Not too many, I'll warrant. And this one belonged to me. How lucky could one girl get?

However, I knew where my duty lay. Pasting a smile on my face, I walked up to Minnie and Ma. "Good morning, Minnie," said I brightly.

She shook her head. "For you, perhaps, Annabelle, but poor Hortense isn't young and healthy and happy as you are."

Hortense was the widowed Mrs. Calhoun. And there was no denying I wasn't she, or that I was young, healthy and relatively happy most of the time. I only smiled some more. Anyhow, according to Betty Lou, Hortense probably wasn't as upset about her husband's passing as she possibly should have been, although if he was the rat I was beginning to believe he was, perhaps she was better off with him dead.

"Well, Minnie dear, we'd best relay our respects to Hortense and get back to the store. Lots of folks are coming in for supplies today, thanks to that dreadful storm last night." Ma kissed Minnie on the cheek and turned to make her way through the throng to Mrs. Calhoun, who sat in state on a big overstuffed chair next to the window.

"By the way, Minnie," I said before I tagged along after Ma, "how'd you get here all the way from the ranch?"

"Libby harnessed the mules to the wagon and drove us," Minnie said, as if taking a wagon ride across a flooded, muddy and possibly quicksandy desert from a ranch twelve miles outside the city limits was all in a day's work. Which it might have been for the powerful Miss Libby. I felt sorry for the mules.

"My goodness. What made you drive all that way through the mud and the floodwaters? You couldn't have heard about Mr.

Calhoun, because the telephone wires were down."

Minnie tapped her head. "I have my ways, as you well know, Annabelle. Your uncle Joe told me there was tragedy afoot at the Calhoun home."

Good heavens. Could it be true? Only Minnie and, I presume, God knew. Maybe Uncle Joe. "Oh. Yes, I see. Well, it's good to see you, Minnie."

All right, I don't believe a person can be faulted for a little white lie if it is used to make another person feel better.

"Take good care of your mother and father, Annabelle," Minnie said, her hazel eyes pinning me with an intensity I found unsettling. "There's evil in the air. Mr. Calhoun isn't the only one who will be affected. I can feel it."

"I'll do my best," I said, and scrammed after Ma.

CHAPTER FOUR

"That was very sweet of you, Susanna," Mrs. Calhoun was saying to Ma when I reached her side, Susanna being my mother's name.

"Oh, Hortense, I was just so sorry to hear about Edgar. If there's anything we can do . . ." Ma's voice drifted out before she'd finished the old tried-and-true indefinite offer of assistance to the bereaved. I must say that Hortense Calhoun didn't look all that bereaved to me, but what did I know?

"Yes. Thank you, dear. I'll be sure to call upon you if we need anything. And I do hope you'll attend the funeral with your family. We'll place a notice in the newspaper." Mrs. Calhoun gave a deep and mournful sigh. Maybe she was more cut up about her husband's death than I'd first supposed. "I don't know what this will mean for the bank, but I'm sure your Richard is terribly upset. Everything must be at sixes and sevens over there right now."

"I'm afraid you may be right," said Ma. "We haven't been in touch with Richard since Mr. Calhoun's demise was . . . discovered." I don't think she wanted to let on that it was I who'd unearthed the tragedy, if unearthed is the right word to use when you've fished someone out of a flooded roadway.

I was also afraid that the bank was in a muddle, too, and that Richard might be in for more trouble than he deserved or needed. Shoot, Richard didn't even like to fish, because he didn't care for hooking worms. Would a man like that commit a

48

cold-blooded murder? I don't think so. Darn it, I *had* to talk to Phil and enlist his help in solving this crime!

"We can't stay long, Hortense," said Ma. "We need to get back to the store. Business is quite brisk, as you can imagine, because of the storm. But we wanted to extend our condolences. I can't imagine what you're going through." Ma had tears in her eyes. She was a truly good woman. I could only aspire to be as decent as she—but not until I'd solved this murder and had a little fun first.

Taking Ma's hand, Mrs. Calhoun, dry-eyed and calm, said, "Thank you so much, dear. Your sympathy means a good deal to me."

Did it? I wondered.

As Ma and I made our way through the throng to the door, I glanced into the big, fancy dining room in the Calhoun home and was surprised to see Herschel Calhoun laughing it up with a couple of his pals. Did he consider his father's death amusing? Even if he did, I should think common decency would lead him to do his guffawing out of the sight of visitors in what was supposed to be a house of mourning.

Hmm. It wasn't unheard of for a son to do in his father if the provocation was great enough. I suspected the Calhoun children were going to be left a lot of loot by their deceased parent. I hadn't really heard any rumors about Herschel being a gambler or whatever, but could he have wanted to speed up his father's end in order to inherit a bundle? Stranger things had happened.

And how was Gladys taking the death of her father? Had she adored him? Or did she think of his death as a laughable circumstance as, evidently, her brother did?

Shoot, maybe the two kids were in cahoots, and they'd both done him in. That was an interesting possibility. I'd have to take it under consideration, and that would mean having a longer chat with Betty Lou Jarvis, who seemed to know what went on in the Calhoun household.

"Annabelle Blue, wherever has your mind gone wandering?"

Ma's voice cut into my thoughts like a sharp knife, and I jumped.

"Help me into the boat, and stop staring off into space," she continued. "Honestly, Annabelle, sometimes I think your head is in the clouds."

I glanced up at said clouds. A pristine blue sky beamed down upon us, frilly little clouds decorating it as though they'd never, ever, in a million years, call on their bullies of water-filled thunderhead cousins to try and drown us out down here in the quiet, dreary town of Rosedale, New Mexico. Liars.

"Sorry, Ma. I was just thinking about the Calhoun family, was all."

"You'd better keep your mind on your own business, young lady. You don't need to be worrying about what's none of your concern."

I helped Ma into the boat, which rocked a little but settled as she did. "Heck, Ma, I found the body. I can't help but be involved in the matter. It *is* my concern. In fact," I said, deciding to tell Ma something she probably wouldn't want to hear, "it's all of our business. Did you know that Chief Vickers told me he's heard Richard and Mr. Calhoun had been arguing lately? I think he thinks Richard is a suspect in Mr. Calhoun's murder."

"*What?*" Ma's screech nearly deafened me.

"Don't rock the boat," I advised sternly and literally. I didn't want my mother to end up in the mud.

"You must have misheard him, Annabelle," said Ma. She gazed up at me with a beseeching look that made me feel bad for spilling the beans.

"I didn't mishear him, Ma. He really said that. He's looking at Richard as a suspect. Well, Richard and a whole lot of other people who hated Mr. Calhoun's guts." Dang. I'd said the word *guts* in front of my mother, who disliked slang. Before she could berate me, I hurried on. "Anyhow, that makes Mr. Calhoun's murder all of our business. I'm not going to allow my brother-in-law to take the blame for someone else's evil deed." I climbed into the boat, took the oars, and began to row us home. The water was starting to recede, and I was mainly slogging my way through deep, sticky mud by that time. It was no darned fun, I can tell you that. "I've got to talk to Phil. I wish the telephone would get back up."

"What does Phil have to do with anything?" Ma asked.

I detected a note of hope in her voice. She wanted Phil and me to get married and settle down. Actually, what she wanted was for *me* to settle down. She thought I read too many adventure books and had begun to expect more from life than it was going to deliver. Nuts to that, and not if I could help it. Not that I'd say so to my mother, whom I loved dearly.

"He can get more information out of the folks at the bank than I can. Because he's a man." I spoke the last sentence with a trace of bitterness.

"You're not going to get involved in investigating this crime, Annabelle Blue. You leave that to the police. I do believe you've begun to think of yourself as some sort of armchair detective, and you're not. You're a young woman who has to help run the store. Keep that in mind, not solving crimes."

"Darn it, Ma, if I don't do something, poor Richard might be sent up the river!"

"Oh, for heaven's sake, Annabelle, don't be so dramatic."

"You won't think I'm being so dramatic when they haul Richard out of the bank in handcuffs."

"That won't happen." Ma's voice held all the confidence I didn't personally possess.

I only huffed. It was tough, rowing through all that mud.

"Well . . ." Ma had begun chewing on her lower lip. "Perhaps

51

you might ask Phil if he wouldn't mind stepping over to the bank when he has time, just to . . . to . . ."

"Ask questions," I supplied.

"Yes. I'm sure that wouldn't hurt anything."

"Good. After I drop you off at the store, I'll row on down to Gunderson's and see if I can enlist Phil in our efforts to help clear Richard's good name." Lord. I could feel my arm muscles growing even as I spoke.

"Don't you think you might be a little too worried about this, Annabelle? Without good reason?"

Not wanting my mother's concern to thwart my trip to see Phil, I said firmly, "No."

Ma only sighed.

Therefore, after I drew the boat up to the boardwalk in front of Blue's and saw that my mother got safely out of the one and onto the other, I continued rowing down Second Street and paid my second visit of the day to Gunderson's. Things had calmed down a lot since my earlier visit, and the place was no longer mobbed with people.

Alone at the counter, Phil looked as if he were counting nails when I walked through the front door. He turned and smiled a big welcoming smile. "Annabelle! Good to see you again. Does your father need something else?"

"I don't think so, but I need to talk to you. Whatever are you doing, Phil?"

He glanced down at the counter, and he blushed a little. I don't know why he was nervous around me, but he was. Ma said he blushed because he cared for me, which made no sense at all to me. "Separating nails. They got jumbled during this morning's rush."

I squinted at the countertop. Sure enough, a whole bunch of nails sat there. "What's the difference between nails?" I asked, always willing to learn something new.

"Size, mainly. Several tens got mixed in with the sevens and sixes, and Pete asked me to sort them out."

Sixes and sevens and tens? Well, I didn't need that much education. "Say, Phil, I need to talk to you."

"Mind if I keep sorting while you talk?"

It sounded to me as if he didn't expect to be participating much in our conversation. He knew me well. "Not as long as you pay attention. But I need your help."

He glanced up, a certain eagerness on his face that I was loath to see vanish, but I wasn't here in pursuit of romance. "It must have been rough on you, finding the body and all this morning. Sorry I was so busy I couldn't help you out with the jitters you must have had. After all, you had to hook him so we could haul him in."

"Yes, it was pretty awful, all right, but I'm not jittery any longer. I need to talk to you about something else."

"Oh?" I could see his guard going up. Sometimes I think he knew me a little too well. "What else?"

"The police think Richard might have killed Mr. Calhoun," I stated baldly, if not quite accurately. "And I need your help in proving them wrong."

After giving me a blank stare for a minute or two, he said, "Why do they think Richard did it?"

"Because, according to Chief Vickers, employees at the bank say Mr. Calhoun and Richard have been having lots of arguments lately."

"About what?"

"*I* don't know!"

"But they're looking at lots of people. I'm sure they only want to eliminate Richard from the list."

"I don't know that, and you don't know that."

"Come on, Annabelle. Richard seems like a real stretch to me."

"Me, too."

"Well, then . . ." Phil shrugged.

"Blast it, Phil Gunderson! You wouldn't be so complacent if *your* brother were under suspicion of murder!"

"Annabelle, I'm sure Richard isn't—"

"He is, too!" Very well, so I'd just stretched the truth a little. Again. "We both know Richard is innocent of the crime, but we're not the police. Shoot, even Pa thinks Chief Vickers is—" I broke off abruptly. Pa hadn't accused the chief of being incompetent; I was the one who feared he was, and my fears hadn't been validated. Yet. "Anyhow, that's why I need you."

"Why me?"

"Because you're a man, and the bank is a man's world." Lord, Phil could be dense sometimes.

"Annabelle, I don't know beans about banking. All's I do in the bank is make deposits and withdrawals for our ranch and for Pete here at the store."

"You don't need to know anything about banking, for heaven's sake. All you need to do is go into the bank and ask people why the chief claims Richard and Mr. Calhoun have been arguing recently." Deciding it might be a good time to pile some more reasons on to my request in order to make it seem more urgent, I added, "Mr. Calhoun was only found murdered this morning, and I've already heard of three or four people who had more reason to kill him than Richard ever did."

"How do you know that?"

"Phil! Can you honestly picture my brother-in-law as a murderer?" The notion was idiotic.

"Well, no, but who are these other people of whom you speak?"

He'd definitely been spending a lot of time with me. Before we took up together, he'd never have put a sentence like that together. See? I was good for him. Or at least for his grammar.

"Mr. Tindall, for one. He said it would be easier to find folks in Rosedale who *did* want Mr. Calhoun dead than those who didn't. Mr. Calhoun gypped him out of his ranch. And Mr. Calhoun cheated Virginia Feather's father out of a bunch of money for some property he didn't even own. Mr. Calhoun, I mean. And Betty Lou Jarvis told me she thought the Calhoun family was probably glad the old man was dead, and she works in their house! Not only that, but I saw Herschel Calhoun *laughing* when Ma and I took Mrs. Calhoun a covered dish on our condolence call." Thinking of Ma's covered dish reminded me it was past lunchtime. I pressed a hand over my empty tummy.

"Playing detective again, are you?" Phil's eyebrows lowered over his gorgeous brown eyes. How come men always get the long, beautiful eyelashes, is what I want to know.

"Darn it, Phil, somebody had better play detective if we don't want to see Richard clapped in the clink because Chief Vickers doesn't want to go to the bother of thoroughly investigating Mr. Calhoun's murder!"

"Oh, for God's—" Phil saw my black frown and heaved a huge sigh. I knew he'd already capitulated to my request. He always did, bless his heart. "Aw, shoot. I think you're nuts to believe the chief would honestly consider Richard as a valid suspect, but all right. I'll go over to the bank and sniff around. But I can't do it this minute. Pete's at the café now, getting us some lunch. I'll snoop at the bank after that."

My stomach growled in a most unladylike manner, but I cleared my throat at the same time, hoping Phil wouldn't notice. "Thanks, Phil. I really appreciate it." I turned to go back to the boat while there was still water enough out there to row through.

"Don't get into any trouble, Annabelle. You know how you're always getting yourself into messes when it comes to stuff like this."

"I do not!" said I, whirling around to scowl at Phil and almost backing into Pete, who'd returned bearing food. "Sorry, Pete."

"No problem, Annabelle. Has my baby brother been giving you grief?" Pete winked at me. He and Phil were the best of friends, as well as brothers, which I thought was swell. They had a younger brother, Davy, who was almost as beastly as my own brother Jack. Naturally, Jack and Davy were pals.

"Not at all," I told Pete. "In fact, he's just agreed to help me out."

"Sir Galahad, that's Phil. Do you need a cape thrown over a puddle so you don't get your feet wet?"

"A cape wouldn't do much good out there in all that mud," I said while Phil flushed furiously. "Anyway, it's nothing like that. Phil can tell you. Maybe you can help, too." Heck, maybe Pete had overheard folks griping about Mr. Calhoun and his wicked ways while he'd rummaged around in his hardware store. Phil was usually stuck on the ranch, way outside of town. Pete was right there in the midst of things.

"Cripes, Annabelle, don't get Pete involved, too."

"Involved in what?"

Oh, my. It smelled as though Pete had bought some barbecued ribs for lunch at the café. I'd bet there was some cabbage salad, too, and maybe some potato salad. My stomach growled again. It was becoming downright angry with me for neglecting it for so long.

"I'll let Phil tell you all about it," said I as I headed out the door and to the boat.

Luckily for all of us, Ma had made two covered dishes while she'd been holed up in the kitchen that morning, and we got to feast on creamed chicken and peas and rice for lunch that day. My tummy was very happy about that.

After lunch, I had to work behind the counter in the store again. Pa had made Jack shovel mud from the walkway running from the house to the store and clean out the stone cooler, a job Jack didn't want to do. I'd never tell him so, but I wouldn't have wanted to do it either, the mud being heavy, sloppy, slippery, dirty and generally icky. When he got through, he'd have to take a bath, something he hated almost as much as he hated working. Still and all, we Blues were lucky in that we had indoor plumbing and hot and cold running water, luxuries most folks in Rosedale couldn't afford. Blue's was a good business, and if Jack didn't care about it continuing to be profitable, I sure did.

Right about closing time, Ma came to the counter to relieve me for a spell, and Myrtle Howell entered the store to ask if I'd like to join her in an ice-cream soda at Pruitt's soda fountain. Ma nodded her approval, so I ducked under the counter and strolled next door with Myrtle.

"How come you don't have to work this afternoon, Myrtle?"

"Mr. Pruitt and Frank told me to close the cosmetics counter. Nobody's coming in today for cosmetics. I guess they're frequenting stores like yours, Mayberry's and Pete Gunderson's. That storm was a whopper."

"What about your folks? Did your house sustain any damage? Those winds were vicious."

"Yes. Ma had just planted a peach tree, and it was pitiful to see her crying over it this morning. The wind knocked it clean out of the ground. Of course, the ground was mud, so it didn't have much of a foothold."

"Oh, dear. I'm sorry to hear that. Our pear tree managed to survive, but the stone cooler flooded. Fortunately, we didn't have much in it. We'll begin receiving the Christmas chocolates and stuff like that any day now. Pa and Jack are cleaning it out right now." I smiled at the thought of my rotten little brother having to work his fingers to the bone while I enjoyed an ice-cream soda at Pruitt's.

By the way, the stone cooler is a little house built of stone.

When I say little, I mean it's about as big as a couple of steamer trunks. It covers a big hole in the ground that's also lined with stones, and in which we keep perishable luxury items like Whitman's Samplers and other delicacies people like to give each other for Christmas, Valentine's Day and Easter. Because it got so hot in Rosedale during the summertime, the stone cooler was the only place where we could keep chocolate so that it wouldn't melt.

"Ma's going to try to save the peach tree," said Myrtle. "It fell over, roots and all, so she might be able prop it up again and keep it alive if she pampers it—and we don't get any more bad storms. But it's certainly weaker than it should be, and winter's coming on."

"Yeah, but we don't generally get snow until December."

"Huh. It snowed in October last year, or did you forget?"

"Oh, boy. Yes, I did forget about that. The weather around here is freakish, isn't it?"

Myrtle heaved a sigh as she climbed onto the soda-fountain stool. Jimmy Bartles, who served behind the soda counter as well as clerking in the store, spotted us and came over. "What'll it be, ladies?"

"I want a chocolate ice-cream soda," I said, my delicious lunch now only a fond memory.

"Same for me," said Myrtle.

So Jimmy mixed ice cream with chocolate syrup and soda water, and plopped two ice-cream sodas in front of us, with straws for sipping.

"Have you heard any more about Mr. Calhoun's murder?" Myrtle asked as she stirred her soda with her straw.

"Only that there are lots of people in town who hated him. That and the fact that Chief Vickers told me to my face that my brother-in-law is a suspect."

"No!"

I grimaced. "Yes. Can you imagine it? Richard MacDougall, who can't even stick a worm on a hook? It's insane, but there it is. But as I said, there are lots of people in town who are probably better suspects."

"How do you know that? Besides Mr. Tindall, I mean." Myrtle took a sip of her soda and added, "Mmmm."

"Because people have talked to me and said so."

"Oh, my. Who?" Myrtle was appropriately avid to hear the dirt.

So I gave her the few names I had at my disposal, then frowned. The list wasn't long and Richard's name might still top the one from which Chief Vickers was working.

"That's all?" Myrtle asked, probably feeling, as I did, that my list was pathetic in its brevity and dearth of details.

"So far. But Phil's going to the bank to ask around and see if there aren't other people who had it in for Mr. Calhoun. I mean . . . I don't mean *other* people as though I think Richard might have done it. In fact, I know he didn't."

"How come?"

I glared at my best friend. "Because I know Richard, and I know he's not a murderer."

"Of course," said Myrtle, who, unlike me, had a pliable and agreeable personality. She didn't care to argue. Well, I didn't either, but I'd sure argue that Richard was no killer if I had to.

And then I espied Betty Lou Jarvis, our friend who worked for the Calhouns, entering Pruitt's. Oh, boy! I fingered the change in my pocket, decided I had enough of it to offer Betty Lou an ice-cream soda, and hailed her from my stool. "Betty Lou! Come and join us!"

Startled, probably because my hail had been quite hearty, Betty Lou whirled around, pressed a hand to her bosom, and saw Myrtle and me on our stools. She walked over to us.

"You scared me out of a year's growth, Annabelle," she said as she neared.

"I'm sorry. But I'd like to treat you to an ice-cream soda if you have time for one."

Betty Lou glanced about, worried, I presume, lest a Calhoun or one of the Calhoun friends see her frittering away working hours. Then she shrugged. "Why not? This day has been horrible. I deserve a soda. Thanks, Annabelle." And she took a stool next to me.

After annoying Jimmy Bartles, who'd been straightening items on a shelf, into coming over and serving us once more, I asked, "How'd you get here, anyway, Betty Lou? Is the water still high?"

"No. Now it's just mud and full of trash." She frowned, the expression marring what was otherwise a very pretty face. "I had to slog through a mile of mud. Good thing I had my rubber boots." She gestured to the door of Pruitt's. "I left 'em outside. Thank God skirts are shorter these days than they used to be. Can you imagine marching through all that mud with a dress down to your feet?"

I could, but that's only because I have an excellent imagination. "I'm sorry you had to walk here. It must have been hard going."

"It was. When I wasn't clinging for dear life to the sides of buildings so I wouldn't slip and fall on my face, I was slopping through ankle-deep mud and water. She shook her head. "But Mrs. Calhoun *had* to have her nerve tonic, and naturally I'm the one who has to get it for her." Her voice carried both disdain and bitterness.

Myrtle shook her head in sympathy. "It's no fun to have to work for selfish people. Not that Mr. Pruitt is selfish, but I know lots of folks are, and they never think about the people who work for them except as paid slaves."

"I'm glad I work at the family business. We're all in it together." Except for Jack, of course. "So how are things at the Calhoun place? Are people still pouring in to offer condolences and stuff like that?"

Betty Lou took a sip of her soda—she'd chosen strawberry—and said, "Lord, yes. I've never opened the door to so many people in my life. And Mrs. Calhoun is in a perfect state because there's no room in the Frigidaire for all the food everyone's been bringing."

"Yes. I can see that might be a problem," I said, thinking that Mrs. Calhoun might consider giving the overflow to some deserving poor folks in town. Mrs. Wilson the seamstress sprang to mind.

"Is she terribly upset about her husband's murder?" asked Myrtle. "Well, I'm sure she must be. I can't imagine losing a loved one like that." She shuddered delicately. She'd recently begun seeing Sonny Clyde, whose family owned the Handlebar Ranch near Tatum, and she was very much in love.

But Betty Lou snorted, taking some of the glow from the moment. "Are you kidding? They all hated the old man. Anyhow—" Betty Lou stopped speaking suddenly and peered around the interior of Pruitt's as if looking for possible eavesdroppers. Myrtle and I hunched closer to her, and she lowered her voice when she continued. "Anyhow," she whispered, "the man was a rat and a philanderer."

Myrtle and I gasped to encourage her.

She didn't need much encouragement. She'd probably been longing to get these revelations off her chest for a long time, but it wasn't considered honorable to gossip about the family one worked for. This must have been a particularly rough day for Betty Lou if it was making her blab like this. She nodded with vigor. "He not only cheated people for a living at his bank, but he's been carrying on an affair with Sadie Dobbs."

Another gasp must have given Betty Lou cause for pleasure. It's always nice to have an attentive and appreciative audience.

Myrtle only spoiled the moment a little bit when she asked, "Who's Sadie Dobbs?"

It was a good question, especially since I didn't know who the woman was, either.

"She's a waitress at the Cowboy Café," said Betty Lou. "But she's not the first one of his dollies, believe me. Why, that man even tried to have his way with *me!*"

"Good heavens!" cried Myrtle. I was sipping my soda, or I'd probably have said something similar. "What did you do to discourage him?"

"Told him I'd tell my brother if he ever did anything like that again, and that Gabe was the best shot in Rosedale." Her smile faded when she realized what she'd said. "But I never told Gabe, and he didn't shoot Mr. Calhoun. Honest. I need that stupid job, even if I hate the Calhouns. But if Mr. Calhoun *had* tried getting at me again, I *would* have told Gabe, and then Gabe would at least have shoved that old buzzard's face in the dirt," she ended defiantly.

"Mercy sakes," I whispered, thinking how nice it would be to have an older brother to protect one.

If he still lived in Rosedale, I suspect George would have protected me if an old pig like Mr. Calhoun had attempted to seduce me. Jack wouldn't care. Pa would, though. Good thing I never got near enough to Mr. Calhoun for him to try anything.

"That's appalling, Betty Lou," said Myrtle, whose face had paled considerably. A sensitive soul, Myrtle.

"So Mr. Calhoun was a two-timing hound," I said, musing and fiddling with my soda straw and thinking I'd just maligned an entire breed of dogs. "What about Herschel and Gladys? When Ma and I were at their house earlier today, I saw Herschel laughing with some friends in the dining room. To me, his behavior didn't seem at all respectful."

"Respectful? Huh. The only thing Herschel and his snotty sister respect is money. They'll probably get a lot of it, too, now that the old man's kicked the bucket."

"I suppose that's so," said I.

"But I'd better fetch Mrs. Calhoun's nerve tonic and get back to the house," said Betty Lou, slipping off her stool. "Mrs. Lovelady was manning the door when I left, and she's probably worn her poor little feet to nubs." She snorted at the thought of Mrs. Lovelady doing actual work. "Thanks again for the soda, Annabelle."

"You're more than welcome. I hope things smooth out at the Calhouns' soon."

Betty Lou gave another snort and walked off toward the pharmacy.

Myrtle and I gazed at each other, and I said, "Sadie Dobbs."

With a nod, Myrtle said, "Yes, indeed."

CHAPTER FIVE

Fortunately for me, the telephone was working again by the time I got back to Blue's. Although I knew it was inappropriate—after all, the man is supposed to do the inviting in a romantic relationship, not that Phil and I had much romance going on—I decided to telephone Phil at the hardware store.

My luck was good. Phil himself answered the 'phone. "Gunderson's Hardware," he said in a harassed-sounding voice.

"You sound busy, Phil. Everything okay?"

"Annabelle?" He perked up some when he said my name. "It's just busy again. The folks who waited for the water to subside are coming in now. Personally, I think it would have been easier to row in the water than wade through the mud."

"It's still awful out there. The mud's feet thick."

"I know," he said with a sigh. "But most of 'em are riding horses."

"Poor horses."

"Yeah. Anything I can do for you, Annabelle?"

"Well . . . I want to know what you find out at the bank when you have a chance to go there, actually, but thought maybe we could chat about it at supper."

"Supper?" Phil sounded blank.

I didn't want to tell him I aimed to do some investigating of Miss—I guess she was a Miss—Sadie Dobbs, supposed mistress of the late Mr. Edgar Calhoun. "I thought maybe it would be nice to take supper together at the Cowboy Café. You know, get out and around a little bit." The words sounded lame to my own ears, and I guess Phil concurred.

"You've got some kind of bee in your bonnet about this Calhoun murder, don't you, Annabelle?"

"Why do you say that?" I tried to sound offended.

"Because I know you. Anyhow, I can't take you to supper tonight. I've got to help Pete get this place organized again. It's a wreck after the rush of business today, and Pete invited me to his house for supper. Maggie's fixing us something special. That's what Pete said. So you'll have to wait until tomorrow for our little discussion."

"You can't tell me anything over the 'phone?" I pleaded.

"Cripes, Annabelle, sometimes I think the only reason you see me at all is so you can get me to help you in your damned schemes."

Oh, dear. It wasn't like Phil to swear. He was clearly mad at me. "I'm sorry, Phil. That's not the only reason I see you. I'm terribly fond of you, and you know that."

"Fond of me," he said, as if being fond of someone was about as low on the scale of romance as a person could get.

"For heaven's sake, I aim to marry you!" I cried indignantly. "Just because I don't want to do it right this minute doesn't mean I don't love you!"

Oh, dear. Had I ever told him I loved him before? I couldn't remember. All I knew at the time was that I'd put my foot in it, and that Phil was the only person on earth I could imagine ever marrying.

However, my words seemed to have a calming effect on Phil himself. "Well . . . thanks, Annabelle. You, too."

From that, I presumed he meant that he loved me, too, only he couldn't say so because the store was full of customers, or maybe Pete was looming behind him.

"Can we get together tomorrow?" I asked, not having the

sense to leave well enough alone. But this investigation affected my family, dang it!

"Tomorrow would be all right. How about lunch at the Cowboy Café?"

"Sounds good to me. Thanks, Phil. And I'm sorry if you think I'm using you for my own purposes. But . . . well, darn it, Richard might be blamed for Mr. Calhoun's murder if we don't find out who really did the crime."

Phil sighed heavily and said, "You really don't think Chief Vickers and his crew are able to do the job? They're trained for this sort of thing, you know."

"I know, I know. But I also know the chief flat out told me Richard is a suspect, and that scares me, Phil. Surely you can understand that."

"I understand, Annabelle." A pause ensued, then he said, "Come over here about eleven-thirty, and I'll treat you to lunch at the café. Is that all right with you? Then we can talk all about what I learn at the bank, if anything."

"Thanks, Phil."

"You're welcome."

He didn't wait for me to say anything else, but hung the receiver back on the hook with what might have been a slam had the receiver been a door. Poor Phil. Was I really an awful person for using him in this way? I honestly did intend to marry him. Someday.

"Annabelle, Hannah and Richard are coming over for supper Friday night."

I turned to find my mother standing at the counter, her face wreathed in smiles. "Really? I'm surpr—Um, that's nice."

"Hannah called as soon as the telephone line was restored to service. She said Richard had a rough day at the bank because of Mr. Calhoun's death, of course, but that she thinks there will be a nice surprise to tell us about."

"Oh, my. I wonder if she's pregnant, too."

"Annabelle!"

"Sorry, Ma." Jeepers, I forgot how old-fashioned my parents were sometimes. Babies were assumed to be blessed events, but you weren't supposed to talk about having them except via euphemism. Sometimes I didn't think I belonged in my own world.

"I'm going to cook a ham. We've got two left in the smokehouse. What else should we have?"

Ham, eh? Ham wasn't my all-time favorite meat, but it beat pickled pigs' feet all hollow. "How about some of those potatoes Miss Libby makes. You know, she slices them thin and layers them with cheese and butter and thinly sliced onions and then pours milk over them and bakes them for a long time. I love those."

"Wonderful idea, Annabelle. I'll fix some pinto beans, and we can have the last of the corn and some fried okra. Maybe I'll make a squash pie for dessert."

"Boy, I wish it was Friday already. That sounds wonderful."

By the way, squash pie tastes exactly like pumpkin pie in case you felt a tremble in your tummy at the thought. Pumpkins are, after all, squash, you know? Only we grew tons of squash in the autumn in our back garden—which hadn't even been visible through the floodwaters this morning as we made our careful way to the store from the house. Butternut squash and acorn squash make the best pies. I mean, you probably wouldn't want a zucchini pie. At least I wouldn't.

"How'd the garden survive the flood?" I asked, my attention having been called to it thanks to Ma's speaking of squash pie.

"It took quite a beating, but the squash seems to be all right. I'm afraid the last of the tomatoes got battered to death."

I'd never tell my mother that I was glad to hear it, but I was. I was so sick of helping her preserve tomatoes and other garden vegetables, I could hardly stand it. Huh. And Jack got mad when he had to wash the store windows and shovel mud. At least he didn't have to stand for hours and hours in a hot kitchen sweating over peeling tomatoes, snapping beans, and chopping everything you can think of for the various relishes Ma fixed. I liked the pickled okra better than anything else she pickled, preferring my cucumbers fresh off the vine, thank you very much. Although I must say that I liked a good dill pickle every once in a while. Anyhow, from what Ma said, there wouldn't be much preserving left to do, thank God.

"Did Hannah tell you anything about what's going on at the bank?"

"Nothing other than that Richard said it had been a hard day and he expects a worse one tomorrow, which I'm sure we can all understand."

"I'm surprised the bank even opened today," said I.

"Oh, it didn't, but the employees who could get there through the floodwaters all arrived, and I guess the board of directors straggled in this afternoon. I expect there will be a lot of reorganizing of staff and that sort of thing."

"What will it all mean to Richard, do you suppose?"

"Mercy sakes, I have no idea." Ma eyed me hard for a moment. "Were you telling me the truth when you said Chief Vickers suspects Richard in Mr. Calhoun's murder?"

"Of course I was!" Indignant didn't half describe my state. Here was my own mother, virtually accusing me of lying to her, and I'd never do that . . . well, not much, anyway. "For heaven's sake, Ma, why would I fib about something that terrible?"

"I'm sorry, Annabelle. It's just so . . . awful that Richard might be suspected of doing something so dreadful. And you do tend to like to get involved in these convoluted problems, you know."

"I don't, either. Not on purpose, anyhow. It isn't my fault if things happen around me. I'd rather not have discovered Mr. Calhoun's body, believe me."

Ma came over to where I stood beside the telephone hanging on the wall and gave me a hug. "I know, dear. I know. I just hope the whole thing is cleared up soon."

"Me, too." Still feeling abused, I didn't soften until about five seconds into her hug, then I hugged her back. I really do love my mother, who's a sweetheart. Small wonder Pa married her.

We ate leftover creamed chicken and peas for supper that night, which was all right by me. It had been an eventful day, and we were all exhausted.

"I've got blisters," announced Jack, sorely aggrieved by having to do manly labor all day long.

"We all have to do our share, son," said Pa, eyeing him somewhat coldly, probably knowing that if he'd been able to, Jack would have skedaddled and left all the hard work to Pa.

"I guess," grumbled Jack.

"Jack Blue, straighten up in your chair and be civil during a family meal," our mother commanded of him.

It was unlike her to be so to-the-point with my awful brother, but I smiled inside that he got what he deserved that night. I didn't dare allow my smile to show, or I'd have been ripped-up at, too. My mother and father believed in fair treatment of all their children. Well, except the ones who had already left the nest. They were treated like gold. Which fact might actually make me consider marrying Phil sooner rather than later.

But no. I'd stick to my guns even if it did mean getting scolded occasionally by one or the other of my parents. I tried like a trouper to behave as a child of William and Susanna Blue should behave, unlike Jack, but every now and then I slipped up.

Besides, I wasn't altogether sure what Phil aimed to do with his life. He was an easygoing sort of fellow, which made sense or he'd never have stuck with me, but did he want to continue on at the Gunderson family ranch way out in the back of beyond, or did he aim to set himself up in trade in Rosedale one day? Perhaps he'd go into the hardware business with his brother Pete. That would be better for me, being a city girl and all, even if the city was Rosedale.

But that's beside the point. After supper, Ma and I did the dishes, Pa read a seed catalog—he'd been thinking about stocking more types of seeds in the store—and Jack read one of the yellow-back novels of which he was so fond. Every now and then Ma made him do the dishes with me, but I hated when that happened, Jack being so horrid and all. He always did something to make the duty even more onerous than it already was, like splash me with water or snap me with the dish towel or smear grease on my clothes. Really, someone ought to do something with boys when they reach a certain age. Stick them in cold storage until they turn twenty-one, maybe.

When the dishes were all washed and dried and put away, I retired to my room to read some more in *Powder and Patch*. I noticed Ma had picked up her workbasket, and was pretty sure she aimed to work on a braided rug or a quilt. It's true what they say about a woman's work never being done—yet one more reason I aimed to put off marriage and motherhood for as long as possible. The notion of not being able to read of an evening because I had to make quilts for the family or braid rugs for the floor after cooking and serving dinner, and all this after a hard day of working in the garden and the kitchen and the store, didn't appeal at all.

I have to admit, however, that it was fun to look down at the braided rug in my room and see bits from my favorite woolen coat from when I was five and Ma's old dress she'd worn to funerals for years and years until she decided to retire it. Not that it wasn't still serving a purpose. Heck, it kept my feet from freezing to death in the wintertime. And so did my old holey flannel pajamas, which were braided into the rug somewhere. Folks in Rosedale, New Mexico, didn't throw things out, by gum.

Fortunately for everyone in town and out of it, although clouds lowered and loomed, no rain came that night. I prayed we'd get no more of the stuff until the appropriate dry spell— say, during spring when the winds were tearing our town to bits and mummifying its inhabitants. The citizens of Rosedale, New Mexico, probably went through more lanolin and hand cream than any other people on earth, barring those in the Sahara Desert.

The next morning after Jack left for school—which meant I'd be free from his evil influence for several hours, bless school—we were able to walk to the store without too much mud impeding our progress. I saw what Ma meant about the garden. It looked as if a giant had stomped it flat, leading me to believe we'd not experienced mere rain and wind but hail, too, during the storm. Usually you can hear hail when it batters down on the roof, but the rain, wind and thunder had been so violent, I didn't even notice when the hail hit. The squash leaves, which are really big, looked as if someone had poked holes in them with the points of sharpened pencils, and Ma shook her head as she passed the pumpkin patch.

"I hope I can save those pumpkins," she muttered, bending over to inspect a pock-marked pumpkin. "They look like someone stuck pins in them. Of course, I can always preserve them, but I was hoping to have some pretty pumpkins to sell for Thanksgiving."

"Careful," I told her. "Better stay on the path." Pa might not yet have built a bridge, but he had laid out paving stones from the house to the store. Jack had grumblingly shoveled mud from them the prior afternoon. "You'll slip in the mud and have to go back and change clothes."

Ma heaved a huge sigh. "I know. But it galls me that the storm did so much damage to everything. I have to put up the rest of the beans and squash, and I can't do that if it's been ruined by rain and hail."

I hoped there wouldn't be too many vegetables to preserve after the ground dried out enough to investigate the garden in detail. If there were, I hoped Ma could preserve them without my help while I manned the counter in the store. We always kept tons and tons of preserved foods in our back room at the store. Ma generally made extra so that she could give some away to people who needed food during the winter months, or sometimes she sold her own preserved goods in the store. A heart of gold. That was what my mother had beating in her chest. Would that I could say the same. However, that morning, I was only eager for lunchtime to come so I could quiz Phil about matters at the bank.

The first person to enter Blue's that morning was Jesse Lee Wilson, who helped out his mother by delivering the newspapers in town. A cheerful redheaded boy about the same age as Jack, he seemed ever so much more responsible and mature than my crummy brother, although that might have been because his family was so poor that everyone had to work or starve. Naturally, due to the flood, no newspapers had been available the preceding day.

"Morning, Jesse Lee. Does anyone know how much rain we got night before last?"

"Says here that we got more than six inches overnight, Miss Annabelle. That's a whole lot of water. No wonder it flooded the town."

"No wonder," I agreed. "Is it still muddy out there?"

"Oh, yeah." Jesse Lee peered down at his feet, which were bare and mud-stained. "I figured it'd be easier to go barefoot than try to keep my shoes from falling apart." That's when I noticed his shoes tied by their laces and hanging about his neck.

Yet another indication of the Wilsons' general neediness, although you'd never find one of them asking anyone for help. Mrs. Wilson had originally come from Switzerland and had married her husband, an aspiring Methodist preacher, after her first husband succumbed to tuberculosis. Mr. Wilson wasn't a young man when he died. In fact, his tombstone proclaims him to have been sixty-three years old. He'd been married to Mrs. Wilson's best friend, who'd died, and then he'd married Mrs. Wilson, I think because he needed someone to take care of his kids from his first marriage. Therefore, when he died, two days after their fifth child was born, Mrs. Wilson was left with thirteen children to rear all by herself as a seamstress. In a three-room house. In Rosedale, New Mexico. What a life! I admired her tremendously, and most of her kids, four of whom were still at home, were really nice. Jesse Lee, for instance, who delivered newspapers before he went to school every day.

Speaking of tuberculosis, which some folks called the white plague, Rosedale had an enormous number of doctors for a town of its size. They'd flocked to Rosedale for the dry climate (with certain notable exceptions) and set up small sanatoriums for consumptives to come for a rest treatment. I don't think there was a true cure for the disease in 1923, although I might well be wrong. All I knew about tuberculosis was that a whole lot of folks came to Rosedale because of it, and I'd read in the newspaper that somebody, in 1882, had isolated the bacillus that caused it.

But this isn't a story about tuberculosis, which no one could deny is a killer, but about another kind of death. "Is there anything in the paper about Mr. Calhoun's murder?" I asked, taking the stack of papers from Jesse Lee.

"Yeah," he said. "I figured lots more people would be buying newspapers today since we couldn't put one out yesterday, so I brought you some extras to sell."

"Good idea. Thanks, Jesse Lee."

"You're welcome. Well, see you, Miss Annabelle. I have to get these papers delivered and go to school."

"Good to see you, Jesse Lee."

"Same here, Miss Annabelle."

And off he went. Industrious child. Perhaps we could exchange him for Jack. It would probably do Jack a lot of good to see how truly poor people had to cope with their condition in life. But I wouldn't inflict him on poor Mrs. Wilson, who had enough on her hands already.

Next to enter was Mr. O'Dell, who didn't appear happy.

"Morning, Mr. O'Dell. Did you get your chicken coop fixed yesterday?"

"Criminy, Miss Annabelle, it was too muddy to do anything yesterday. Damned birds—sorry, Miss Annabelle—anyhow, Mrs. O'Dell found most of the birds, but we had to lock 'em in the cellar. It was flooded too, but they roosted in the rafters. The place will have to be ploughed out, it's such a mess of feathers, mud and chicken sh—droppings." He shook his head in disgust. "I'll have to rebuild the coop today, but it's going to be a damned—uh, darned muddy job, and I'm not looking forward to it."

"Why don't the city fathers build a dam?" I asked, honestly curious.

"Beats the hell—heck out of me," he said. "I need another can of pomade. It's not easy to sell land when the weather doesn't cooperate, either."

He continued to mutter and grumble while he found his preferred brand of pomade and slapped it on the counter. Mr. O'Dell dealt primarily with farming and ranching land, and I could imagine having the entire desert flood the way it had might interfere with his business.

Speaking of business . . . "Say, Mr. O'Dell, did you have any dealings with Mr. Calhoun at the Farmer's and Rancher's Bank?"

"Some," he said as he counted out sixty-three cents from the change in his pocket. "When I couldn't help it."

Interesting comment.

"I hear he wasn't always the most honest man in the world." I tried to sound innocent.

"Honest? Ed Calhoun? Don't make me laugh! He was crooked as a dog's hind leg." He huffed to add weight to his words.

"I've heard from others that he took advantage of folks. Mr. Tindall claims he swindled him out of his ranch, and another person said her father gave him money for a piece of property Mr. Calhoun didn't even own."

"Huh. I remember that. The wording on the contract was so vague, it would have taken an army of lawyers to straighten it out. Well, got to get to the office. Thanks, Miss Annabelle." He spied the stack of newspapers and grabbed one. "Here." He handed me a nickel, and was off again.

And, since nobody else entered the store, I grabbed a newspaper myself and decided to read all about Mr. Calhoun—although I doubted very much if the editors at the newspaper would tell the truth about him.

CHAPTER SIX

Whoo boy, was I right about the editors of the *Rosedale Daily Record* soft-pedaling Mr. Calhoun's dirty dealings. According to the paper, he'd been a pillar of the community, a fond father and a beloved husband, and had belonged to every civic organization Rosedale had to offer including Woodmen of the World, the Rotary Club, the Chamber of Commerce and the Freemasons. Huh. And here I'd thought all those organizations had rules and regulations and that their members were supposed to be above reproach. Shows how much I knew about anything.

A delivery van arrived shortly before eleven o'clock. I was surprised to see it, since automobile traffic was scarce after floods. Most vehicles got bogged down in the mud, but this one didn't even slither as it pulled up in front of the boardwalk. I recognized the delivery man, a fellow named Mr. Juarez, and greeted him as he walked into the store in sturdy boots. He was burdened with several bolts of fabric Ma must have ordered.

"Gee, Mr. Juarez, how'd you get your truck through the mud out there?"

He grinned. "Put chains on the tires. Works for ice. Why not mud?"

Smart man, Mr. Juarez. "I'm surprised to see you doing deliveries today."

He shook his head and grunted as he plunked the bolts on the counter. "Teddy couldn't get into town. I'm the only one available." Years and years ago, Mr. Juarez had built his delivery company right next to the railroad yard, so that he could pick up shipments and deliver them wherever they needed to go in town. Teddy, whose family lived outside the city limits, was his primary hired worker.

"I'll go get Ma. Have you been all over town, or are there still places you can't get to?"

"Can't go much farther east than the railroad station, but the west is clearing up pretty good."

"I see. I expect the mud will dry up in another day or two."

"Especially if the wind starts howling." Hauling a big handkerchief from his pocket and wiping his perspiring brow, Mr. Juarez said, "Anyhow, I sure hope so, Miss Annabelle. Gonna have to work all weekend getting the deliveries made. Stuff has piled up."

"I don't suppose the trains are running yet."

"Not yet. Probably pretty soon. Bet the tracks outside of town need repair."

"I'm sure they do."

"After the trains are running again, we'll be really busy, what with all the delays in getting merchandise here. People will be yelling for their stuff. I just heard Gunderson's is out of lumber, and his customers are hollering for it."

"Oh, dear. Poor Pete and Phil."

What a nonsensical place to live, this Rosedale, New Mexico, in the middle of a desert where nothing lived but cactus, coyotes, rattlesnakes and cattle. When we weren't in danger of being blown off the face of the earth during the spring windy season, we almost always flooded in the summertime—and occasionally in November, too, as this present storm proved—we fried during the worst heat in the world, and half the time we got snow in October or April, when it spoiled the fruit on the few trees people managed to baby through the rest of the year. I could only remember two or three white Christmases. And it's no good telling me that Jesus was probably born in a desert much like this one. I wanted my hometown to look like a Currier and Ives print at Christmas, darn it.

Oh, well. Ma was separating sewing notions when I went into the back room and told her the fabric delivery was here.

"So soon? I didn't expect Mr. Juarez to be able to get around until sometime next week."

"He put chains on his tires. Says it works for ice, why not mud?"

Ma laughed as she rose and shook out her skirt. "Why not, indeed?"

By the time Ma had paid Mr. Juarez and they'd had a good jaw, it was almost time for me to meet Phil at the Cowboy Café, so I asked Ma if I could be excused for lunch a little early. She eyed me speculatively. "And why do you need to take off early for lunch, young lady? If you're going to play detective—"

"Ma! Phil asked me to take lunch with him at the Cowboy Café." I tried to appear injured and I guess I succeeded, because Ma's smile softened.

"Isn't that sweet of him? You know, Annabelle, you're not likely to meet a better young man anywhere than Phil Gunderson."

"You're right," I said, bracing myself for the lecture to come.

"I know you want to see some of the world before you marry poor Phil and settle down, but don't you think you're being a little unfair to him?"

"Shoot, Ma, he can go adventuring with me, can't he?"

"Annabelle, a young man has to make his way in the world. He can't be haring off to this place and that just because his wife has an itch to visit foreign climes."

"What if I want to make *my* way in the world? Who says I can't . . . I don't know. Be a companion to some old lady in

78

New York City? At least I'd get to see Central Park and maybe go to a play on Broadway. Or at least maybe I could visit George in Alhambra once before I die."

Shaking her head, Ma said, "Annabelle, sometimes I despair of you."

Her words struck me to the heart, and I felt guilty as I left the store and walked to Gunderson's. Luckily for Rosedale's residents, although we didn't have dams to prevent floods, most busy intersections had wooden bridges crossing them that city crews kept swept, so one could walk across the street via the bridge if the street happened to be caked with slippery mud. Didn't work during the floods themselves, of course, since the bridges, too, were generally underwater, and afterwards they were too gooey to cross until the city workers cleaned them off. There weren't bridges at every intersection, but at least I didn't have to get myself all dirty walking to Gunderson's, although I did have to go three blocks out of my way to get to a bridge. Stupid town.

It was only as I walked those three extra blocks that I thought about my appearance, far too late to do anything about not having my glad rags on. I looked down at my blue checked day dress, which was fine for working in the store, but not exactly a gown suitable for sending a would-be husband 'round the bend with romantic notions. But that was probably just as well because, as Ma said, I didn't want to give Phil false encouragement. At least I'd taken off my apron and hung it on the hook in the back room.

Was I treating him shabbily? I hoped not.

Too late to think about that now. I was already at Gunderson's, where Phil waited for me just outside the door. His smile would have brightened the day, if the day hadn't already been bright, the sun shining down upon us as if it had never allowed a cloud to sully its face.

"Hey, Annabelle. You're a sight for sore eyes."

"Hey, Phil." I allowed him to greet me with a discreet kiss on the cheek. It wasn't wise to do anything more than that in full daylight in the middle of town unless I wanted people telephoning my parents and tattling on me. Not that I'd ever do anything naughty. Girls who did that ended up married with babies before they were ready for either marriage or motherhood. "Mr. Juarez told me your customers are grumbling about Gunderson's being out of lumber."

Phil heaved a huge sigh. "Yeah. And the trains aren't running yet. Pete put in an order weeks ago, but God alone knows when it'll get here. In the meantime, folks are steamed. What with the condition of the roads, you can't even get to the mountains to chop your own wood."

"Face it, Phil. We live in the middle of nowhere."

"Yeah," he said, shoving his hands into his pockets after making sure he was on the outside of the boardwalk as a gentleman should be, "we do."

"I'd like to visit my brother in California one day."

"That would be nice."

I couldn't tell if he meant it or not. When I glanced at him, he appeared a little gloomy. "What's the matter, Phil? You can't be all that upset about the lumber. That's nobody's fault but God's."

"I'm not gloomy. Not about the lumber, anyhow."

"What's the matter, then?"

He scuffed his foot on the boardwalk. "Aw, Annabelle, sometimes I don't think you care for me at all."

Nuts. I didn't want to have to go reassuring Phil of my love and loyalty. Not when I wanted to concentrate on finding Mr. Calhoun's murderer. Therefore, I took his arm and gave it a squeeze. "You know that's not true, Phil. I aim to marry you one day. I'd never marry anyone I didn't care for. A lot."

Very well, so it was a weak reassurance. Besides, I had to be really careful or he'd give me up and go on to more fruitful pastures. So to speak. I'd had a scare not a month ago when I'd thought he was falling for a gorgeous woman who was in town for a tent revival. I'd been jealous, and the feeling wasn't one I cared to experience again.

Fortunately for me, we were already at the café, so Phil opened the door for me. Told you he was a gentleman. The place was full of folks we knew from town and others who were only passing through and had been caught by the floodwaters.

Blanche Wheeler, who owned and ran the place with her husband Jerome, met us at the door. A large, robust woman with bushy red hair, she was as friendly and kind as anybody. She served as an interesting contrast to her husband, who did the cooking. Jerome was so thin, you wouldn't even notice him if you saw him standing sideways, and he always frowned. Not that he was mean or anything. He just let his wife do the talking, which she did with gusto. She had a laugh that would make the grumpiest of people grin, if only behind their hands if they didn't want anyone to see. "Howdy, Phil. Hey, Miss Annabelle."

"Hey, Mrs. Wheeler. It looks like business is booming."

She grimaced. "It surely is. I'm glad to take the extra money, but I'll be gladder still when the drummers can get out of town. I'm sick of hearing them whine."

"Well," I said, feeling a stab of sympathy for the poor drummers, "you have to admit there's not a lot to do in Rosedale after you've conducted your business in town."

"You're right about that," said Mrs. Wheeler. "Looks like there's a free table over there. We're short of supplies like everybody else after that awful flood, but we have good barbecued ribs and pickled cabbage salad and potato salad." Good old cabbages and potatoes. Even during perilous times, folks had plenty of those two commodities.

By the way, the ribs of which Mrs. Wheeler spoke, and of which I aimed to partake, were good old beef ribs. I understand in other parts of the country folks barbecued pork ribs, and I'm sure they're tasty, too, but we ate beef. I guess it was out of some sort of loyalty to the reason the town was here in the first place. Or maybe not. All's I know is that they were absolutely delicious, and my mouth was already watering.

I glanced around the place. It was full of diners, but the person I wanted to see and talk to was Sadie Dobbs. I asked Mrs. Wheeler, "Is Sadie Dobbs working today?"

"She's working her fingers to the bone, poor thing. We've never been this busy. Well, not since rodeo season, anyhow." Then she gave one of her big bellowing laughs, rodeo season having been a mere month earlier.

So we sat at the only free table in the place, and pretty soon Sadie Dobbs sidled up to us, pad and pencil in hand. The Cowboy Café didn't go in for fancy things like menus. If you didn't like ribs, steaks, sandwiches or potato salad, you had to take yourself and your dining tastes elsewhere; elsewhere being one of the hotels in town, and their restaurants were too expensive for the likes of Phil and me.

"Morning," said Sadie, not sounding at all interested in us, the morning or anything else.

I studied her face and noticed that she appeared a little puffy around the eyes. Hmm. What did that mean? Had she been crying for her dead lover? For that matter, had she truly loved Mr. Calhoun, whom most folks found quite unlovable? Or was she only sad because she'd lost her sugar daddy, a vulgar term my mother would slap my face for saying. But I was only thinking it, so it didn't count.

Phil glanced at me and I nodded. He told Sadie, "We'll take the ribs, cabbage and potato salad. And I'll take coffee." He tilted his head toward me, and I nodded again.

"Right," said Sadie, and she sashayed off.

Dang it, how was I going to interrogate the woman if she was working all the time? I didn't know her. I couldn't just bark a bunch of questions at her as she served our lunch, could I? Puzzled, I fiddled with the flatware on the table, which was covered with an oilcloth that either Mrs. Wheeler or Sadie had wiped off after the last diner at the table had vacated the premises. Although the Cowboy Café was a busy place, Mrs. Wheeler made sure it was clean and tidy.

"So, tell me, Annabelle, why'd you *really* want to come here today?" asked Phil.

His words startled me, and I nearly broke my neck lifting my head to stare at him. "What do you mean?"

"I meant what I said. How come you really wanted to come here today? Don't bother telling me because you crave my company. I know you too well for that. And it's not just so I could tell you about what I learned at the bank, either, because I could have come to your house to do that when I pick you up to go to the pictures tomorrow night."

Blast. I'd been caught. Well, since Phil had already agreed to help in my . . . I mean *the* investigation, I figured I might as well tell him the truth. "Betty Lou Jarvis told me Mr. Calhoun and Sadie Dobbs had been having a . . . a love affair. She's the waitress who just took our order. I was hoping to get to talk to her, but it doesn't look like that's going to happen. At least not now."

After glancing around the jam-packed café, Phil said, "Sure doesn't. Boy, Annabelle, you sure know how to make a guy feel special, you know that?"

I took his hand across the table. "I'm sorry, Phil. I know it seems like I'm only interested in solving the Calhoun murder, and I know you don't think I have any business butting into the case at all, but you have to understand that we Blues have a huge stake in the matter. Chief Vickers might actually arrest my brother-in-law if nobody better shows up. Surely you can understand why I need to . . . to . . ." Darn. I hated the word that popped into my head. But I said it anyway. ". . . meddle."

"I don't believe the chief would arrest Richard unless he had a darned good reason, Annabelle."

"When he talked to me, he sounded as if he thinks he *has* a good reason, Phil. Don't you see that? According to what Chief Vickers told me, Richard and Mr. Calhoun were forever having arguments at the bank, which means they disagreed about something, and it must have been important because Richard wouldn't fight with his boss unless he had a good reason. He's too much of a stuffed shirt to jeopardize his job without whatever it was about being really important."

"You really have a way with words. You know that?"

I could feel my cheeks heat. Or maybe the heat came from the crowded café. Naw. I was blushing. "Well, he is a stuffed shirt, Phil. Even you must know that."

"All right, all right. Your brother-in-law is boring, but he's in peril so we have to rescue him. Do I have that right?"

"Exactly," I said, happy that Phil seemed to be on my side at last.

"But what I'm going to tell you doesn't look good for him."

My bubble burst with a soggy pop. "What do you mean?"

"According to the fellows at the bank, Mr. Calhoun and Richard didn't merely argue, they yelled at each other. Everyone could hear them hollering even through Calhoun's closed office door. This had been going on for a couple of weeks before Calhoun was killed, and nobody knows why, although—this will make you happy—they're all on Richard's side. The bank's trustees are meeting to go over the books right now. If they find Mr. Calhoun's been fiddling with the books, that'll still look bad for Richard, because it'll give him a motive to have killed him, although he'd probably just have reported him to the trustees. But if Mr. Calhoun threatened him with anything, I guess Richard might have . . . well, you know."

"What could he have threatened Richard with?"

"How should I know? That's all I could find out. Nobody knew any specifics or they'd have told me. They don't want Richard to get into trouble. They all hated Calhoun and are hoping Richard will step in to fill his shoes."

"Crumb."

"The only other piece of information I came away with probably doesn't mean anything."

"What is it? Anything at all might help."

"The man who works at the shoe store? Firman Meeks? He spent a long time talking with Mr. Calhoun in his office a couple of weeks ago. That's just about the same time Richard and Mr. Calhoun started being on such bad terms."

I wrinkled my nose. "Firman Meeks? Is he that ferret-faced guy who's kind of stooped and wears those ugly checked suits?"

Phil clearly didn't care for my description of Mr. Meeks because he rolled his eyes. "Yes, although what his face and his clothes have to do with anything, I don't know."

"I was only trying to place him," said I, feeling defensive.

"He was probably only applying for a loan or something. I think he's seeing your friend Betty Lou. Maybe he wants to buy a house and set up housekeeping with her."

"Betty Lou is seeing a drip like him?"

"Annabelle." Phil had on his most disapproving expression, and I guess I hadn't been very polite. Besides, a girl in Rosedale didn't have much to choose from. If Betty Lou found Mr. Meeks amiable, who was I to quibble?

"Sorry." Boy, what a discouraging investigation this had been so far.

Our lunches came then, and my stomach took the opportunity to growl. Fortunately, there was so much noise from chitchat in the café, no one noticed. At least I hope they didn't.

Lunch was delicious, and bless Phil's heart, he paid for it, which made me feel guilty again since I'd all but forced him into taking me to the café that day. On the way out, I passed by Sadie Dobbs. Since she wasn't holding any dishes in her arms or anything, I did something impulsive. Phil would tell you I'm always doing impulsive stuff, but that's not true. Anyhow, I stopped and spoke to her.

She turned and stared at me as if I had two heads, I guess because she wasn't accustomed to being spoken to by people she didn't know. She was a pretty girl, not much older than me, which gave me pause, since Mr. Calhoun had been an old coot. The notion of him and her doing intimate things together was . . . unpleasant to say the least.

"Miss Dobbs?"

I heard Phil grumble, "Annabelle . . ."

I ignored him.

"Yes?"

Sadie Dobbs wore more makeup than most of the girls I knew, but I aimed to withhold judgment until I knew her better. If she'd let me, that is. "Would it be all right if I came by after you get off work and have a few words with you?"

"A few words? Why?"

"It's about an important matter I can't go into here and now. What time do you get off work?"

Still gaping at me as if she thought I was insane, or maybe some religious zealot who aimed to witness to her, she hesitated. "Well . . . I don't know."

"I promise I won't take much of your time."

"Oh, all right. But right now I have work to do. As you can see." She swept her arm out in a gesture meant to encompass the packed café and darned near clobbered a customer.

"Right. What time do you get off work?"

"Today I'll probably have to work late. Maybe seven? Are you the girl who works at the grocery store up the street?"

"That's me, all right." I gave her a big smile and stuck out my hand. "Annabelle Blue."

"Huh." She gave me a limp handshake. "Sadie Dobbs."

"Thank you *very* much for agreeing to see me, Miss Dobbs. I'll come by at seven."

"All right." And she walked off, looking as dubious about a proposed meeting as anyone could.

"Jeez, Annabelle, you just bull your way in, don't you?" grumbled Phil as we exited the restaurant and walked back toward Gunderson's.

"Darn it, Phil, I need to find out who killed Mr. Calhoun. Even you say it looks bad for Richard. I need to gather all the information I can."

"Because you don't trust the police to do their job."

I felt like stamping my foot, but I was an adult so I didn't. "Listen, unless Chief Vickers is a whole lot smarter than I think he is, the murder might very well be pinned on Richard. Even you found evidence against him."

With a shrug, Phil said, "I wouldn't exactly call what I heard evidence. Anyhow, maybe he did do it."

"Phil Gunderson! He didn't!"

"Don't have a fit, Annabelle."

"Richard would never kill anyone."

Phil held his hands up as if he were surrendering to a bandit. "All right. I don't want to argue with you. Will you still go to the pictures with me tomorrow, or are you mad at me now?"

"No, I'm not mad at you," I told him, lying through my teeth. I was not only mad at Phil but scared to death. If Phil considered Richard even a remote candidate as murderer, things looked really bad for my brother-in-law. "And I'll . . . oh, wait a minute."

"Here it comes," muttered Phil.

"No it doesn't," I snapped. "I forgot that Ma told me Richard and Hannah are coming to supper tomorrow night. Maybe Saturday would be better. Would that be all right with you?"

"I guess so. When's the funeral? Do you know?"

"I haven't looked at the obits in the paper yet today. Heck, the arrangements probably aren't in today's paper anyway. I sure read a whole lot of lies about Mr. Calhoun, though."

"Lies?"

"Yeah. According to the *Record*, Mr. Calhoun had a heart of gold and never did a bad thing in his life."

"And you know better?"

"The man's been dead for a day, and already I've met three people who've accused him of cheating them or people they know and one who equated him with Satan. I've told you this before now, Phil. Why are you being so obstreperous?"

"I don't even know what that means, but if it means I think you're nuts to pursue a criminal investigation on your own—especially one that involves murder—then I'm being whatever that word is because I don't want anything bad to happen to you. For the good Lord's sake, Annabelle, use the brain God gave you!"

"Blast you, Phil Gunderson, I *am* using my brain! That's why I'm not going to quit until I've cleared Richard of any implication in that horrible man's death. Even if the police never arrest him, unless the true killer is found, people will always look at Richard with suspicion, and that's not fair!"

"Right."

And Phil opened the door to his brother's hardware store without a glance back at me and disappeared inside, leaving me standing there on the boardwalk and feeling as if my last friend on earth had deserted me.

CHAPTER SEVEN

I felt pretty gloomy for the rest of that day, but I did manage to slip on my coat and sneak out of the house after supper a little before seven o'clock and hurry to the Cowboy Café to speak with Sadie Dobbs. I hoped she'd meant it when she'd told me to come by at that time.

During November in Rosedale, New Mexico—well, I guess in most places—night comes early. Unfortunately for us residents of Rosedale, streetlights were a thing of the future. Talk about your basic pitch-black night. I took one of those battery-powered flashlight things with me, but my footing was still iffy, and the boardwalk, which had swollen in spots during the recent downpour, tried to trip me up several times. Shady lumps showed up on the periphery of my sight, and I jumped every now and then, thinking someone was looming at me. The moon was almost gone, and what little there was of it was clouded over. No stars twinkled down upon yours truly. It was dark. Black-dark. Scary-dark.

However, I finally got to the bridge, crossed it, and made my way to the Cowboy Café at approximately the correct time. A single light still burned in the café's window, and I was surprised but very happy when I saw Sadie Dobbs, wrapped in what looked like a very old coat, leaning against the building and smoking a cigarette. Don't ask me why, but her smoking shocked me almost as much as the notion of her having an affair with Mr. Calhoun. According to the newspapers and magazines, the decade in which we lived was supposed to be roaring, what with illegal liquor and short skirts (and short hair) and gang warfare and stuff like that in other parts of the country. But Rosedale was a backwater, most folks took Prohibition seriously, and ladies didn't smoke. Anyhow, Sadie had short dark hair, bobbed into the latest style, and I'd noticed earlier in the day that she had pretty brown eyes, enhanced by heavy makeup.

Not that I'd allow being shocked to stop me. "Thank you so much for meeting me, Miss Dobbs," said I as I approached her.

She tossed her cigarette aside and said, "Oh, for God's sake, call me Sadie. Unless you're going to preach at me. If that's the case, I'm walking right now."

"No. I'm not going to preach at you. And please call me Annabelle." Although I'd just as soon my parents had named me something else. But they hadn't, so I was stuck with Annabelle. "I just wanted to ask you a couple of questions."

"About what?"

I took a deep breath and took the plunge. "About Mr. Edgar Calhoun."

And darned if she didn't break down and start crying. Right there on the boardwalk. I felt like a worm. "Oh, crumb, Sadie, I'm sorry. I didn't mean to hurt your feelings."

She waved away my apology, grabbed a hankie from her ancient coat pocket, and blew her nose. "It's all right," she said thickly. "Everyone else in this stupid town has been eyeing me as if they consider me no better than a damned whore. At least you're willing to talk to me."

Shocked again—ladies not only didn't smoke, they also didn't swear or say words like *whore*—I patted her on the back and said, "I'm trying very hard to determine who could have killed Mr. Calhoun."

Over the handkerchief, which she still had pressed to her

face, she peered at me with watery eyes. "The coppers have already talked to me. I couldn't tell them anything except that Edgar was kind to me. And he *was*, damn it! It's hard for a girl to make it on her own. I suppose you have a nice family and everything?" Her tone was bitter.

"Yes," I admitted. I decided she didn't need to know about my stinky brother, since she seemed to have bigger problems even than a lousy brother to deal with. "And I'm sorry you're having a hard time. Are you on your own in the world?" Gee, that sounded dramatic. But still, I felt a little sorry for the poor girl, especially if she'd been desperate enough to fall for a creep like Mr. Calhoun.

"My parents are dead, and I don't have any other relations who are worth spit."

Ew. "You aren't from here, are you?"

She glanced around, although, as I said, she couldn't see anything because night had fallen and covered the whole town like an ebony blanket. "God, no. Why would anybody want to live here?"

Good question. "Well, lots of cattle ranchers and farmers live in the area. It's good for that, I guess."

"Why are you here?"

"Because my family is here."

"But don't you want to better yourself?" I think she shuddered, although I couldn't really see well enough to tell. "I can't imagine a young man or woman actually *wanting* to live in this place."

"Better myself? Is that what you're doing?" I didn't mean to sound snotty, but really. I wasn't overly fond of my hometown, but I didn't like it when outsiders criticized it. "Is that why you started . . . um, seeing Mr. Calhoun?"

"Yes!" she said, sounding about as stormy as the weather a couple of nights ago. "Yes, that's why I started seeing him. He gave me things. He gave me money. He was nice to me! I was saving money to go to California."

"Oh. You have plans to move to California? My brother lives there."

"Lucky him," she said savagely. "I want to get into the pictures, but in order to do that you have to be in New York or California. California's closer to where I come from."

"Where's that?"

"Lubbock, Texas. It's almost as pitiful as Rosedale, New Mexico."

"Ah. And you're working your way west?" Sounded to me as if she'd chosen a hard path, but I wasn't about to judge her, even if I thought having affairs with married men wasn't proper. As my very kindhearted mother was wont to say, one never knows what another person is going through at any given time, so it's always best to give them the benefit of the doubt. So I tried to do that. With Miss Dobbs. Miss Libby'd already earned my distaste twenty times over.

"Trying to," she said, blowing her nose again and straightening up. "I was crushed when I learned of Edgar's death. Like I said, he was good to me."

Yeah? What about his wife and children? Did she ever think about what he might be depriving them of when he gave her money and presents? Naturally, I didn't ask.

She might have been reading my mind. "And you can blame me all you want for running around with a married man. His wife treated him like dirt, and his kids are spoiled brats who don't give two figs for him. All they ever wanted from him was his money. At least I treated him good. And he returned the favor."

"I see. And do you have any idea who might have shot him?"

"No. If I did, I'd shoot *him*."

Volatile female, Sadie Dobbs. "Mr. Calhoun never talked

about having any enemies or anything like that?"

"Well, there was a guy who worked at his bank who was giving him grief. Richard something-or-other, I think his name was."

Egad. I didn't like the sound of that.

"And another guy, the guy who owns the car dealership? Mr. Calhoun said he'd been giving him a hard time."

I hate pronouns. It was so hard to know who was giving whom a hard time in Sadie's sentence. So I asked. "You mean Mr. Calhoun was giving Mr. Contreras a bad time, or the other way around?"

She looked at me blankly, then said, "Oh. The car guy was giving Eddie a bad time."

Eddie? Shoot, it was hard for me to envision Mr. Calhoun as an Eddie. I didn't say so. "I see. Do you know why that was?"

"Something about a loan he didn't want to pay." She shrugged. "I don't know. I didn't pay any attention when he talked about business. It was boring."

To her, maybe. But I wished that night, as I stood on the boardwalk with her, that she'd taken notes. "Hmm. Maybe I should go talk to Armando tomorrow."

"Whoever Armando is."

"The car guy," I said to enlighten her. "Did Mr. Calhoun mention any other names? In any context at all?"

Another shrug. "I can't remember. He complained about a lot of people not liking him."

Big help. "Well, thanks for talking to me, Sadie. I appreciate your time. If you can think of anything else—a name, an incident, anything at all—please let me know. I work behind the counter at Blue's six days a week."

"All right," she said, sounding sorry I aimed to leave.

I guess she didn't have any friends in town, poor thing. "Or if you just want to come in and pass the time of day, feel free. I'm almost always there. Well, except when I go to the library or something like that."

"Why are you interested in Edgar's death?" she asked at last. I was surprised she'd waited so long.

"Because the Richard of whom you spoke is my brother-in-law, and I'm afraid the police suspect him of killing Mr. Calhoun. But I know he didn't do it and am trying to figure out who did."

"How come you're sure he didn't do it?"

I decided to tell her the truth. "Because my brother-in-law, Richard MacDougall, is the stuffiest, most boring man on the face of the earth. He'd faint dead away if somebody ever even handed him a gun. He'd never shoot one."

"Jeez, you don't sound like you like him much. Why bother trying to clear him?"

"Because I love my sister Hannah, who's married to him. Besides, even though he's uninspiring, he's not a bad man, and it would be an egregious miscarriage of justice if the police arrested him for a murder he didn't commit."

"Yeah?"

Sadie appeared a teensy bit confused. I guess she didn't care much for ten-dollar words. Well, that didn't matter. She could figure it out for herself. "Yes. I truly appreciate your willingness to talk to me, Sadie." Something occurred to me. "Say, where do you live?" Rosedale wasn't bursting with apartment buildings.

"I'm renting a room from Mr. and Mrs. O'Dell. It's a little apartment over their stable. It's not much, but it'll do me until I save enough to move on."

"I see. Well, good luck to you. I hope you make it to California. And don't forget to come and see me if you need to talk or if you remember any names or anything like that."

"I will." And she turned to walk off.

"Wait a minute," said I, compassion compelling me. "Don't you have a flashlight or anything?"

I heard a huge sigh. "No. I know where the O'Dell place is. I can probably feel my way there."

Have I mentioned it was dark? Well, it was. Impenetrably dark. Dark as soot. Dark as a black boot.

"Why don't I walk with you? We can use my flashlight, and it'll be easier to avoid mud puddles and stuff like that."

A silence greeted this offer. Then Sadie said, "Well, if you're sure you don't mind. I've been meaning to get a flashlight or at least carry a lantern with me, but I didn't think I'd have to work this late today. Thanks, Miss Blue."

"Annabelle," I corrected her. And I flipped on my flashlight once more and led the way to the O'Dells' home, which wasn't too far from the café, on South Washington Avenue.

Luckily for us, Washington, like Lee, was where the wealthier element in town lived, and it had a paved sidewalk. Stairs from the boardwalk led down to it. It was a good thing Sadie had taken me up on my offer, because there were still perilous spots where vegetation had clumped up. Whoever'd had the bright idea to import Russian thistles to the United States should have had to walk with us that gloomy night. Huge piles of tumbleweeds, looking as though they'd been woven together by a herd of spiders once we got close enough to see them, blocked the sidewalk and we had to shove them aside, covering ourselves with mud and prickles in the process, to get to the O'Dells' place. Even without piles of tumbleweeds, the night was darker than the inside of a cow and it was difficult for us to see anything until we'd plowed into it.

"Shoot," I muttered after we'd manhandled one gigantic alp of tangled tumbleweeds, "how'd you manage to get to work this morning? Were these piles here then?"

"No. I guess someone plowed the road and pushed them up onto the sidewalk."

"Stupid town," I muttered.

Sadie barked a short laugh. "Exactly my thoughts."

So there you go. We both thought Rosedale was a stupid place to live, even though I didn't like hearing her opinion expressed aloud.

I left her at the stable and did my best to light her way with my flashlight as she tiptoed through it and went to the stairs to her apartment. The O'Dell place had been hit hard by the storm, and the stable remained a mess. I guess Mr. O'Dell had been concentrating on his chicken coop and flooded basement. He'd better work on the stable next, or poor Sadie was going to have a hard time maneuvering through the muck in order to get to work on the morrow.

During the summertime when we got floods, the water dried up pretty quickly, both because the weather was so hot and because the cyclonic winds sucked the moisture out of the ground, not to mention Rosedale's residents, in a day or so. These freakish autumn storms took longer to dry out because the weather remained cool. I hoped that by Saturday, when Phil picked me up to go to the flickers, we wouldn't have to avoid mud on our way. In fact, it would be pretty keen if he drove the Model T Ford he'd recently bought from his brother. Pretty soon a body would be able to buy an automobile, if he wanted one, from Armando Contreras—to whom I needed to talk soon.

As I walked home, staring eagle-eyed into the thin beam of light leading my way and hoping I wouldn't trip over something and fall flat on my face, I thought about Sadie Dobbs. Poor girl. I knew she'd done a bad thing by carrying on with Mr. Calhoun, but I still couldn't help but feel for her. Heck, she probably wouldn't even dare go to the funeral—and so far she seemed to be the only person in town who genuinely grieved Mr. Calhoun's passing—and that included his family.

Speaking of which . . . after I got home again, I asked Ma,

"Has anyone telephoned to give you the particulars on the Calhoun funeral?" I could probably read about them in tomorrow's newspaper, but I was curious.

"Yes. Mrs. Howell called a while ago. The funeral's going to be held on Monday afternoon at South Park Cemetery after a short service at the Presbyterian Church. Two o'clock. We'll close the store for a couple of hours."

That was customary. Everyone who was anybody rated a store-closing so people could attend his or her funeral. I was sure Mr. Pruitt would close his store, too, so Myrtle would be able to attend the obsequies.

"Will there be a get-together at the Calhoun home after the burial?"

"Yes."

That, too, was typical. It was almost akin to holding a party for the deceased, only he wouldn't be there to enjoy it. I wondered if his children and wife would. Enjoy the party, I mean. I aimed to look very closely at the attendees at that reception.

"Where were you, Annabelle? All of a sudden, you were gone when I looked for you after the dishes were done."

"I just went out for a little walk," I told my mother.

"A *walk?* In this weather in these conditions? Are you out of your mind?"

"No, I'm not out of my mind, and yes, I took a walk." That wasn't much of a lie. "I felt a little headachy, and walks generally help headaches." That was almost true.

"She probably went out to smooch with Phil now that he's staying in town," said Jack, proving once again that he was not merely obnoxious, but wrong.

"I did not!"

"Jack, that's enough," Ma said, bless her.

"Why else would she go outside in the middle of November

when it's all cold and dark and muddy?" Jack asked, sticking his tongue out at me in the process.

"What I do is none of your business," I told him. "I'm going to go read in my room now, Ma. Do you need me to do anything first?" Virtue was my middle name. Actually, my middle name was Grace, but what the heck.

"No thank you, Annabelle. I'm going to darn some socks, but you go on and read."

Shoot. One more example of a woman's work never being done.

At that moment, Pa came into the house through the back door. He scraped his boots off, grumbling as he did so. "Blasted mud. I hate autumn storms."

See what I mean? If you have to live in a place that floods, make sure it's a place that's hot and dry most of the time. And windy. The winds are really good at drying up mud and water. Say, I just thought of a good reason to live in Rosedale! When we got flooded out, the water didn't remain around long enough, even in the fall, so that things got moldy. Very well, maybe it's not a big virtue, but it's a virtue nonetheless.

"Is everything all right now, William?" Ma asked him.

"Yeah. I think so."

"What were you doing, Pa?" I asked.

"Putting a strip of rubber around the door to the stone cooler. Trying to make it more weather-tight so it won't flood so easily in the future."

"Good idea." I eyed my indolent brother, attempting to figure out why Pa hadn't roped him into helping. That question was answered a moment later when Mayberry Zink, my sister Zilpha's husband, followed Pa into the house.

"Hey, Mayberry," I told him, smiling. I really liked him. Not only was he a good-hearted fellow, but he had a sense of humor my other brother-in-law lacked. Also, he was helpful and knew how to do things. Witness the present circumstance.

"Hey, Annabelle. Where've you been?"

So how come my absence was such a hot topic of conversation that evening? "Just went outside for a bit."

"She was smooching with Phil," said Jack, snickering.

"Stop that right now, Jack," Pa said. Thank God. Once Pa began giving orders, even Jack paid attention. Most of the time.

"I only went for a walk," I said, eyeing my brother with loathing. To change the subject, I said, "How's Zilpha doing? She was pretty sick last time I talked to her."

"She's feeling better now," said Mayberry, beaming at the prospect of becoming a papa. He'd make a good one; I felt it in my bones.

"I'm glad to hear that."

"Have some cake, you men. You deserve it after all the work you've done on the cooler." Ma bustled off to the kitchen, and I decided to put off my reading for a while, until I found out what kind of cake she was offering.

This turned out to be a wise move on my part, because Ma took down the coconut cake she must have baked that very night while I was out chatting with Sadie Dobbs. I love coconut cake, but I wasn't sure she should be giving us all slices of it. Had she baked the cake instead of a squash pie for Richard and Hannah's dinner on Friday?

"May I have a piece?" I asked hesitantly, not wanting to seem piggish. "I'm surprised you're letting anyone eat this before tomorrow night."

Ma heaved a sigh. "I forgot Richard doesn't like coconut until I'd already frosted the stupid thing. So we might as well eat it up, and I'll make something else for tomorrow night."

"I thought you were going to make a squash pie."

"I was, but I'm going to be making a lot of those for Thanksgiving and Christmas, and I don't want everyone to be tired of them. I only wish I'd remembered Richard's aversion to coconut before I made this cake."

God bless Richard and his pickiness—and Ma's forgetfulness. The cake was delicious, and it went down really well with a glass of milk. Even my obnoxious brother complimented our mother on the cake's overall delectability. If that's a word.

"Thank you all," said Ma, executing a curtsey. "But now I don't know what kind of cake to make for dessert tomorrow."

Jack, who was a connoisseur of all things sweet, instantly offered suggestions. "Chocolate! Or marble. Or that kind with the pineapple on the bottom."

"Hmm," said Ma, musing as she chewed. "Pineapple upside-down cake isn't sophisticated enough for Richard, I fear."

She was probably right. I don't know where Ma got the recipe for it, but I loved it. However, she made it in a cast-iron skillet, and I guess that put it in a category too humble for Richard.

"If Richard can't eat what's put before him in our house, he can eat somewhere else," growled Pa, who didn't care for people putting on airs.

"I know that, dear," said Ma, patting his hand.

"Richard's an all-right guy," said Mayberry, who seemed to like everyone. That's probably why everybody liked him. "Although I know what you mean. But he's not really snooty. He just has to dress up and act that way for his job." He swallowed a bite of cake and a sip of milk. "Speaking of which, Zilpha and Hannah have been on the telephone most of the day today talking about Mr. Calhoun's murder. Hannah's scared to death the police are going to pin it on Richard, and that's flat stupid."

"I agree," said I. I was going to go on and say I was doing some investigative work on the case myself, but common sense smacked me upside the head and I held my tongue. Neither Ma nor Pa would countenance me going around asking snoopy questions of Rosedale's citizens, even if my rudeness was for a good cause.

Pa shook his head. "I don't think Richard even owns a gun. He never goes hunting. Besides, he would no more shoot a man in cold blood than I would."

"Exactly," said Mayberry. "Say, Susanna"—Ma had told both of her sons-in-law and her daughter-in-law to call her Susanna, mainly because that was her name—"I don't suppose I could take a piece of that wonderful cake home to your daughter, could I? She might like a little snack. If it don't make her sick, of course, but she's mainly sick in the mornings."

Even after I'd had an adventure or two, succumbed to the inevitable and married Phil, I was going to think long and hard before I had any kids. Not only was the process of getting them into this world sickening and painful, but with my luck, I'd end up with a monster like Jack. I'd have to discuss this matter with Phil when the time seemed appropriate.

"Of course. I'll pack up two pieces. One for Zilpha and another for you, Mayberry. You deserve it after coming to the rescue with that rubber stripping."

"Thanks. I hope it does the job."

"Me too," growled Pa, who didn't like having his regular routine messed up by storms and floods and so forth.

After Mayberry left for home, Ma and I cleaned up the cake plates and glasses, and I finally retired to my room. I'd finished *Powder and Patch* and moved on to *The Breaking Point*, by Mary Roberts Rinehart, the last book in my stack. Time for another trip to the library. Maybe tomorrow. After I talked to Armando Contreras.

CHAPTER EIGHT

Ma solved the problem of dessert Friday night by making floating island, which consisted of fluffy little baked meringues on a sea of soft custard. Another of my favorites. Not only that, but there was enough coconut cake left over from last night's snacking to have at lunch that day. Life was good. So was lunch. And there was still one teensy piece of coconut cake leftover.

However, that didn't negate the problem of clearing my brother-in-law in the case of Mr. Calhoun's murder.

Therefore, in the early afternoon when I asked Ma if I could take off for a little bit and walk to the library, praying the streets between our house and the Carnegie Library on Third and Richardson were dry enough to walk upon, and she agreed, I made a wee stop at Armando Contreras's business, which was soon to be called the Contreras Motor Works, on my way. Before Richard made the loan to Armando, if you wanted to buy a machine, you had to go all the way to El Paso, Albuquerque or Santa Fe, and everyone was looking forward to the grand opening in January 1924.

I was lucky in the mud department. A brisk wind had blown through overnight and dried up most of the remaining water. The unpaved streets now looked as if they were built of big, uneven brown paving stones, all cracked and ragged. There were a few muddy spots toward the curbs, but I managed to o'erleap them, as Shakespeare might have said. Or maybe that was Charlotte Bronte in *Jane Eyre*. Well, I don't suppose it matters. Leaping wasn't much fun, since I carried a heavy bag full of books, but I did it anyway.

Armando's wife Josephine, who looked as if she'd been trying to pick up leftover storm debris, met me at one of the gasoline pumps when I walked onto what was planned to be the car dealership's lot. It might be fun to own an automobile, but at the moment I was happy to be allowed to drive my parents' Model T when I could. Jack resented the fact that I was allowed to drive and he wasn't. But, for heaven's sake, he was only twelve. And it wasn't as if we lived on a ranch or a farm where kids were allowed to drive tractors and things because they were actually helping their parents with the family business. Jack just wanted to drive for the heck of it. He was *such* a louse.

"Hey, Annabelle. Wasn't that a storm we had?"

"It sure was. Did you guys have any damage?"

Josephine gave a grimace and waved at the lot, upon which sat several automobiles already, although the Contrerases didn't aim to begin selling them for another couple of months. "I'll say we did. The hail dented a Ford and an Oldsmobile in several spots. Armando is trying to figure out how much we'll have to reduce the prices on them so people will still buy the machines."

"Golly, Josephine, I'm sorry to hear that." It had never occurred to me that an automobile dealer's business might be hurt by hail, but it made sense.

"Some days this place leaks money," she said in a sour voice. "Other times it's a gold mine. We about break even, all things considered. When the dealership opens, I expect we'll start making more money."

"I'm glad of that, and discounting for dents is probably better than losing sales altogether. Say, is Armando here? I have a couple of questions to ask him."

Josephine, a nice woman, who was plump and friendly—and whom I'd believed had been carrying on a torrid affair with my brother-in-law Richard only a month before, about which I was glad to have been proved wrong—said, "Sure is. Go along to the office. Buying a car, are you? We can give you a good deal on a Ford with hail dents on the hood." She laughed heartily.

I joined in. We both knew that clerking at my parents' store didn't pay me enough to afford a car, even a dented one. "Sure. I'll buy one for me, and maybe I'll get one for Jack. With any luck, he'd drive himself off Mescalero Ridge and we'll be rid of him forever." Unkind, Annabelle. Still, one couldn't help but dream of happier times.

"You only wish," said Josephine, who had a younger brother of her own. "Say, Annabelle, Armando said you're the one who found Mr. Calhoun's body. That must have been a shock."

"It was. Actually, that's why I want to talk to Armando."

"About finding the body?"

"No. I'm afraid the police are thinking about accusing Richard as the killer, and I need to find out more about Mr. Calhoun's business dealings. So far, I've heard he was a real crook."

Josephine snorted. "You can say that again. Go ahead. Mando can tell you all about the loan Richard got us for this dealership and how Mr. Calhoun tried to take it over and nearly made us lose the place."

"Good Lord, really?"

"Really. And we're not the only ones in town he messed with. The man was a criminal and should have been locked up. Of course, then his family would have been humiliated. It wouldn't surprise me if one of them bumped him off before the cops could get at him."

"Interesting theory, and one I've considered. All I know for sure is that Richard didn't do it."

Shaking her head and grinning, Josephine said, "No. I can't quite picture Richard shooting anybody."

She chuckled, and I walked over to the office where Armando sat, working on a long row of figures. Ugh. Math. My least favorite subject in school. Too bad I had to use it at work. He glanced up from his figures and seemed relieved to see me. Guess he didn't care much for math either.

"Hey, Annabelle. Whatcha got in the bag?"

He waved me to a chair in front of his desk, and I sat, plunking my book bag on my lap. What a relief! My poor arm was aching. "Books. I'm on my way to the library, but I wanted to stop by here and ask you a few questions about Mr. Calhoun."

"That son of a b—buck."

No hiding his feelings in the Calhoun department. "Josephine said something about him taking over the loan Richard arranged for you to buy the car dealership."

"He sure did. Then he called in the loan. It took Richard and me both, along with Mr. Jaffa—"

"The lawyer?"

"That's the one. I had to hire him, but he was worth the money. Calhoun backed off once I got a lawyer on my side. I don't think Calhoun fiddling with Richard's loan sat well with your brother-in-law."

"I'm sure it didn't, although I didn't know about it until you and Josephine told me."

"Well, we're not the only folks in town Calhoun tried to cheat, believe me. I don't blame somebody for shooting the bast— buzzard in the back."

"Yeah, Mr. Tindall said Calhoun cheated him out of his ranch. Do you have any idea how he might have done that?"

"Probably some fancy financial footwork like he tried with me. Josephine and me, we're lucky because the gasoline station's done real good—until that damned storm, anyhow. Sorry, Annabelle. But we could afford to hire Mr. Jaffa. But Tindall . . . well, most of the ranchers hereabouts are only hanging on by their fingernails. I know there are some big outfits, like your friend Phil Gunderson's place, but most of 'em are small potatoes, and it wouldn't take much to make 'em lose everything. It makes me sick to know that folks like Calhoun, who already have everything, try to cheat people who don't have the bucks to fight back."

"Me too."

He shook his head, and I shook my head, and we sat there in silent contemplation of the evils of certain people, until I decided I'd rested long enough and stood, heaving my bag up with me.

"You must read a lot," Armando commented.

"I do. But I think I'm going to go a little easier on the books today. I don't mind walking to the library more often if it'll lighten my load on the way back. I'm going to have shoulders like a football player's pretty soon if I keep this up."

"You any good at arithmetic?" he asked out of the blue.

"Lousy," I said with the utmost truth.

"Too bad. Do you think if I reduced the price of a machine ten dollars per dent, folks would go for it?"

"I don't know, but it sounds like a good deal to me. If you find one that has five or six hundred dents in it, let me know, will you?"

Armando laughed, and I left his office, walked across the lot, waved good-bye to Josephine, who waved back, and tramped on up the street to the library, where I didn't go easier on the books, darn it. Then I had to carry them all back home again.

"I think I'm going to sew another handle on my book bag," I told Ma when I reentered the store. "That way I can sling a handle over each shoulder and maybe this bag won't feel so heavy."

Ma shook her head. "I swear, Annabelle, I'm surprised that little library has enough books to satisfy you, you read so many of them."

"Naw. They manage to keep up with me. Miss Whitesmith is always holding new books for me, bless her."

"I'm glad you have a friend in Miss Whitesmith. I suppose there are lots of worse habits a person can have than reading."

Yeah. Like trying to cheat innocent people out of their livelihoods. I didn't say that, because the comment might have prompted questions from Ma that I didn't want to answer.

"Take over the counter now, please, Annabelle. I'm going to the house to get dinner started. I made the floating island this morning, but I have to cut the okra and get the potatoes ready to go in the oven. I'll slip the ham in now." She glanced at the clock, which said it was now two-thirty in the afternoon. "It's a big one and will take some time. And those potatoes take a lot of time, too."

"What time's dinner?"

"Six."

"Oh, boy, I can hardly wait. In fact, I'm hungry now."

"Well, eat a pickle from the barrel," said Ma as she bustled off.

Hmm. I was hoping for that last teensy piece of coconut cake, but you can't have everything. A pickle and a couple of crackers from the appropriate barrels staved off the pangs of starvation, and I managed to make it through the rest of the day.

That evening shortly after Jack and I locked up the store and closed the shutters—Jack's job, and he did it for once without complaint—Hannah and Richard showed up at the house, Richard carrying a bouquet of chrysanthemums for Ma.

"Oh, how nice!" said Ma, taking the flowers and glancing at me.

I went to the cupboard and got down a vase and filled it with water. Then, while Ma fussed around the kitchen—I'd already set the table in the dining room, but, by informal tradition, everyone in the extended family gathered in the kitchen before meals—I snipped stems and stripped leaves and listened as Richard told us about his harrowing couple of days at the bank.

"It was pretty awful," said he. Hannah held his hand, to give him comfort I suppose. "The shock of Mr. Calhoun's death affected all of us. The trustees met to go over the books, and they balanced out all right."

I noticed, from my position at the sink, that his brow furrowed, so I asked a pointed question. "You don't look as if you believe the trustees or the books, Richard. Why is that?"

Shooting me a frown, he nevertheless answered my question. "Well, I don't suppose it's a secret any longer that Mr. Calhoun and I have been having our differences lately. I'd have been willing to swear that he'd been doctoring the books somehow, but it looks as if I was wrong about that, because the bank's records balanced perfectly."

"That's odd, because I hear he's been cheating people right and left," I said, earning another frown from my brother-in-law. "Armando Contreras said Mr. Calhoun bollixed up the loan you arranged for the car dealership, and that it took you and Mr. Jaffa to straighten everything out."

This time Ma and Pa frowned at me, too. "Have you been nosing around about this Calhoun thing, Annabelle?" Pa demanded. "Because, if you have—"

"No!" I lied. Passionately, by gum. "But I saw Josephine and Armando on my way to the library today, and we naturally talked about Mr. Calhoun, because Armando was there when I bumped into the body." The mere notion of which still made me break out in gooseflesh.

But then I began to think about Armando Contreras. He'd

told me his problem had been solved via Mr. Jaffa and Richard, but what the heck had he been doing at the scene of the crime when I discovered the body? For that matter, how long had Mr. Calhoun been in the water? It was possible that Armando had visited Gunderson's for some supplies he needed to fix something other than hail-battered vehicles. Or he might have been taking breakfast at the Cowboy Café, but I didn't know either of those things for a fact. Which meant I was a really rotten investigator. Heck, I could have asked Phil if Armando had been in the hardware store that morning, and I could have asked Armando himself if he'd taken breakfast at the café. I sure had a lot to learn about this detectival stuff.

"Anyway, Armando isn't the only one. Mr. Tindall told me that Mr. Calhoun cheated him out of his ranch, right there with Mr. Calhoun floating on Second Street."

"Annabelle!"

"Sorry, Ma. But it's the truth. The more people I talk to, the more of Mr. Calhoun's enemies seem to pop out of the woodwork."

"I'm afraid you're right, Annabelle," said Richard with what sounded like a heartfelt sigh. "And I'm afraid the police think I'm the main one."

"Oh, Richard, please stop saying that!" cried Hannah, squeezing the hand she held.

"I'm worried anyhow, sweetheart. Chief Vickers grilled me like a fish. Fortunately, the trustees don't seem to share his opinion, because they've made me interim president of the bank." He couldn't suppress a smile of triumph.

"Richard! That's wonderful!" Ma cried.

"Congratulations, son," said Pa, sticking out his hand for Richard to shake. Richard had to get it back from Hannah first, but that didn't take long.

"That's my Richard," cooed Hannah. From which, I presumed the presidency of the bank brought with it a raise in pay. Not that I'd ask or anything. Besides, Hannah loved Richard. She didn't just love his money.

"I only hope I can keep the job and not be arrested for murder. So far it doesn't seem to me as though the police are looking awfully hard for suspects other than me."

"That's not quite fair, Richard," I said, carefully placing chrysanthemums in the vase. They were really pretty, and I took them out to the dining room and put the vase in the center of the table. "I'm sure they're looking at everyone. Heck, I've heard lots of people say they didn't like Mr. Calhoun because Mr. Calhoun cheated them in one way or another."

"That's true, although in a way I don't blame the chief for suspecting me," said Richard as if he didn't like admitting it. "Any number of people would have told him that Mr. Calhoun and I have been having words—loud words—at the bank recently. Now I wish I'd kept my voice down. But it made me so darned mad to know he was swindling people."

"He swindled people?" Pa quirked an eyebrow. "Can you prove that? If that's so, you should have gone to the police before somebody took the matter out of your hands and shot the son of a gun."

"But I couldn't find any proof," Richard said, his voice kind of whiny.

Since I read a lot of detective fiction and had seen this sort of thing in books, I said, "If he was a crook—and so far everyone thinks he was—and if the bank's books look pristine, maybe he was keeping his crooked records somewhere else. Could he have been embezzling money from the bank too?"

"Annabelle!" cried Ma, appalled that I could even think such things.

But Richard, who looked kind of pale, said, "I thought he was, actually. Embezzling money, I mean. But there again, the bank's books were clean, so I guess I was wrong."

"I doubt it," said I. "Everybody knows he was a crook. If he was really devious and smart about it, he was probably embezzling and cheating people and keeping a second set of books somewhere else."

"You have a vivid imagination, Annabelle," said Richard, curse him. He was trying to humor me, but I wasn't in the mood to be humored.

"Would you rather be arrested for murder or have the police find a second set of books?"

"Annabelle!" Ma again.

"But, Ma, it's the truth. Chief Vickers might arrest Richard for the murder if somebody doesn't find proof of Mr. Calhoun's wrongdoings and come up with some more viable suspects."

"Lord," whispered Richard. "I'm afraid you're right."

"Hmm. How does a person go about doing something like that? Keeping doctored books, I mean?" asked Ma as she manhandled the ham out of the oven and set it in its cast-iron roasting pan on top of the stove with quite a bang.

"If I knew that, I'd have told the police," said Richard. "But I can't tell you how many people have complained to me that Mr. Calhoun had cheated them in one way or another. Mr. Contreras was lucky he could afford a lawyer."

"Yeah," said I, adding my two cents. "Poor Mr. Tindall wasn't so lucky."

But it was time to shovel the okra, which Ma had coated with cornmeal and fried, and which I loved, into a serving dish, put the ham on a platter, take the potatoes out of the oven and carefully set them on the trivet waiting for them on the dining room table, set out the corn and pinto beans, and for all of us to sit down.

What a meal! My mother is a wonderful cook. I do a fair bit of cooking myself, but for some reason, Ma's meals always taste better than mine. Maybe that's because she does all the work.

Conversation around the dinner table veered away from Mr. Calhoun, death not being deemed appropriate for dinner-table chitchat, but the storm gave us a wealth of material to work from. That and Jack's schoolwork, which hadn't been up to par lately.

"You'd better hit those books harder, Jack," said Richard. "You'll want to be able to get a good job when you leave school. Why, if your grades are good enough, you can even go to college."

That comment hit a sore spot with yours truly because I'd wanted to go to college, but neither Ma nor Pa thought it worthwhile for a girl to get a higher education since girls were supposed to marry and rear families, and who needs a higher education for that? I considered this reasoning pure bunkum, but I couldn't afford tuition on my own, so I had to abide by my parents' rules and read a lot. Anyhow, they weren't alone in their feelings. Most of the folks in Rosedale held similar archaic beliefs.

As for Jack, he looked as though he wanted to say something to the effect that he'd rather die than end up in a musty old bank like Richard, but he held his tongue. I knew, because he'd told me, that Jack wanted to be a cowboy. This, even though he knew the romanticized pictures of cowboys he read in Zane Grey's novels were total manure. A cowboy's job was hot and hard and dusty, they didn't make any money, and by the time they were old enough to know better, they were, most of them, too banged up to do anything else. Idiot brother.

Anyhow, I didn't care a fig about Jack's grades. Musing about a second set of records got me to thinking, though. If the books at the bank were clean, then Mr. Calhoun must have kept the other set of books (to be honest, I wasn't even sure what the word "books" meant in this context) in another location, and the only location I could think of was his home. How could I, Annabelle Blue, who wasn't well acquainted with the Calhoun family, get into their house and snoop around long enough to uncover a second set of books and maybe some incriminating papers?

This was going to take some deep thought—and probably some help from Phil, who'd be loath to give it, he being so fussy about things like breaking into other people's houses and so forth. Nevertheless, I determined I'd talk to him about it the next day, when we'd be seeing the Harold Lloyd flicker at the Pecos Theater on Main Street.

I worked half days on Saturdays, so I had plenty of time to consider how I intended to wheedle Phil into helping me with the Calhoun business. Phil showed up in plenty of time to come in and chat with my mother and father, who looked upon him with great approval. In fact, I got the feeling sometimes that they considered him something of my own personal savior— which sounds blasphemous—because they were afraid that what with my odd ways, love of reading, and insistence upon prying into other people's business, I might end up an old maid. As if a woman remaining unmarried were some sort of sin.

As we walked through the black, black night to the Pecos Theater, aided by the light of Phil's flashlight, I decided to bull ahead and take the consequences if Phil rebelled.

"Say, Phil, are you going to Mr. Calhoun's funeral on Monday?"

"Yeah. Pete and I are closing the store for a couple of hours so we can attend. My folks are coming from the ranch with Davy."

"Great. That way Davy and Jack can disrupt the service, create havoc and embarrass both our families."

"Pa won't let him do that," said Phil, although I could hear his smile. He knew, as I did, that his brother and mine were a couple of brats, especially when they got together.

"I expect Pa will keep a tight rein on Jack, too. At least I hope he will."

Taking my hand in his, probably because it was dark and nobody could see, Phil said, "I hope so, too. Those two would probably jump into the grave for the fun of it if left to their own devices."

"They probably would." I hesitated a second and then proffered my request. "Say, Phil, while we're at the funeral, would you be willing to speak with Herschel Calhoun for me? I want to find out what kind of father Mr. Calhoun was and if his family really misses him or if they're glad he's dead."

"I can't ask a question like that! For the good Lord's sake, Annabelle—"

"You don't just come out and ask, Phil. For the Lord's sake yourself! Be subtle. I aim to question Gladys, because I need to find out who killed her father before the police nab Richard. Darn it, can't you do that one tiny thing for me?"

Although I couldn't see his face, I knew Phil was rolling his eyes because he always did when I asked his help on projects like this one.

I went on, "It's not hard to talk to people, Phil, and it's certainly not difficult to get a feel for how Herschel felt about his father. Heck, if my own father died, the entire family would be devastated and crying for days, but when Ma and I took our covered dish to the Calhouns the day of his death, none of them seemed particularly cut up that he'd been shot in the back. If that had happened to anyone else's husband and father, the entire family would be in tears, don't you think? Heck, even Betty Lou Jarvis said none of them cared when he died, and she works for them."

"Cripes, Annabelle."

"Please, Phil? It won't be difficult, and I *really* need to know."

"You're not the damned police," he growled.

"No, I'm not. The police aren't doing their job." I didn't know that for a fact, but I didn't want to take any chances. "Do you *want* to see my brother-in-law arrested for a murder he didn't commit and watch my family fall apart because of it?"

"Of course I don't."

"Well, then?"

"Oh, for . . . all right. I'll talk to Herschel."

"Thank you, Phil."

He was grumpy for the rest of the evening, even though I let him kiss me when he took me home after the flicker—which was pretty funny, although my mind was swirling around other topics during the whole show.

CHAPTER NINE

On Monday afternoon, we closed Blue's Dry Goods and Mercantile Emporium at a little before two o'clock and drove to the Presbyterian Church, which the Calhoun family had attended. Well, I guess they still did, except for the deceased Mr. Calhoun. Normally we would have walked there, but we had to go to the cemetery after the service, so we took the car. Pa drove, probably to avoid an argument between Jack and me.

The place was full of flowers, primarily chrysanthemums since they were blooming at the time, although there were also bouquets of hothouse roses here and there. I guess the Calhoun family could afford such expensive floral arrangements, although I wasn't sure where they'd got them. Maybe somebody in town had a hothouse, because I don't think the train tracks had been repaired by then. Anyway, who ever heard of cut flowers being delivered by train?

The service, everyone agreed, was lovely, and no mention was made by the preacher of the way by which Mr. Calhoun had met his end. Mrs. Calhoun, Herschel and Gladys sat in the front pew, naturally. The two females were clad in black, as was deemed appropriate for the family of the deceased. No one else sat with them, from which I gathered that none of their other relatives lived close enough to get there in time for the funeral, Rosedale being so out-of-the-way. My family sat with Phil's family, taking up an entire two pews in the church, there were so many of us. The contrast between our numbers and the Cal-

houns' struck me, and I felt a little sorry for those three isolated
people sitting all by themselves in that front pew—but not sorry
enough to soften my attitude toward the deceased.

As I'd suspected would happen, Sadie Dobbs didn't attend
the service. Of course, she had to work at the café, which
couldn't afford to close for a couple of hours for anybody's
funeral. Still, I doubted she'd have attended anyway, after what
she'd said about people looking at her as if she were a . . . well,
you know.

Then a long line of cars, wagons and buggies followed the
hearse and the Calhouns' family Oldsmobile—the only other
people in town who owned such a fancy car were Richard and
Hannah, who had a Cadillac—to South Park Cemetery, where
the man was buried in earth still mushy from last week's flood.
Then we all trooped back to the Calhoun place on Lee Avenue.

Phil and I walked into the house together. Betty Lou Jarvis
was the official door-opener, I reckon, since it was she who let
us in, and it was only then that I realized she hadn't been at the
funeral.

"Because I had to get the house ready for all the guests.
There's enough food for an army stacked up on the dining
room table. I had to put all that out, too," she muttered when I
asked her about it.

I got the feeling she felt a trifle abused, not that she'd cared
for Mr. Calhoun because she hadn't, but because almost
everybody else in town got a break and she didn't. Can't say as
I blamed her for her attitude.

"All right, Phil, let's mingle. When you sense the time is
right, go talk to Herschel."

"Criminy, Annabelle," he muttered.

But he'd agreed to do it, a fact of which I reminded him.
Phil, being the honorable young man he was, would never back
out on a promise.

I began my mingling in the dining room, where lingered dainty little finger sandwiches with their crusts cut off, small savory pies filled with a chicken mixture that I liked a whole lot, bowls of olives and pickles, a platter with rolls and butter, and loads of other foodstuffs. I filled a plate and began to roam. A punch bowl sat at the end of the table surrounded by little etched crystal cups, but I didn't take any of the punch then, as I needed a hand free in order to grab my nibbles.

Naturally, since she was my best friend, Myrtle wanted to hang out with me. That was all right. It would probably make talking with Gladys easier, since it wouldn't feel so unnatural to approach her with my condolences and my questions with a friend at hand.

"These little chicken pies are delicious," said Myrtle at one point.

"They sure are. Do you know if Betty Lou cooks for them, or does Mrs. Calhoun do the cooking?"

"Be serious, Annabelle," said Betty Lou, who was at that very moment passing us with a tray filled with goodies, overhearing my question. "I do all the cooking. *And* all the cleaning. That woman doesn't do anything but go to club and committee meetings."

"Really?" I was chewing, so I couldn't say more than that until I swallowed, then I said, "I'm really sorry you have to work here, Betty Lou."

She sniffed with meaning. "So am I. Wish my family owned a store or a ranch or something so I could work at their business."

"You probably wouldn't like working on a ranch," I pointed out. "Ranches are so isolated."

With a sigh, Betty Lou said, "I guess you're right. Maybe I could get a job at a store in town. Firman says they need clerks at a couple of the hotels. I wonder if they'd hire a girl as a hotel desk clerk."

Oddly enough, Rosedale supported three fairly large hotels, primarily because, as a cattle hub, folks from back east and up north and out west traveled here for business reasons. Then there were the folks on the Chautauqua Circuit who visited occasionally. Heck, William Jennings Bryan even visited Rosedale once. Talked for hours and hours and stirred up some interest in an overall lackluster town for a couple of days. He didn't mention his feverish opposition to Darwin's theory of evolution, which I'd learned about in school. That had been moderately disappointing, but at least we got to stare at and listen to a famous man for a while.

"It might be interesting to clerk at a hotel," I said. "You could meet lots of different people. Say, do you know where Gladys is? I want to pay my respects."

"Huh. Her majesty is in the parlor, I expect, sopping up the sympathy. As if she cared about the old goat."

"Thanks, I'll—" And then something Betty Lou had said finally penetrated my thick skull. "Say, Betty Lou, did you say Firman told you about the hotels needing clerks? Do you mean the shoe-store man?"

"That's the one." Betty Lou's face went all soft for a minute.

So Phil had been right about the two of them seeing each other. Boy, you never could tell about love, could you? Even in Rosedale, I should think Betty Lou could do better than a man who looked like a weasel and wore ugly checked suits. Oh, well. Love, according to people who should know—authors and poets and the like—was not merely blind, but a tricky business entirely.

Myrtle and I made our way to the parlor and discovered Betty Lou had been absolutely correct. Mrs. Calhoun sat in one expensive chair, holding court with the older people in town, and Gladys sat in another, likewise engaged, only with younger folks. Myrtle and I wandered over to the Gladys contingent. She was speaking in a subdued voice and didn't seem to be saying much.

119

"Thank you, Phyllis. I appreciate your concern. Thank you for coming, Louise. And thanks for the flowers. They're very pretty." Standard stuff. We waited our turn in the line that had formed in front of Gladys, eating all the while.

Finally I managed to get close to Gladys. It was fortunate that I'd polished off the sandwiches, pies, and so forth, so I wouldn't have to converse with her between bites.

"I'm so sorry about your father, Miss Calhoun," I gushed. We weren't on first-name terms.

"Thank you, Miss . . ."

"Blue," I said. "Annabelle Blue."

"Ah, yes. From the grocery store. Well, thank you, Miss Blue."

"I'm sure you'll miss him terribly."

"Um . . . certainly." Her eyes squinched up. She wasn't aw-fully pretty, although she did have lovely, thick brown hair that shone as if she brushed it a hundred times before she went to bed every night, as my mother was always telling me I should do. "Say, aren't you the girl who found the body?"

There went that chill up my spine. "Yes. I was. And it wasn't any fun, either, I can tell you."

"I'm sure it wasn't." Then she said something that almost surprised the socks off me. "It wasn't any fun living with him, either." She glanced quickly around. "Don't tell anyone I said that. Please."

"I'll never tell," I said, crossing the fingers of my right hand behind my back. "Was he difficult to get along with or some-thing?"

"Difficult?" Gladys gave a wry snort of laughter. "He was a tyrant and a bully. But I really should keep the line moving. It was kind of you to come to the funeral, Miss Blue, and I'm sorry you had to be the one who found my father's body."

If this weren't such a crowded room, I'd have loved to ques-tion her further, but she had a good point. I kept being bumped in the back, and Myrtle was tugging on my arm. "Please take care of yourself and your mother," I said in parting. Don't ask me why I said that, because I don't know.

"Thank you, Miss Blue. That should be much easier now." She sniffed once, then turned to greet the next person.

"Oh, my, Annabelle, that was interesting." Myrtle, holding her empty plate, appeared avid.

"It sure was. I guess the man was no more cared for at home than he was in the community." Except for poor Sadie Dobbs. "But let's get some of that punch before it's all gone. I ate so much, I probably won't be able to eat dinner tonight."

"Me, too," said Myrtle.

I'd noticed her glancing a little feverishly around the room and supposed her to be looking for her gentleman friend, Sonny Clyde.

"I doubt that Sonny came to the funeral," I said as I poured out a cup of punch for Myrtle. "Their ranch is clear over near Tatum, and I don't think they had much to do with the Calhouns."

"I'm afraid you're right," said Myrtle with a mournful little sigh.

"We'd better be going, Annabelle. Your father wants to open the store now." I jumped a bit, not having seen Ma approaching us.

Drat! I hadn't had a chance to talk to Phil about Herschel. "All right, Ma. Do you mind if I say good-bye to Phil?"

A frown creased my mother's brow, but she said, "All right, but don't be long. People still need to do their shopping for the week, so we need to reopen the store."

"I won't be long," I promised. To Myrtle I said, "I'll talk to you later, Myrtle. We can discuss what we learned here today."

As I scurried off searching for Phil, I heard Myrtle ask, "We learned something?" Dang it, was I the only person in Rosedale who cared who killed Mr. Calhoun? Maybe I was. It would be a different story if Chief Vickers led Richard out of the bank in handcuffs, but by then it might be too late.

I heard a couple of interesting snippets of conversation as I wove my way through the throng and wished I could stop and eavesdrop, but I couldn't take the time. However, I was mighty interested in a few people's comments:

". . . crook if ever there was one. I'm glad he's dead."

". . . stole that ranch right out from under him, Calhoun did."

". . . charged outrageous interest. Wonder what's going to happen to those loans now."

". . . what the will's going to say about things. Don't know if he had anything left to leave."

That last one fascinated me particularly, but there wasn't any way I could learn more about Mr. Calhoun's will just then.

Frustrated, I finally found Phil in a back parlor, still eating and nowhere near Herschel Calhoun. I wasn't too pleased when I walked up to him. "Well?" I demanded. "Have you talked to Herschel?"

"Cripes, Annabelle. I haven't had a chance yet. Give a fellow a break, can't you?"

"No, I can't!" I said, stamping my foot. Childish, I know, but who's perfect? "My brother-in-law's life might be at stake here!"

"Keep your voice down. I'll talk to him as soon as I finish up this . . . stuff." Phil nodded at his plate.

"All right. But come over to Blue's when you can and let me know what you learn. Pa wants to get us back to the store now, so I can't wait for your convenience."

"Don't get all fussed up, Annabelle. I'll visit you at the store before I go back to Pete's."

"Thank you." I turned on my heel and marched out to the

Model T, where my family waited for me in undisguised impatience.

"Took you long enough to say good-bye to your gentleman friend," said Jack in the obnoxious singsong voice he uses when he wants to be particularly annoying.

Pa gave him a halfhearted whap on the head, and I sniffed.

"I had a difficult time finding him in the swarm of people, and I only said good-bye." I held my chin up so far, I'd have drowned if it had started raining. No chance of that, though. Last week's thunderstorm was a freak of nature and wouldn't be repeated any time soon. We all hoped so, anyhow.

The rest of the day was pretty boring. A few folks came in for groceries and canned goods after they left the Calhouns' place, and I managed to chat with a few of them, but nobody had any interesting information about the family to impart. It occurred to me that Betty Lou Jarvis might be able to help me get into the house one night so I could search for money and doctored books. Which reminded me . . .

"Say, Phil," I said when he came in to spill the goods about Herschel Calhoun. "What exactly are 'books,' anyway?"

He looked at me slanty-eyed for a second before his gaze fell to the novel lying on the counter: *The Great Impersonation*, by E. Phillips Oppenheim.

"Oh, for heaven's sake, I know what a *book* is!" I said, irked. "What I want to know is what people are talking about when they said the bank's books are clean. What kinds of books are they talking about? I know it might sound like a stupid question, but I overheard somebody at the funeral get-together say that he thought Mr. Calhoun might have a second set of books hidden somewhere that would show how he'd cheated people. Those kinds of books." Okay, so I lied again. Sue me.

"Ah. I see. You're talking about account books. Ledgers of debits and credits. Income and outgo, so to speak."

"Hmm. So, if the bank's books tally correctly, then Mr. Calhoun must have another set of ledgers somewhere else. Is that what you mean?"

"No, but I take it that's what *you* mean," Phil said. He sounded annoyed, but I don't see why he should have.

"Well, never mind about that," I said. "Tell me what you gathered from talking with Herschel." I almost blurted out that Gladys seemed to be glad her father was gone, but that, as the lawyers say, might have been leading the witness, so I gulped back my impulse.

"What I gathered is that Herschel is a spoiled brat who's glad his old man is dead, and he's looking forward to inheriting a whole lot of money once the will's read. I'm surprised that hasn't been done already, by the way."

"Why's that?"

With a shrug, Phil said, "Generally, shortly after a person's death, lawyers tell the family what the will of the deceased has in store for them."

"Doesn't this count as shortly after his death? After all, for two days, the town was almost impossible to navigate. Maybe the lawyer's office was closed or something."

"Maybe."

"Do you know who the lawyer is?"

"No, and whoever he is, he isn't going to allow you to sit in while the will's read," snapped my intended, who for some unaccountable reason seemed to be peeved with me that day.

"Why are you being so grumpy, Phil? It wasn't *that* hard to talk to Herschel, was it?"

"It wasn't hard at all. What was hard was standing there listening to him brag and blow."

"Oh. He sounds like an unpleasant person."

"Like I said, he's a spoiled brat."

"Isn't he kind of old to be a spoiled brat?"

"Age has nothing to do with it. I got the feeling his sister's a spoiled brat, too."

Mercy, Phil had certainly taken a dislike to Herschel. He seldom said mean things about people. However, I suspected he was correct about the Calhoun family. "Betty Lou Jarvis said pretty much the same thing to me, only in different words. They don't sound like people I'd like to be chummy with."

"Huh. I doubt they'd consider you chum material. They're too good for the rest of us, to hear Herschel talk."

"He sounds like a real pill."

"He is. Are you satisfied? May I get back to work now?"

"Yes, Phil, and thank you very much. I appreciate this a whole lot."

"I'll bet." With that, Phil heeled around, slapped his hat on his head and stomped out of the store.

"I do!" I hollered, but he didn't turn around or anything. Nuts. I hoped I hadn't made an enemy of my very best male friend in town. Oh, well. Nothing I could do about it at that moment, because I was stuck behind the counter at the store and folks continued to come in and buy things.

Because we'd all stuffed ourselves at the Calhouns' post-funeral reception, Ma made a ham sandwich for Pa, and left Jack and me to our own devices. I wasn't hungry, although I did make a trip to the kitchen around midnight when hunger pangs woke me up. So I got the ham out of the Frigidaire, which Pa had bought about three years earlier, got the bread from the bread box, cut it and slapped some mustard on it, and made myself my own ham sandwich. As I sat at the kitchen table nibbling on it, Ma came out and joined me. Naturally, I'd been contemplating things I'd overheard at the Calhouns' house and the things Phil had told me about Herschel. I glanced up at her. "Hey, Ma. You hungry, too?"

"I thought I'd have a little leftover floating island. It's soggy, but I'm sure it'll still taste good."

"I'm sure it will. I love that stuff."

"Yes, I know you do." Ma smiled at me in a way that let me know she loved her youngest daughter. I thought that was sweet. I was lucky in my parents, and I knew it.

"So what did you think of the funeral and the reception?" I asked around a bite of ham and mustard.

With a sigh, Ma set herself on a chair and her bowl on the table. She took a tiny bite of soggy meringue before answering. "Oh, I don't know, Annabelle. I know the Calhouns are a prominent family, and that they probably have more money than God—"

This statement shocked me, but I didn't let on.

"—but I'm glad I'm a plain old Blue. I think we're ever so much happier than the Calhouns are."

"I think so, too. Heck, nobody'd ever want to shoot Pa in the back. He's always helping people. From everything I've been able to gather so far, Mr. Calhoun made it his life's work to cheat people."

Ma gave me a hard stare. "Annabelle Blue, you're not snooping into the murder, are you? That's the business of the police department. Besides, if someone shot Mr. Calhoun, a rich and important man, do you think that person would hesitate to do away with a nosy girl?"

Well, crumb, I hadn't thought of my inquiries in exactly that way before. "I'm not snooping, Ma," I fibbed. "I just don't want them to fix their attention on Richard."

"You don't know that they are, Annabelle. As much as I know you'd like him to, Chief Vickers isn't about to give you daily updates on the police investigation."

Boy, wasn't that the truth? "I know it, Ma. I'm just a little bit worried about Richard, is all."

"Fine. Worry all you want, but I think you're taking Chief Vickers's interest in Richard far too seriously. Naturally, he had to question all the people who worked at Mr. Calhoun's bank." She pointed her spoon at me. "You are *not* to meddle in the business, Annabelle Blue."

She sounded quite firm in this command, so I didn't bother arguing with her.

Still and all, I aimed to have a chat with Betty Lou Jarvis as soon as I could.

CHAPTER TEN

Luckily for me, Betty Lou made a trip to Blue's the very next day in order to get some fabric and sewing notions for Mrs. Calhoun.

"They can't just dye their old clothes," she said in a derisive voice. "Their majesties have to have all new black duds made up."

"She doesn't patronize Miss Petty's Fancy Dresses?"

"Buy *store-bought* goods?" Betty Lou lifted her eyebrows in a you've-got-to-be-kidding expression. "Not for the likes of their majesties. Nothing but the best for them. Mrs. Wilson, and *only* Mrs. Wilson, will make clothes for the Calhoun ladies."

"I see. Well, we have lots of fabrics. Ma carries a variety in black just for funeral attire."

"At least Mrs. Wilson will make some money this week, and that's a good thing," said Betty Lou, heading toward the fabric section of the store.

Ducking under the counter, I followed her. "Did Mrs. Calhoun give you a budget? Or can you spend as much as you want?"

She grinned at that. "No. As a matter of fact, I've been directed to get the cheapest fabrics I can find, as long as they don't *look* cheap. Evidently, the will was read after the funeral, and Herschel's been raging around the house like a rabid polecat. Mrs. Calhoun has been in tears all day, and Gladys is sulking in her room and declares she'll be darned if she'll wear black for her father, who wasn't worth the space he took up on earth. Those were her exact words."

My eyes had widened. "You mean he didn't leave them a fortune?"

Shrugging, Betty Lou fingered some black wool crepe. "I guess not. Naturally, I wasn't invited in to hear the reading." She snickered when she went on. "Herschel's afraid he'll have to get a *job*. Lord, wouldn't that serve him right?"

"You don't like him, either?"

"He's a total pill. Thinks he's God's gift to everyone, and he's really a whiny crybaby. Gladys is no better. She's as stuck-up as a girl can be."

I shook my head. "What a family."

"You said it. When I told Firman about the will and the family's reaction, he said he wasn't surprised. Firman talked to Mr. Calhoun about a loan to get a house"—here she blushed, and again I recalled the insignificant Firman Meeks. But to each her own—"because we want to get married. Firman said Mr. Calhoun was a hard man and difficult to deal with. Firman said he thought Mr. Calhoun was probably piling up money somewhere and aimed to take off with his honey and leave the family flat."

"Goodness! That thought hadn't ever occurred to me."

"Me, neither. But if either Gladys or Herschel got wind of his plans, I can see either one of them plugging the old buzzard."

"Gee, I wonder where he kept his money, if that's what he'd been planning. According to Phil and Richard, he may have kept a second set of books detailing his illegal transactions somewhere other than the bank, because the bank's books are clean."

"Really? Well, I wouldn't put it past him. He was truly awful, Annabelle."

"I believe you. Say, Betty Lou, if Mr. Calhoun *was* planning a bolt, he probably kept his stolen money and doctored books in his house somewhere. Did he have an office or anything?"

"Oh, yes. Kept the door locked, too, and I don't think anyone's found the key yet."

"Hmm." I'd read books in which people picked locks, but none of them gave specifics on how to go about the process. Perhaps I needed to make another trip to the library.

"But Herschel busted out a window, and the police looked through the old man's desk and cabinets and didn't find anything. Then Herschel went through everything after the police left, but he didn't find anything either."

Bother. Still and all, neither the police nor Herschel struck me as the sharpest tacks in the box. Perhaps they didn't think to look for loose floorboards or secret compartments and other stuff like that. Then, greatly daring, I sucked in a huge breath and said, "Um, Betty Lou, do you think you could sneak me a key to the house? I'd like to go over that room myself and see if I can find anything. Bet I'm a better searcher than Herschel and the police."

"Heck, Annabelle, I'd be happy to lend you the key to the house, but you won't need it. They replaced the glass in that window yesterday, and I can just leave it unlocked one night and let you in if you really want to snoop around." She eyed me sharply. "Why do you want to, though? What's it to you if the old goat stashed a bunch of money somewhere? You don't aim to steal it, do you?"

"Good Lord, no!" I cried, horrified at the very notion. "I just need to find out Mr. Calhoun's secrets regarding his illegal dealings so that I can find out who the killer is. Otherwise, I'm afraid the police are going to fix their attention on Richard MacDougall, my brother-in-law."

"Oh, golly. Why would they do that?"

I heaved a largish sigh. "Richard works at the bank, and he

and Mr. Calhoun had been having very loud disagreements about the way the bank was being managed recently. The police have him in their sights."

"But Mr. Calhoun cheated everybody in the whole town!"

"I know, but I can't help but worry about Richard."

"Still?" Betty Lou asked, moving on to some black cotton. "I mean, I can understand why they might have fixed on your brother-in-law at first, but surely they've been investigating the matter since last Thursday. Don't you think so? Lots of folks in town carried a grudge against Mr. Calhoun."

"You might be right. Did the police do a really thorough search of Mr. Calhoun's office?"

Betty Lou shrugged. "I wouldn't say so. Not to my knowledge anyway, and unfortunately, I live there."

"See? That's what I mean. I don't think they're looking hard enough for anyone other than Richard."

"You might be right. This is Rosedale, after all. None of our elected officials seem to work very hard."

Harsh, but probably true. "Maybe I'll pay a call on Chief Vickers. He probably won't tell me anything, but if they've dropped Richard from their list of suspects, he might say that much."

"Frankly, Annabelle, I don't see your brother-in-law shooting anyone. He and your sister are too snooty to do stuff like that."

It pained me to hear Betty Lou say that about my own sister . . . but she was right. "Yeah. I know."

She apparently didn't hold Hannah's snootiness against me, because she said, "So when do you want to do this breaking and entering? I'll unlock the window tonight if you want to do it then. The family is usually in bed by eleven, unless Herschel is out drinking with his pals."

"He drinks?"

"Good Lord, yes." Betty Lou looked at me as if she considered me a ninny.

Still and all, I know it sounds ridiculous, but I wasn't accustomed to people flagrantly flaunting Prohibition laws as Herschel Calhoun seemed to be doing. A wastrel. That's what Pa would call him, and he appeared to be correct in Herschel's case.

As it turned out, reasons to visit Chief Vickers multiplied shortly after Betty Lou left Blue's. Later on that day, Ma, who had been in the kitchen preserving squash, hurried into the store, agitated as all get-out. I'm not sure where Pa was at the time, although I suspected he was visiting local ranchers and farmers, making deals and finding out what would be needed the next time he placed an order with the big warehouses in Dallas, Texas, for seeds, manure, pesticides, lineament, horn and udder balm, sheep dip and so forth. There was a whole lot to this farming and ranching business that most folks didn't think about unless they had to, and Pa had to.

"What's the matter, Ma?" I asked, shocked to see her wringing her hands and darned near in tears. I rushed over to her and hugged her.

She threw her arms around me and very nearly squished me in her anxiety. "Oh, Annabelle, Hannah just telephoned. The police have taken Richard down to the station to question him some more. They still consider him a suspect in Mr. Calhoun's death. They took him out of the bank in front of everyone!"

I goggled at my mother. "They hauled him out in handcuffs?"

Ma gave me a moue of irritation and let go of me. "Of course not. But they escorted him out of the bank and to the police station. Isn't that bad enough?"

"Yes. It is bad enough." Blast the idiotic police department!

"Hannah's so worried," said Ma, her irritation with me forgotten.

My own irritation seemed to grow as hers subsided. "It's so stupid of them to pick on Richard."

"I know it!" Ma began to cry.

My mother never cried. At least not in front of me. The fact that she'd let her emotions get her down really worried me. The police must truly be on Richard's tail unless Hannah had overly dramatized the situation. She did that on occasion. "What did Hannah say, Ma? Maybe it's not as bad as she made out."

Sniffling and grabbing a handkerchief from an apron pocket, Ma said, "Hannah tried to put up a brave front, but I could tell she was worried to death, Annabelle. I can't believe this! Surely there are others who are more likely suspects than Richard to have killed that man. Why, from what you've told me, he cheated nearly everyone in town. Why are they still looking at Richard?"

"Well . . . I'm not sure." But I thought I understood. Richard was right there at the bank, visible, and was known to have been in conflict with Calhoun. He was easy. They'd have to dig harder and farther to find other suspects with other motives and, while I don't mean to disparage the man, Chief Vickers wasn't much of a digger. He kind of focused on the obvious, if you know what I mean. I'd seen him in action before—or perhaps I mean inaction—and I knew these things.

"Try not to worry, Ma. I'm going to visit Chief Vickers and see if I can prod him some."

"No, you will not!" my mother cried.

"Why not? I know lots of stuff now that I didn't know before about Mr. Calhoun, and maybe if the chief knew about them, too, he might just start looking harder at other people."

"You are not going to involve yourself in a police investigation, Annabelle Blue," my mother told me, her eyes, formerly full of tears, now snapping fire.

It was difficult, but I held on to my own temper. Because I couldn't help myself, I did ask her, "Do you *want* to see Richard hanged for a murder he didn't commit, Ma?"

I think she had a hard time of it not to smack me upside the head as Pa was forever doing to Jack. After a tense moment, her shoulders drooped. "Of course I don't. But I don't want you prying into this mess either."

"It won't be prying to ask the police chief to please look at other suspects! Heck, I'll even give him some names and some reasons they could have hated Mr. Calhoun."

"Annabelle, sometimes I think you're impossible."

And vice versa, although I'd never say so. One doesn't say stuff like that to one's mother, although the reverse of that rule clearly doesn't apply. Nobody ever said life was fair. "So you won't scream and holler at me if I have a little chat with the chief?"

After a pause and a heavy sigh, Ma finally said, "No. I won't scream and holler. But please don't antagonize the man. That wouldn't do any of us any good, and especially not Richard."

"Honest, Ma, I do have a couple of grains of common sense and more than two brain cells to rub together. I definitely won't antagonize Chief Vickers. All I want to do is ask him some questions and give him some names and reasons."

"And just how did you come by this information you aim to impart to the chief, Annabelle?" Ma appeared suspicious. "You've been prying, haven't you?"

"No, I haven't been prying! All I've done is ask a few people a few questions, and I've discovered lots of folks who had reason to hate Mr. Calhoun. Heck, I didn't even have to ask most of them. They just came out and told me."

After squinting at me for another moment or two, Ma said, "Very well. When do you aim to do this interrogation of the police chief?"

"Are you through canning stuff? I could go now if you don't need to go back to the house for anything."

She heaved another sigh. "Very well." She thought of something. "And while you're out, will you stop by the shoe store and see if they have any leather slippers in your father's size? His slippers are a disgrace, and I want to get him new ones for Christmas. Might as well look now and find out if I'll have to order from the Sears and Roebuck catalog." She shook her head. "If I have to order them, they'll never arrive in time for Christmas."

Oh, boy! Another opportunity to snoop, and my own mother had instigated it. I really and truly wanted to get a good look at Firman Meeks and see what Betty Lou Jarvis saw in the man. Maybe he had charms I hadn't noticed. I hid my joy.

"Sure. What size does he wear?"

"Eleven."

"I'll be happy to look for slippers for Pa. Want my apron?"

"Why not?"

So I took off my apron and handed it to my drooping mother. I felt sorry for her because I know this latest news had hit her hard. As it had me, although I'd anticipated something of the sort. Blast Chief Vickers, anyhow! It's too bad the crime had taken place in town, because Sheriff Greene, who handled matters in the county but outside the city limits, was a much better—or perhaps merely a more enthusiastic—investigator.

A crisp wind blew the dirt around outside, clouds hovered in the sky—although they didn't look like the thunderhead variety—and I put a sweater on over my blue skirt and white shirtwaist before I left.

The shoe store, which was called Chewling's because it was owned by Mr. Otis Chewling, came before the police department, so I dipped inside and ran smack into Mae Shenkel, the high school principal's daughter, along with her friend, Ruby Bond. Ruby had been best friends with a girl named Hazel Fish, who'd been killed the month before, and I was glad to see she'd found a new friend. Both of them were nice girls, and Mae was very pretty and looked kind of like Mary Pickford, although I think her head was stuffed with cotton wool. Mae's head, not Mary's. Talk about not being the sharpest tack in the box; sometimes I thought Mae had been left out of the box entirely. But she was pretty, and that mattered more than brains. Unfair, but true.

I understood that she was seeing Bruce Lovelady, whose father owned an investment firm in Rosedale, and who was poised to step into his father's shoes any old time now. So they'd probably be set for life if they married. I couldn't repress a small shudder. Not that I disliked Bruce or anything, but the thought of marriage affected me almost as much as thinking about Mr. Calhoun's body bobbing in those floodwaters. I didn't know any interesting gossip about Ruby or I'd pass that along, too. She mainly lingered in Mae's shadow.

"Hey, Mae. Hey, Ruby. How are things going for the two of you?"

"Oh, Annabelle, it's so nice to see you," Mae gushed. "Look what I just got from Bruce." She flashed her left hand in front of me, and nearly blinded me with the rock on her finger.

"Wow, Mae, that's beautiful!" I thought it was gaudy, but I was a polite person. "So he's popped the question, has he?"

"Yes." She clasped her hands to her bosom as if she considered Bruce her own personal knight in shining armor. "How about you and Phil? Are you engaged yet?"

Aw, jeez. "Nope. Not yet. I don't want to marry for a while." I didn't tell her why.

"You'd better not let him dangle for too long, Annabelle," Mae said with a mischievous grin. "He's a good-looking fellow and might just get away from you."

I smiled. The notion of Phil falling madly in love with someone else and marrying her did give me a pang—a big one. Nevertheless, a girl has to abide by her principles, and my guiding principle at that time was getting out of Rosedale at least once before I married Phil and stopped living. "I'll try not to let that happen," I told Mae. Which reminded me that I'd do well to enlist Phil's services that night to stand guard whilst I rifled through Mr. Calhoun's home office. I turned to Ruby. "How are you doing, Ruby?"

"I'm fine, thanks. I'm sorry you had to find that body, Annabelle. That must have been awful for you."

"Yes. It was." There went that shiver, kind of like ants crawling up my spine. "Are you getting married, too?" That was probably a stupid question under the circumstances—I'm sure she'd have told me instantly if she was engaged—but I wanted to change the subject.

"No wedding on the horizon for me," she said sadly. "But I'm going to be Mae's maid of honor."

"Good for you." I tried to sound enthusiastic. "Are you looking for shoes today?" Yet another stupid question. After all, we now stood together in a shoe store.

"I'm looking for things for my trousseau," said Mae, her smile lighting up the place.

Whatever a trousseau was. I'm sure Hannah or Zilpha could tell me. Or even Ma, probably. "That's nice."

"We're going to be getting the invitations back from the engraver soon, and you'll get one, Annabelle. In fact, your whole family will be invited."

"That's very nice of you," I said, meaning it. There was always lots of food after a wedding, at the reception, and I enjoyed food, especially if neither Ma nor I had to cook it.

"May I help you?" came a quiet voice from behind me.

Firman Meeks. I turned and smiled at the man. "Thank you. I need to look for some slippers for my father. Leather slippers."

"Well, we'll see you later, Annabelle," Mae said, as she and Ruby headed for the door. I noticed they were both carrying several brown-paper parcels. Stuff for Mae's trousseau, undoubtedly.

"See you," I called after them. Then I fixed my attention on Firman Meeks. Pointed chin and nose, small eyes, nondescript hair greased back and parted in the middle, he was rubbing his hands together in a manner that reminded me of Uriah Heep. What in the world did Betty Lou Jarvis see in this man?

"Leather slippers?" he said. "I'm sure we can find something for you. Do you know your father's shoe size?"

"Eleven, my mother told me. She wants to give him new slippers for Christmas." Why was I babbling to this man? I supposed it was because I wanted to examine him closely, and I couldn't just come out and ask him why in the world Betty Lou Jarvis would want to go out with him, much less marry him.

"Your father has a large foot."

"Does he? Well, he's a big man." I glanced down at Mr. Meeks's feet, which were shod in small shoes that were pointy like his nose and chin.

"I see. Here is our selection of slippers. If we don't have the one you need in his size, I'm sure I can order some for you."

"Thank you." Huh. We could order them for ourselves, but I guess he wanted the store to get its commission. As a merchant myself—or at least the daughter of one—I could understand that.

Mr. Meeks led me over to a shelf holding a variety of men's slippers. They were mostly leather, unlike the ladies' slippers, which sat right underneath them on a lower shelf. The ladies' slippers were made of anything from leather to fluffy pink stuff that I didn't know how to classify. I picked up a man's slipper. These were really slippers, in that you'd slip your feet into them and then they'd slap the floor behind you when you walked in them because they didn't have backs. Pa'd hate them.

"How much are these?" I asked, feeling I should.

"Two dollars."

Shoot. That was a lot of money for a couple of backless slippers. "I see." I put those back on the shelf and picked up a pair that seemed more likely. They were lined with sheepskin and were enclosed so that a guy's heels wouldn't be left to flap in the cold.

"These seem nice," I said. Then I dropped a snooping comment into the conversation. "I understand you applied for a loan at the bank and didn't much care for Mr. Calhoun. Betty Lou Jarvis told me." I added that last part because he seemed to be stiffening. I guess it was a nosy question.

"Yes, I did. And yes, I didn't care for Mr. Calhoun." Mr. Meeks's voice seemed a little chillier than it had been.

"Lots of people didn't like him, although I don't know why anyone would shoot him in the back like that."

"I'm sure I couldn't say."

Oh, dear. I was clearly getting on the man's nerves. "I'm sorry if I sound nosy. I guess it's because I'm the person who found the body. It was . . . not a pleasant experience. And I can't seem to get Mr. Calhoun and his activities out of my mind." I feared *out of my mind* might be a little too apropos to my present stumbling attempts to draw Mr. Meeks out.

"I regret you had such a terrible experience. Miss Jarvis and I haven't really discussed Mr. Calhoun, however, although I did mention to her that I didn't care for the man after I spoke with him at the bank."

Oh, boy, I'd definitely ruffled his feathers this time. Or his fur. Both ferrets and weasels had fur. Not that it matters what he looked like, although I still questioned Betty Lou's choice. What mattered was that I was a truly an abysmal interrogator, and I hadn't even been bent on interrogating this specimen. I'd only wanted to discover what Betty Lou found to love in him. However, in my defense, I was a rank amateur. I'm sure the police were more suave in their questioning practices—well, some police. "How much are these?" I asked, a sense of failure making me feel inept and silly.

"Three dollars. They're lined with fleece, as you can see, and this is top-grade leather."

"Ah. I see. Well, I'll tell my mother. I don't know if she wants to spend that much, but they're nice slippers. Do you have them in size eleven?"

"I'll be happy to check the back room for you."

He sure didn't look happy as he took off for the back room to look for fleece-lined slippers in a size eleven. Nuts. I honestly hadn't meant to annoy the fellow.

I poked around the store while he was gone. There were some really pretty shoes there, but I didn't need new shoes, more's the pity. Not that I could have afforded them if did need them. What money I earned at the store, I saved. For future adventures. Anyhow, I had shoes for work and shoes for church, and that's all I really needed. I was fingering a pair of beautiful black patent-leather evening shoes with cross-strapping when Mr. Meeks rejoined me. Where in the world, do you suppose, would a person wear shoes like that in a place like Rosedale? A wedding, maybe? Well, never mind.

"Yes, we do have those slippers in a size eleven," he said to me, his smile not doing much for his face.

Usually when people smile, their expressions soften, but his didn't. I hoped to heck he was nicer around Betty Lou than he was in the store. Cripes, I might just have to go out and get another man for her if she couldn't find anyone better than this one on her own.

"Thank you very much for looking. I appreciate it. I'll let my mother know. They're really nice slippers."

"My pleasure." It wasn't, though. I could tell.

Then, because it just occurred to me and I figured I couldn't irritate him any more than I already had, I sucked in my breath and asked a bold question. "Say, Mr. Meeks, you aren't from around here, are you?"

He stiffened slightly. "I moved to Rosedale from the Midwest about a year and a half ago, although I don't know why my former residence is of interest to you?"

"Oh, I don't know. It just puzzles me when people move to Rosedale, I guess. I can't imagine why anyone would want to."

That comment seemed to relax him. He even chuckled for about half a second. "I see. Yes. Rosedale is rather out of the way, but I came to dislike the city. Too much hustle and bustle for me."

"We don't get much hustle and bustle here, that's for sure. Well, except when they drive the cattle down Second Street."

"Yes, and I enjoy the wide open spaces. So different from Chicago."

Chicago, eh? Where all the bootleggers lived? Well, Chicago and New York. But I doubted Mr. Meeks was a bootlegger. Weren't they all Italians? Meeks didn't sound like an Italian name to me, and he didn't look like any of the gangsters whose pictures ended up in the newspapers.

Because it was almost true, and because our conversation seemed to have turned a corner, I sighed and said, "I'd love to visit Chicago someday. Or any other big city, for that matter. Just to see what it's like, you know?"

"I'm sure that's a common wish if one is born and reared in so small a place as Rosedale. Rosedale is so out of the way. Isolated, as it were."

He sounded as if he considered our isolation to be a good thing. He was sure right about it, too. Even if you traveled two hundred miles, you'd end up in El Paso or Albuquerque or Santa Fe, and they weren't exactly Chicago, you know?

"My brother lives in Alhambra, California. That's near Los Angeles. If I ever get to travel, it'll probably be there."

"I'm sure California is nicer than Illinois," said Mr. Meeks. "At least the weather is better."

"I'm sure you're right. Well, thank you very much."

"Certainly. I trust your mother will like the slippers."

"Thank you. I'm sure she will. Say," I added, inspiration—or something—having struck, "would you mind measuring my feet? I was looking at that lovely pair of patent-leather shoes over there"—I pointed to the ones I meant—"and thinking they might be nice for church." Actually, they looked as if they'd be right at home at a ladies' tea at Mrs. Calhoun's house. Or maybe a dance hall.

"Of course. Please have a seat."

So I did, and Mr. Meeks got out the foot-measuring device all shoe salesmen use, I took off my right work shoe and stuck my stockinged foot onto the measurer. As Mr. Meeks took measurements of my right and then my left foot, I said, "My name is Annabelle Blue, by the way. My parents own Blue's Dry Goods and Mercantile Emporium a couple of blocks west of here on Second."

"I see. As you may have learned from Miss Jarvis, my name is Meeks. Firman Meeks."

"Yes. Betty Lou told me."

"You have a great interest in the business of others, Miss Blue."

Oh, my. Chilly. Very chilly. "I'm sorry. I didn't mean to step on your toes."

I thought the comment was kind of funny, but Mr. Meeks only gave it a strained smile and said, "Let me see if I can find a pair of those shoes in your size."

"Thank you."

Lord. You'd think I didn't have the sense God gave a goose, the way I was going about this questioning stuff. As I waited for Mr. Meeks to come back with or without the shoes, I wished I could talk to Micah Tindall. At least he was a local man, and easy to talk to. Or Armando again. He had a hot temper, and I hoped to goodness he wasn't the killer, but at least he liked to converse. Firman Meeks . . . well, let me just repeat that I didn't see what Betty Lou liked about him.

But he was back again. "I'm very sorry, Miss Blue, but we don't have that particular shoe in your size. Would you like me to order a pair for you?"

"Oh, no, thanks. I'd hate for you to order it and then not like it or the fit or something." Blithering. I was blithering. Darn it!

"That wouldn't be a problem. Your foot is of average size, Miss Blue, and if you found the shoes uncomfortable, I'm sure we could sell them to someone else."

"Ah. Well, that's good. But . . ." Shoot. Now what? Oh, well. "Yes, then, please do order them. I'll come in . . . when will they get here?"

"In approximately a month."

"Okay. Thanks. I'll visit you again in a month and see if I like them when they arrive. And I'll ask Ma about the slippers."

"Very good, I'm sure."

"Thank you." And I skedaddled out of the shoe store, feeling Firman Meeks's squinty-eyed gaze following me as I left. Jeepers. Maybe he was the world's nicest man, but I couldn't really see him and Betty Lou together. Then again, what did I know? Not much, is what.

CHAPTER ELEVEN

On my way to the police department, I was trying to decide if I didn't like Firman Meeks because he looked like a weasel or if I just didn't appreciate his manner. The conclusion I came to was that Meeks's manner put me off. Heck, I served the public, too, in my position as clerk in my parents' store, but I treated everyone in a friendly, agreeable manner. I didn't sidle up to them and get stiff and snooty when they asked me questions.

On the other hand, the guy was from Chicago. Maybe people from Chicago just naturally acted differently from those of us who'd been born and reared right here in Rosedale, where everyone knew you from birth and vice versa. Having the entire town know you and your business occasionally gets irritating, but one becomes used to it if one is subjected to it from the cradle on. One even learns how to circumvent interference, if one is clever—or lucky. Therefore, because I liked Betty Lou Jarvis and wanted her to be happy in her choice of a gentleman, I decided to give Firman Meeks the benefit of the doubt. Mind you, that wouldn't stop me from looking around and seeing if I couldn't find her somebody I liked better.

However, once I got to the police department, I had to stop thinking about Betty Lou and Firman Meeks and concentrate on the task at hand, which was to try to persuade Chief Vickers that Richard was the least likely person in Rosedale to have killed Mr. Calhoun.

I opened the door and marched in. The deputy at the desk, a

fellow with whom I'd gone to school, Martin Rogers, and who'd recently joined the force, glanced up from the desk behind which he sat and smiled at me. "Hey, Annabelle."

"Hey, Martin. Is the chief available? I'd like to speak to him for a few minutes if he's not busy."

"What about?" asked Martin, curse him.

"The Calhoun case. As you can imagine, it's important to my family, especially since I hear the chief brought my brother-in-law down here for questioning this very morning."

Martin folded his hands on a pile of papers on his desk. "Yes, well, what is it you want to say to the chief, Annabelle?"

"What I want to tell the chief is what I want to tell the chief, Martin, not you." I was becoming annoyed at this clear attempt to keep me from my goal. "I'm a citizen of Rosedale, and I should think I'd be allowed to speak to the chief if I want to. Are you trying to keep me from him? Why is that, Martin?"

"Hold on, Annabelle. I'm not trying to keep you from the chief. But as you can imagine, he's a really busy man."

"So am I. Well, I'm not a man, but you know what I mean. And I've been deputized by my family to talk to the chief, so let me at him. Or do I have to make an appointment? For heaven's sake, Martin, I'm the one who found Mr. Calhoun's body!"

"I know. Hold on a minute, Annabelle. I'll see if he can see you." He left his desk and went through a door leading to the back of the police station.

Fuming, I browsed the "wanted" posters tacked to the walls of the lobby. Criminals, criminals, criminals. Who'd want to be a criminal? I didn't understand. Heck, I'd have to go to a good deal of hard work to get *into* trouble, yet according to the descriptions I read on the posters, there were tons of folks in the good old USA who couldn't stay out of trouble to save themselves. Why was that? It seemed so easy just to follow the rules and obey the law. Life was simple that way. You didn't have to go around looking over your shoulder to check if the police might be chasing you. I guess bootleggers made a lot of money, but they also got killed a lot—well, not more than once each, but you know what I mean. Sounded like a lot of anxiety and stress and bother to me. I'd rather read a good book, relax and be normal than have to worry about being caught, arrested and flung in the clink, even if I got rich in the process. Heck, if you were in the clink, you couldn't enjoy your ill-gotten gains, could you?

Perhaps I lacked a certain type of imagination required for criminal work, although I had plenty—my mother would say too much—imagination for other things. The lack of criminality in my personal character might be what made me so crummy at the interrogation of people. Witness my late confrontation with the mild-mannered but ferret-like Firman Meeks. He wasn't a suspect, but only the fellow a friend was sweet on, and I'd only talked to him to see if he was good enough for her—and it didn't even matter what *I* thought. Betty Lou was the one who'd be stuck with him if they married and bought the house he'd gone to the bank to get a loan for.

Fudge. After perusing the "wanted" posters, I plunked myself down in one of the hard wooden chairs lining the shabby lobby of the police department. It galled me that citizens of Rosedale, New Mexico, one of the smallest towns in the world, should have to go through intimidation and questioning in order to speak to their police chief. Darn it, we citizens were the ones who'd elected him! Well, I personally didn't, not being quite old enough to vote yet, but if anybody from the PD gave me any more grief, I'd be darned if I'd vote for Vickers next time an election was held.

Or was the police chief hired by the city councilmen? Bother. I didn't know. Either the sheriff or the police chief was an elected official, but I couldn't remember which was which. I really needed to study this stuff if I planned to do any more investigations. Which I didn't, but still . . .

"Miss Annabelle," Chief Vickers said in a jovial voice, coming into the lobby to greet me. "Martin tells me you want to talk to me. Come in. Come in."

Very well, maybe I would vote for him. But only if he found the real killer of Mr. Calhoun and didn't pin the crime on my brother-in-law.

"Thanks for seeing me, Chief," I said as I followed him into his office.

"Not at all. Not at all. I understand you want to chat with me about the Calhoun case."

He gestured for me to take a chair opposite his desk, so I did. This one was hard and uncomfortable, too, but I guess one shouldn't expect luxury in a police department. "Yes, I do. I understand you brought Richard, my brother-in-law, down here for more questioning this morning."

"Yes, we did. However, as you must know, I can't tell you any more than that. We need to keep a lid on ongoing investigations."

"Is that so? Well, I want you to know that Richard isn't the only person in this town who had grievances against Mr. Calhoun."

"I know that, Miss Annabelle. No one knows it better than I."

Hmm. That took the wind out of my sails for a second, but I forged onward. "Well, then, I don't understand why you're not bringing in Micah Tindall or Armando Contreras or Mr. Feather or any number of other people whom Mr. Calhoun swindled. Or his mistress, Sadie Dobbs." I felt my face flame when I said the word *mistress*. Nevertheless, I forged on. "Or his family. Heck, they all hated him. Maybe one of them decided to do the world a favor and plug him."

"I must say you use colorful language, Miss Annabelle."

"It may be colorful, but it's also the truth. Richard MacDougall is the least likely of all the people in Rosedale to have committed cold-blooded murder, Chief Vickers, and you know that. He and Mr. Calhoun were having arguments at the bank because Richard didn't approve of the way Mr. Calhoun was treating his banking clients."

"I can't discuss an ongoing investigation, Annabelle. You know that. However, you probably will be happy to know that we've interviewed Miss Dobbs and the other people you mentioned. Mr. MacDougall is as of much interest to us as anyone else. He even owns a firearm that corresponds to the caliber of the murder weapon."

Although I hate to admit it, I goggled at the man. "*Richard?* Owns a *gun?* I don't believe it."

"Believe it. We found it when we searched his home."

"And are you sure it was his?"

"He denied owning the weapon," the chief said, although I don't think he wanted to.

"Well, then," I said, throwing my arms in the air. "There you go. It was planted in Richard and Hannah's house by whoever did the deed. Listen, Chief Vickers, I know Richard MacDougall. He hates guns."

"There's no getting around the fact that a weapon was found in his home."

"It wasn't his gun," I said stubbornly. "Anyhow, more than half the folks in Rosedale own guns! Didn't you find guns in any of the other suspects' homes?"

The chief grimaced. "I've already told you too much, Miss Annabelle. I know this case is of interest to you because your brother-in-law is involved—"

"He is not!"

Chief Vickers sighed heavily. "He's as much involved as Mr.

Tindall or any of the others. And yes, we found weapons in many other homes, too."

"Well, then," I said, and didn't know what to say next.

The chief's shoulders sagged slightly. "You'll be pleased to know we're investigating all the others who had weapons of a similar caliber. After all, as you're probably aware, possession is—"

"Nine tenths of the law. Yeah, I know that."

I must have looked discouraged, because the chief said, "We're working every angle we can find, Miss Annabelle."

"Are you investigating Armando Contreras and Mr. Feather?"

The chief let out a gusty sigh. "Yes, Miss Annabelle. We're talking to Mr. Contreras and Mr. Feather, among many, many others."

"What about the rest of the Calhoun family? My friend, Betty Lou Jarvis, works and cooks for the Calhoun family. She told me they all hated him and she wouldn't be surprised if one of his kids did him in."

After staring at me for several seconds, making me want to squirm, Chief Vickers wrote this interesting item down on his pad. He shook his head. "Thank you, Miss Annabelle. We'll take this bit of . . . information into consideration."

He wanted to thank me for spreading gossip; I could tell. Because I really did feel as though I'd been blabbing over the back fence or something, I said defensively, "Well, if anyone should know how that family works, it's Betty Lou. She even lives in the same house with them."

The chief sighed. "Anyone else you can think of who we should look at, Miss Annabelle?" he asked politely, probably to make me feel less foolish than I did.

"Not that I've heard about, but at the funeral I heard lots of people say they were glad Calhoun was dead, and I'm sure there were good reasons for their comments." After hesitating for a second, I said, "You might want to talk to Sadie Dobbs again. She told me he gave her money sometimes, and he might have given her money he'd embezzled from the bank—"

"Embezzled!" The chief's roar made me jump. "Tell me exactly how you know the man was embezzling bank funds, Miss Annabelle."

Dang. "Well, I can't prove it, because I don't know anything. Richard said the bank's books were clean, but if they were clean, Calhoun must have been keeping the money he chiseled out of his victims somewhere else. It only makes sense."

"We've done a thorough investigation at the bank and at his home, Miss Annabelle. Nothing seems amiss. As for Miss Dobbs, we have no reason to believe Mr. Calhoun gave her anything but some cash and presents. I know you don't want Mr. MacDougall to be guilty, but we really do know how to do our job."

Chief Vickers rose from his chair, signaling that our chat was over. "Thank you for dropping by, Miss Annabelle."

Bet he didn't mean that. "Thank you for paying attention to what I said, Chief. I *know* Richard didn't kill Mr. Calhoun."

"Yes, well, we'll see." And he saw me to the door.

"I'll be back if I hear of anyone else who might have a motive," I promised—or maybe it was more of a threat.

"Thank you. We always appreciate it when citizens are eager to help us do our job," said the chief, lying through his teeth.

Hmm. As I walked west on the boardwalk, I considered my day so far. I hadn't done awfully well at getting information out of Firman Meeks. I wondered where a person who was interested in such things could get training in investigative techniques. Perhaps I should join the police department, if they allowed females in. Police departments probably taught a person how to ask questions effectively and get good results. All I seemed to do was stumble around and antagonize people.

My mother would faint dead away if I tried to do anything so outrageous as join a police department anywhere at all, much less in Rosedale. My father would probably disown me. Nuts. It didn't seem fair to me that women weren't welcomed into police departments the world over. We were ever so much more perceptive than men. For the most part, anyway.

Before I went back to Blue's, I decided to pay Phil a visit at the hardware store. He was going to hate what I was going to ask him to do, but I was pretty sure he'd do it anyway. Phil nearly always did what I asked him—and nearly as often hated every minute of it. But I really did want to get him to watch out for danger and/or interlopers that night when I rifled through Mr. Calhoun's home office.

"You're going to *what*?" Phil actually roared at me. "Annabelle Blue, are you out of your mind?" He ran his fingers through his hair as he added that last part. "But of course, you are. I already know that. And you think you know better than the police and God Himself about criminal investigation, too."

"That's not fair, Phil," I said, hurt to the core. "I'm a lousy investigator, but at least I'm doing some investigating. That's more than the police seem to be doing! Why, did you know that Chief Vickers hauled Richard into his office this very morning?"

Phil sagged against the counter of his brother's store. "From what I've heard, they've had half the men in town in there to question them about Mr. Calhoun. Richard's not the only one."

"But he's the only one connected to my family, Phil! Wouldn't you want to discover the truth if the police suspected Pete of a dastardly crime?"

"Dastardly," muttered Phil, clearly believing I was overreacting to circumstances.

"It was a dastardly crime," I said, defending my choice of words.

"Yes, yes, I know. And yes, I'd want to find out the truth if

Pete were suspected of something like murder. But I'll be horn-swoggled if I'll abet you in breaking into the Calhoun place and poking around in things that are none of your business."

"Darn it, Phil, this *is* my business! Richard's my brother-in-law!"

"Criminy, Annabelle, you just won't give up, will you? Police matters are best left to people who know how to conduct them. Besides, you've got work of your own to do. It's better to butt out of police business."

"Nonsense. I've talked to Betty Lou Jarvis, and she told me the police didn't conduct anywhere near a thorough search of the Calhoun house. Anyhow, you don't have to abet or break into anything. I just want you to stand guard outside the window and warn me if anybody seems to be moving around in or out of the house. And I won't have to break in, either, because Betty Lou is leaving the window unlocked for me."

"Oh, for cripes' sake," moaned Phil.

"Please, Phil? I'll appreciate you forever." I considered batting my eyelashes at him, but gave up the notion as too stupid a thing to do. I didn't like it when girls played up to men using their feminine wiles, because I consider such tactics demeaning.

"I'll just bet," he grumbled. Then he squinted square into my eyes. "You're going to do this idiotic stunt whether I go with you or not, aren't you?"

"Well . . . yes. I have to, Phil! Even *you* must see that."

"I don't see anything of the kind."

"Darn it, I just came from Chief Vickers's office, and he *still* thinks Richard did it." Very well, so that was kind of an exaggeration.

After heaving a gigantic sigh, turning around twice, slamming his fist against the wall—which brought Pete out of the back room; Pete only glanced at the two of us, grinned, and went back again—he gave up. "Damnation, I just hate it that you can always talk me into doing crazy stuff like this."

I thought it was one of his more sterling qualities, but I didn't say so. "Oh, *thank* you, Phil! You won't regret it. I promise you won't. You'll feel like a hero when the real killer is caught and Richard can go back to living his life without worrying again. And Hannah, too," I added, as a conscientious sister should.

"Nuts," muttered Phil. "What time do you want to do this stupid thing?"

A moment's thought gave me the appropriate answer. "I do believe these searches are traditionally undertaken at midnight."

Phil gave me a hard look. "This isn't a game, Annabelle."

"I know it's not. That's why I'm doing it."

"Aw . . . shucks." I think he wanted to use another, less proper, word.

"And if the family is still up and about at midnight, we can just wait a while."

"Great. I've always wanted to lurk outside somebody's house in the middle of a cold November night. There's a new moon tonight and it's supposed to be cloudy, which means it will be darker than sin. Wonder if it'll rain. That would add zest to the atmosphere."

"Quit being so grumpy," I advised. "I truly appreciate your help in this, Phil."

"Yeah, yeah. You always say you appreciate me. You never show it, though."

Stunned, I cried, "Phil! That's not so! You know I appreciate you!"

"As a collaborator," he groused.

"As much, much more than that," said I stoutly. "You're the man I intend to marry one day, after all."

"God help me."

I left after that.

As it turned out, I didn't get the opportunity to rifle through

Edgar Calhoun's home office that evening. Oh, we started out all right, Phil and me. He came to the front door shortly before midnight, wearing a heavy fleece-lined jacket, work boots, gloves, and his hat pulled low.

"Thanks, Phil. Looks like it's cold out there."

"Duh," he said.

I went back for my gloves, a scarf and my own heavy coat, then rejoined him at the front door. I was remiss in not inviting him inside to wait in the warmth of the house, what there was left of it—warmth, I mean, not the house—but I didn't want any of my family to hear his heavy boots clomping on the floorboards.

Luckily, since he was right and blackness loomed all about us, we'd both thought to bring our flashlights. Phil took my arm and guided me to the store. Even with two flashlights, it was difficult to see much, but we walked around the store and headed down the boardwalk toward Lee Avenue.

Shadows lined us on both sides, looming darkly, appearing ominous, and I couldn't help but remember that there was a killer somewhere on the loose in our dumpy little town. We also made a whole lot of noise, blast it.

"I didn't realize how loud our shoes would sound on the boardwalk."

"It's the middle of a freezing-cold night," Phil reminded me. "We're the only fools outside in it."

"I hope nobody hears us and investigates."

"Not many people live on Second here. It's all businesses. Anyhow, when we get to Lee, we'll be walking on the street, and we won't make so much noise."

"I suppose so." I still didn't like it, though. For all I knew, the chief might have taken his duties seriously and have a stake-out—I think that's the correct word—on the Calhoun place. And then there was that murderer-on-the-loose thing. I felt creepier by the second.

Nevertheless, we made our way to Lee, walked down the steps to the street—I nearly broke my neck when I missed the last step because I couldn't see it—and took off north toward the Calhoun house. Once we got there, I sucked in a deep breath and told Phil the plan I'd made out in my head before he came to get me. One doesn't like to break and enter without a plan, after all.

"Walk with me to the back of the house where the office is."

Phil lifted his flashlight, I suppose to see his way to the back of the house, but I smacked his arm to lower the light. "Don't do that! We don't want anyone to know we're here."

"Hell, Annabelle, it's as dark as onyx out here. How are you going to find your way back there without your flashlight?"

I thought *onyx* was quite a poetic turn of phrase for the generally prosaic Phil, but I didn't bother to say so then. "Betty Lou told me exactly where it is. We can find it if I only turn on my flashlight once or twice." I hoped. There were a few leafless bushes around the house, and I didn't fancy falling into any of them. But that was negative thinking, and I didn't say so. "Then you wait outside while I climb in the window. You might have to boost me."

Phil grunted.

Only we never quite made it to Mr. Calhoun's office in the back of the house. That's because I turned off my flashlight, turned, walked several paces in what I believed was the right direction, tripped, stumbled and almost fell flat on top of Herschel Calhoun's body before we got there. If Phil hadn't been there to catch me, I'm sure I would have driven the knife into his back even deeper than it had already been driven. As it was, I ended on my hands and knees, straddling the body. Talk about a rude encounter!

CHAPTER TWELVE

Phil and I sat shivering in the police chief's office. Oh, very well, I was shivering. I'm not sure about Phil, who hadn't sat but sort of prowled around the office. Anyhow, while the weather was brisk, my shivers had more to do with finding another dead Calhoun than they did the weather.

"All right," said Chief Vickers, still looking unhappy at having been called out of his warm bed on a bitter November night. "You say you were out for a stroll? In the middle of the night?"

With a glare at me, Phil said, "Yes."

I knew that simple answer wouldn't hold up under more intense questioning, so even though I yet suffered from shock, distress and leftover horror, I forced my brain into action. "I couldn't sleep. Too many things have been plaguing me lately. So Phil walked with me for a while. He was doing a kindness for a friend."

"I see. And you and your friend just happened to walk to the Calhouns' house?"

"Yes!" I said, incensed that he sounded so suspicious of our actions. After all, *we* didn't kill anyone. "Darn it, Chief, I'm worried about Richard, and fretting about him has me in a fidget. I couldn't sleep, and Phil was kind enough to come over and walk with me for a while. We walked past the Calhouns' place because . . . because . . . I don't know why we did. I guess because I've been thinking about them so much. Anyhow, it wasn't a conscious decision. We just turned north on Lee because we did."

"So you and Phil here went for a walk in the pitch dark on a cold, moonless night," said the chief, his skepticism clear for all to hear. Fortunately, the only folks there besides him were Phil and me. "Did he sense your inability to sleep by divine intervention or magic? Did he even have a clue about your restlessness before he showed up at your door?"

I didn't like the tone of his voice one little bit. However, his sarcasm made me straighten my spine some. "No. I telephoned him at his brother's house."

"I'm sure Pete and his wife appreciated that a whole lot."

"I answered the telephone," said Phil, surprising me, as he wasn't generally one for perpetrating lies. In this case, though, I guess he figured he'd better.

"And no one else heard it ring?"

"No." Phil was firm.

Although my spine was a trifle stiffer than it had been when I first sat in the chief's office, I still felt mighty shaky. After I'd nearly fallen on top of Herschel Calhoun, my shriek of alarm had roused the rest of the Calhoun family, not to mention neighbors on both sides of their house and across the street. Lanterns were lit everywhere (the electric company stopped service at midnight), and folks flocked to see what had caused such an uproar in the middle of the night.

Naturally, as soon as they saw Herschel's body, more cries of fright and agitation were raised, and somebody must have called the chief's house because he showed up not long after that. When he heard it had been I who had fallen over the body while out for an evening stroll with Phil, he'd looked at me sharply and asked us both to visit the police station with him as soon as the coroner and the undertaker were through with their business.

We'd had a couple of hard frosts by that time of year, and there were fallen leaves all over the place, including some stick-

ing to my coat and scarf and hands. I brushed them off as well
as I could. All at once, the terror I'd felt about a murderer being on the loose while Phil and I walked to the Calhouns' house
seemed more real even than it had while we'd been walking. I
wanted to wash my hands, not primarily because of the leaves
and dirt on them, but because I'd been in close contact with a
dead body, and I was pretty sure I had blood on my hands,
although it was too dark to tell for sure. I'm not sure how
coroners and undertakers ever get used to their jobs. Not that it
matters. I sure wasn't going to become a coroner or an
undertaker. At that point, even joining the police force was a
stretch.

I don't know how long the coroner and the undertaker stayed
at the scene, but it seemed like forever. Then Chief Vickers left
his second in command, Frank Parker, who looked as though
he'd put his uniform jacket on over his pajama top, to guard the
scene. Frank also hadn't bothered to brush his hair, which stuck
out all over the place, and he appeared to be still half asleep. Yet
another reason to rethink my desire to join a police department.
I'd forgotten that you had to be available at all hours of the day
and night in order to do the job properly.

Mrs. Calhoun had nearly fainted when she saw her precious
son lying in the front yard of her home with a knife in his back,
and it had taken a couple of her neighbors to get her into the
house, weeping and sagging against them. Gladys showed up,
too, in a pretty pink dressing gown, her face pale and ghastly as
she stared down at the body of her late brother. More neighbors
attached themselves to her and led her indoors. There was a lot
of fumbling around because, even though there were lots of
lanterns available, the light from them only lit patches of the
moonless night, and folks blundered into bushes and flower
beds and each other as they attempted to help the two women.

In other words, chaos ensued after my initial discovery of the body, and I'm not sure what time it was when we got to the police chief's office. I only knew it was awfully late, and I also hoped Chief Vickers wouldn't telephone my parents.

By the way, Chief Vickers had a wonderful hound dog named Harley. Harley had helped the chief on many a search. The fact that Harley wasn't needed in this instance didn't lessen my wish that he were there so I'd have something warm and friendly to pet.

"Nobody besides you heard the telephone ringing. I see," said the chief. He turned to me. "And so you invited Phil to take a walk with you?"

"Yes. To clear my mind."

"To clear your mind." The chief cocked an eyebrow first at me and then at Phil.

"You know Annabelle," muttered Phil under his breath, the rat.

I shot him a glower, but the chief sighed and said, "Yes, I do know Miss Annabelle." He turned to me. "Listen, Miss Annabelle, I understand that you're worried about your brother-in-law. I'm not surprised about that. But don't forget that we haven't stopped looking at other suspects."

Eyeing him narrowly, I said, "Well, then, why did you have to haul Richard to the police station? He has a position at the bank to uphold, you know."

"Annabelle," said Phil in a warning tone. To heck with him. This was important.

"We brought many suspects to the station for questioning." Chief Vickers scratched his head. "Now who the devil—sorry, Miss Annabelle—would have reason to kill Herschel? From everything we've learned, Mr. Calhoun was a shrewd customer—"

"He was a crook," I corrected. Phil rolled his eyes, and the chief sighed again.

"Yes, so many folks have told me. It might interest you to know that we've found no indication of dirty tactics in his business records, however," said the chief.

"Well, of course you haven't! What you need to do is talk to the people he swindled!"

"We are doing exactly that, Miss Annabelle." The chief sounded mildly irritated. Maybe more than mildly.

"Oh, crumb!" I was so frustrated by that time, I darned near cried. But I wouldn't allow myself to do that. Not in front of these two brutes. So I stated the obvious. "Clearly, Calhoun would keep clean records at the bank. He was probably keeping a second set of books somewhere else."

"Where else?"

I frowned. "I don't know. Somewhere."

"Right." The chief rubbed a hand across his face. "Anyhow, while Mr. Calhoun might have had something going on that was a little shady, I don't know why anyone'd kill his son."

"Maybe he was in on his father's financial shenanigans," I suggested.

"Except we haven't found proof of any shenanigans."

Aw, nuts. *Everybody* knew Calhoun had been a hound dog— with apologies to Harley, who'd never cheated anybody that I knew about—and a criminal. It seemed incredible to me that not an ounce of proof of his shenanigans had been found yet. "Have you talked to Armando Contreras?" I demanded. "He had to hire a lawyer to get him out of the mess Mr. Calhoun got him in when Calhoun tried to call in the loan Richard had arranged for him."

"Yes, indeed. We've spoken to Mr. Contreras."

"Well? What did he say?"

"That Mr. Calhoun had called in his loan. The bank can do that, you know."

"But . . . but that's not fair!"

"It doesn't sound fair to me, either, but it was legal. Even Mr. Jaffa said so."

"I thought Mr. Jaffa was the one who made Mr. Calhoun back off."

"He did. But that doesn't mean there was anything crooked about the matter. It was low-down mean, but that's different."

"Fudge!" I no longer felt like crying. What I wanted to do at that moment was resurrect Edgar Calhoun and kill him myself.

The chief heaved a big sigh. "Listen, Miss Annabelle and Phil, why don't you go home now. Phil, you can see her to her door, right?"

"Right," said Phil. He'd continued pacing the office as the chief and I spoke. Now he came over to where I sat huddled in my uncomfortable wooden chair. "You ready to go home, Annabelle?"

"I guess so."

"Try to stay out of trouble," advised Chief Vickers. "We're going to start looking hard at *you*, Miss Annabelle, if you keep stumbling over bodies."

I think he was trying to be funny, but I didn't laugh. "I will," I said stolidly. Then I took Phil's arm, which was stiff. I got the feeling he didn't want to support me any longer that night, and that made my heart plummet.

"We'll probably have to talk some more tomorrow, Miss Annabelle," the chief warned. "I'll need to get a signed statement from you, since you're the one who found the body. So you might want to let your folks know what happened."

Oh, joy. Exactly what I wanted to do. Pa would be furious. So would Ma. Jack, the fiend, would be aggrieved that it had been I and not he who'd found yet another body. I'd be just as happy to give over body-finding to him, except that it would have made him swellheaded, and he was already difficult enough to bear.

161

Phil and I walked in silence for several minutes in the gloomy darkness. Our flashlights illuminated pinpricks of the boardwalk, but I still felt creepy, what with shadows glowering behind, beside and in front of us. I also knew Phil was mad at me, although I think his anger was unjustified. After all, I hadn't asked him to come with me in order to find another murder victim. I'd been hoping he'd just stand watch while I went through Mr. Calhoun's home office. But now he blamed me for getting him into yet another pickle. I kind of felt like crying again, although I'm not sure why. Phil's annoyance? Shock at having found Herschel's body? Exhaustion? Being scared by walking at night in a town where two murders had been committed?

Probably all of those things contributed to my puny state. That and the thought of telling my parents I'd been out prowling in the middle of the night with a man whom everyone expected me to marry. They might think we'd been doing something untoward, and we hadn't. Well . . . I guess finding murdered people might be considered untoward, but you know what I mean—and we hadn't been doing any such thing. Heck, Phil would probably have been delighted if we had been. Now he was just mad at me.

"I'm sorry I got you into this mess, Phil," I said after we'd been walking for a while, picking our ways carefully along the shadowy boardwalk.

"Me, too," he said, his voice snapping in the chilly air.

"It's not my fault we found Herschel." I regret to say my voice sounded whiny. "That's not what I expected, darn it."

"No, you just wanted to break into someone's house and go rifling through their private records."

"But it would have been for a good cause!"

"Right."

Silence surrounded us again, except for the clomping of our

shoes on the boardwalk. Then I sniffed and said, "At least I don't see how the chief can pin Herschel's murder on Richard."

"Huh."

Phil's mood and Herschel's murder didn't negate the fact that I wanted to go through that darned office, but I hesitated to bring up the subject with Phil. He was really on edge, and if I pushed him too hard he might just explode all over me. He was an easygoing fellow most of the time, but when pushed too far, he could show a hellish temper. I'd only ever seen him really angry once or twice, and I'd just as soon not be the one to provoke him into a temper fit a third time.

Crumb. I didn't know what to do. Perhaps Betty Lou Jarvis might be willing to act as scout when I tried the office ploy again.

And how was I going to break the news to my parents that I'd found another murdered man?

Lord, life could be difficult sometimes.

We got to my house after what seemed like an entirely too-long walk, and Phil said a curt good night when we finally made it through the pitchy black to the door to the house. Feeling lower than dirt, I first went to the bathroom and washed my hands about three hundred times. Then I made my way to my room. When I looked at the clock on my bedside table, I learned it was almost three o'clock in the morning. I'd never been awake so late on purpose before in my life. This time wasn't on purpose, either, come to think of it. I sat with a whump on my bed and tried to think of some way to tell my parents what had happened, without making them angry.

After considering the matter one way and another and upside and down, I came to the discouraging conclusion that there was no way to do it. They were going to be hurt and furious that I'd sneaked out of the house. Neither one of them would buy into the notion that I was only out for a stroll with Phil because I couldn't sleep. They'd accuse me of butting into police business. Curse it! If only we'd found Herschel's body on the Second Street boardwalk, my tale of merely being out for a walk would be so much more believable.

But we hadn't. We'd found him at his home, which meant that Phil and I had deliberately walked up Lee Avenue, and there was only one reason to do that, and it was to visit the Calhoun place. Oh, boy. I was really in for it this time.

Moodily, I rose from my bed, took off my coat, which still had leaves and muck clinging to it, and hung it in the closet, then climbed out of the rest of my clothes and into my nightgown. When I flopped back on the bed and pulled the covers over my head, I wished I'd never have to wake up and face what was sure to come at me in the morning.

I almost didn't. Wake up in the morning, I mean. I overslept. This seldom happened, because my mother would wake me up so that I could work in the store. I don't know why she didn't wake me up that morning . . . well, I didn't know why until she stormed into my room around tennish, and then I learned the reason for her prior forbearance.

"Annabelle Blue, you get out of that bed this instant!"

I blinked and tried to focus my gummy eyes on her. "What? What?"

"I was going to wake you up earlier but you looked peaked, and I thought you might not be feeling well. I'd heard you get up a couple of times last night. But now Chief Vickers is in the kitchen, and I *know* why you were up and about, and I'm ashamed to call you my daughter! Get up and put your robe on and get to the kitchen right this minute!"

Oh, Lordy. Offhand, I couldn't recall ever seeing my mother so angry, not even with Jack when he was behaving his worst. Generally speaking, when Ma was upset with her children she'd get all sorrowful and unhappy, and we'd behave ourselves in order not to put that expression on her face again. And never before, in all my nineteen years, had she ever told me she was ashamed of me.

"Ma, I'm really—"

"Don't you go telling me how sorry you are, either, Annabelle Blue. You were nosing into somebody else's business, and look what's come of it! That a daughter of mine should discover not one, but *two* bodies in my own town in a matter of a few days is . . . is . . . well, I just don't know what to think. I can't imagine what your father is going to say!"

Oh, Lordy again. "Pa doesn't know?" I croaked, thinking I really did feel rather unwell. But Ma would never believe me if I told her I was sick. Anyhow, even being sick wouldn't get me out of the trouble I'd got myself into.

"Not yet," she snapped. "He's gone to Dexter on business. But when he gets back, you'd best prepare yourself, young woman."

I wanted to cry again. "Did Jack go to school this morning?" I asked with hope sagging somewhere around my ankles.

"Yes, although you don't deserve to get off so easily."

My good fortune wouldn't last, and we both knew it. "I'll be right there, Ma," I told her, keeping my voice steady with a major effort.

"See that you are." Darned if she didn't slam my door on her way back to the kitchen. My mother. Slamming doors. Oh, boy, this was bad.

If I was in bed, Ma was in the kitchen, Pa was in Dexter, and Jack was at school, who was minding the store? That thought kept my mind away from uglier matters as I arose and shuffled into some clothes. I rushed as fast as I could, because Ma had told me to merely put on a robe, but I simply couldn't face the chief and the wrath of my mother in a robe and nightgown. So I flung on a skirt and shirtwaist, brushed my hair and knotted it on top of my head, and headed to the kitchen in my slippers. I felt like pure hell.

Ma was still angry with me when I tiptoed into the kitchen. She glared at me and said, "Sit yourself down, young lady."

I sat. I could have used a cup of coffee, but I didn't dare ask or get myself one. I did nod to the chief.

Fortunately for me, Chief Vickers was a gentleman of the old school, and I could tell he felt sorry for me. "Don't be too hard on her, Susanna. She had a rough night, and she and Mr. Gunderson were only being curious."

"Curious! Well, I guess she *was* curious! And she managed to fall over another body. I can't believe this nonsense!"

Odd how she'd fixed on the precise verb to describe how I'd discovered Herschel Calhoun. I didn't say so.

"Why don't you get Annabelle a cup of coffee, Susanna? She looks like she needs it."

"She doesn't deserve your kindness, Chief Vickers," said Ma, crushing me to the heart. But she did as he'd suggested and plunked a mug in front of me.

"Thanks, Ma," I whispered, almost not daring to say that much with her in this mood.

"You're welcome." Then she stood there, her fists on her hips, and frowned at me. "I swear, Annabelle Blue." Her voice was nominally gentler, and I took some courage from that. "Of all our children, you were the one who never gave Will or me a moment's trouble. But look at you now! Snooping around in the middle of the night. Finding bodies everywhere you go. I just don't understand it."

"I don't either," I said softly. "And I never wanted to upset you or Pa. Honest, Ma. But I couldn't sleep, and I called Phil, and we walked and . . . well, and we found Herschel's body."

"And that's another thing, young lady. Calling boys in the middle of the night! Why, I never heard of such a thing! What do you think people are going to say when they learn you've been walking around Rosedale with Phil Gunderson in the middle of the night?"

Straightening, I said with more firmness in my voice than I'd heretofore been able to summon, "Anyone who knows Phil and me will know we'd never do anything to bring shame on our families." That was a powerful statement, and I was proud of myself for thinking of it—even if it wasn't exactly true.

"She's got a point there, Susanna," said the chief, bless him. "I don't suspect the two of them of doing anything worse than poking around where they don't belong. They weren't up to anything else."

"That's right," I said. I longed to ask Ma who was minding the store but didn't dare, since minding the store was my job.

"Well, I suppose that's something," grumbled Ma. "But I need to get back to the store, Chief. I left everything unlocked when you came in. I was that upset." She turned to me again. "When you finish talking with the chief and eat something for breakfast, you get yourself to the store, Annabelle Blue. You're shirking your duty."

"I didn't mean to," I told her. "I thought you'd wake me up in time to get to work."

She snorted. "And here I thought you might be sick." She shook her head. "But you'd been out prowling in the middle of the night. No wonder you looked so sickly when I went in to wake you up earlier." And then, to add thorns to my crown, she said, "I'd expect such antics from Jack, Annabelle, but I *never* thought you'd do anything so addlebrained." And off she went, leaving me with the chief, feeling every bit as sickly as she'd thought I was.

CHAPTER THIRTEEN

The chief didn't stay long. I couldn't tell him anything more than I'd told him the night before, and I maintained the lie about telephoning Phil. I didn't dare admit I'd been going to sneak into the Calhouns' house and look through papers that didn't belong to me. I hoped Phil would stand firm on that issue too. I expected he would, since he didn't want to look like an idiot any more than I did.

Because I still considered my interest in the investigation relevant, even though no one else did, I asked, "You said you spoke to Micah Tindall, Chief Vickers."

The chief heaved a bigger-than-ordinary sigh, but he answered me. "Yes, I spoke to him. What he said is none of your business, young lady."

"I suppose not. But I feel sorry for him."

"I do, too. But it looks as if he's going to be all right. His cousin, Jerry Murdoch, is going to give him a job in his tinsmithing business."

"I didn't know Mr. Tindall was a tinsmith."

"Jerry's offered to teach him."

"It's nice of Mr. Murdoch to teach him a new trade and give him a position."

"You know us folks in Rosedale, Miss Annabelle. We look after our own."

"Yes. I guess we do." Most of the time. "Anyhow, Mr. Tindall going into the tinsmithing business doesn't explain who might have killed Herschel Calhoun."

"No. It doesn't."

"And Mr. Feather?"

"Yes, Miss Annabelle."

I could tell he was getting irked. My shoulders slumped. "And you've talked to Sadie Dobbs?" I asked, even though I knew he had.

"Young lady, this investigation has nothing to do with you. I don't know how many times I've already told you that."

"But—"

The chief held up a hand, and I shut my mouth. "I know. You're worried about your brother-in-law. I'll talk to Miss Dobbs again today, but you don't really think she had anything to do with killing the goose that laid the golden egg, so to speak, do you?"

"No. Probably not. And I guess Herschel being killed sort of lets him off the hook for killing his father." Boy, Richard couldn't catch a break for love nor money. "But who could have killed Herschel?"

"At this point, I have no idea. One thing's for certain, though, and it's that *you* need to stay out of the business. If what happened last night didn't teach you that much, you're not as bright as everyone says."

People thought I was bright? That was a new one on me. All I'd been hearing lately was how stupid I was. I said, "Thanks, Chief," because I couldn't think of anything else to say.

Then I fixed some toast and bacon, although my tummy hurt from humiliation and anguish. The notion I'd riled my mother so much that she'd told me she was ashamed of me curdled my innards. While I felt justified—sort of—in what I'd aimed to do the night before, I also didn't believe she'd wronged me. The thing I did wrong was to get caught. I'd never have been caught if somebody hadn't murdered Herschel Calhoun. And I couldn't for the life of me figure out who might have done that evil deed.

At any rate, it wasn't more than about a half hour after Ma had roused me from my bed that I entered the store, full of fear and trepidation and still tired from my overnight experiences.

She eyed me with disfavor when I appeared. I'd braided my hair, washed my face, and given myself a quick sponge bath, not wanting to keep her waiting any longer than necessary. My hands still hurt from where they'd scraped over leaves and dirt the night before. "Well? What did you and the chief talk about?"

"Only about what happened last night. And I asked him—" Uh-oh. It occurred to me I ought not tell her I'd asked about the ongoing investigation. "I asked him who he thought might have killed Herschel."

Ma sniffed. "And what did he say?"

Shaking my head, I said, "Not much. It's difficult to imagine someone killing both father and son. I mean, the father I can understand—"

"Annabelle!"

"Well, darn it, Ma, I can. Mr. Calhoun was a crook. Even Richard thinks so. Heck, I thought Herschel might have killed Mr. Calhoun, actually, but it sure doesn't look like that now."

"Why would a son kill his own father?"

"From what Gladys told me and from what Herschel told Phil, Mr. Calhoun was a tyrant at home. Plus, he was running around on his wife."

"Annabelle Blue!"

I lifted my hands in a gesture of defeat. "I can't help the truth, Ma. He was seeing Sadie Dobbs. That's not my fault. It's his. Or it was."

Her eyes narrowing and, I think, in spite of her better nature, she asked, "Who's Sadie Dobbs?"

"She's a waitress at the Cowboy Café. I spoke to her a little bit the other day—"

"Annabelle . . ."

"I wasn't interfering with the police! I only talked to her." Lifting my bib apron from its hook, I pulled it over my head and tied it behind my back. "As far as I can tell, she's the only one who's sorry the older Mr. Calhoun is dead. I don't think she even knew Herschel."

"It's a puzzling problem," said Ma, sounding as if she were almost ready to forgive me for being interested in what was, after all, at least a fascinating mystery and one, moreover, that directly affected her own family. "Um, Annabelle . . ." Her sentence trickled out before she'd finished it, from which I gathered she wanted to ask me something about the investigation but didn't want to let go of her anger quite yet.

I waited her out, only lifting an eyebrow in query.

Finally she just up and said, "Does the chief still suspect Richard? Even after the death of Herschel?"

"Well, I'm afraid he might still suspect him, Ma, although he's interviewing lots of people who had more reason to kill Mr. Calhoun than Richard ever did. Besides, even Chief Vickers must believe the same person killed both men, and why would Richard kill Herschel?" Dang it, I *had* to get into the Calhoun house and go through that office!

"I have no idea." Ma appeared genuinely upset. "Poor Hannah. She's in a state, Annabelle, and I don't blame her. Even if Richard is completely exonerated—and I'm sure he will be—all this attention from the police can't be good for his career."

"I know. That's another thing that worries me."

"How horrible to have your own husband suspected of murder," Ma muttered.

I'm assuming Ma didn't know this from personal experience, Pa having been a pillar of the community without a blot against his name from the moment of his birth or thereabouts. "Yes. I'm sure it must be. I'm sorry for Hannah and Richard both. And," I added to be fair, "the Tindalls and Mr. Contreras and

Mr. Feather and whoever else the police are looking at."

"Yes, indeed." Ma heaved one of the huger sighs I'd ever heard and said, "I've been preparing orders folks have telephoned in, Annabelle. Will you please deliver them?"

Would I? Oh, boy! I loved delivering things, because that meant I got to drive the Model T and chat with friends. I hoped the Calhouns would be on the delivery schedule.

"Sure. Who gets what?"

"Mr. Farley needs you to take six yards of white linen and some white embroidery thread to the church."

Mr. Farley was the minister of the Methodist Episcopal Church, North, which we Blues attended faithfully every Sunday.

"How come he needs fabric and embroidery thread? He's not taking up sewing, is he?"

I felt a tiny bit encouraged when Ma laughed. "No. The altar guild is planning to make and embroider new altar cloths for the Easter season."

"Oh. That's nice. All white, eh?"

"Well, we have those nice purple ones Mrs. Wilson made for the Lenten season. When Easter Day arrives, the white ones will replace those old yellowish ones they've been using since the last century."

"I see." I hadn't quite figured out which colors went with which seasons, although I did then recollect that the preacher always covered the cross with purple cloth from Lent up until Easter Sunday, when the cross was revealed in all its emptiness and white replaced purple on the altar and dais. But Ma was right: the white altar cloths had turned yellow several years prior, and it would be nice to have shiny white altar cloths to replace the old ones.

"Mr. Chewling needs a package of receipt pads delivered to the shoe store."

Hmm. The shoe store and Firman Meeks again. "Do you want me to pick up those slippers for Pa?" I'd told her about the open-backed slippers for two dollars and the fleece-lined ones for three dollars, and she'd frowned.

She did so again now. "I haven't made up my mind. They're awfully expensive."

"True. But I'll be at the shoe store today."

She waved a hand in the air. "I'm still deciding about the slippers. Mrs. Calhoun wants another five yards of black poplin and more thread."

"Huh. I'm surprised she didn't send Betty Lou to fetch them."

"I understand that Betty Lou is needed at the Calhoun home to take in covered dishes. I made a squash pie before I opened the store this morning, so you can take that along with you when you deliver the fabric. We need to keep up the proprieties." Ma shook her head and frowned. "That poor family. I should go with you to offer my condolences, but there'd be no one left to watch the store if I did, so please convey my sympathy."

"I certainly will." Boy, I didn't think I'd be able to get back to the Calhoun place so easily. This must be a blessing from heaven! Or maybe from the other place. At any rate, I'd be able to talk to Betty Lou and ask her to stand watch when I went through Mr. Calhoun's desk.

"While I was making pies, I fixed one for Pete and his family, so you can drop that one off on your way." She eyed me keenly. "But don't linger with your young man, Annabelle. I don't want people to get the wrong idea about you two." She shook her head. "Imagine telephoning Phil Gunderson in the middle of the night. People are going to talk, you know."

Fudge. I didn't want people to talk about Phil and me, mainly because we hadn't done a single, solitary thing that was worth talking about. Well, except for finding another body. "There's nothing to talk about," I said, feeling abused and mistreated.

"That's as may be. Appearances tend to belie your words, however, so hold your head high and behave yourself. If you do, the talk will die down."

"I sure hope so. Poor Phil. He doesn't deserve to be talked about."

"I suggest you think about that before you make another midnight telephone call, young lady."

"I will," I said humbly. Heck, I hadn't called him in the first place. We'd made arrangements ahead of time. But I couldn't say that, either. Talk about talk! If folks knew we'd arranged to meet at midnight, the gossip would last forever.

"And please stop by the butcher and get a pound of round steak from Mr. Deutsch on your way back home. I'm making Swiss steak for supper tonight."

"Yum. I love Swiss steak."

"So does your father." She tapped her cheek. "Let me see. Is there anything else we need?"

As I couldn't answer her question, I remained silent.

"I guess that's it, Annabelle. But it's freezing cold out there, so you'd best get your coat and scarf and gloves."

"Will do. Be right back."

So I returned to my room, where I took out the coat I'd worn the previous evening. Ma was right about the cold. Riding in the machine would make me even chillier because of the wind in my face, so I wrapped the scarf around my head, and fetched some gloves that were leather and wouldn't interfere with my handling of the steering wheel and gear lever.

Then, after I loaded the Model T, I set out, deciding to visit Phil first and apologize once more for getting him into last night's muddle.

Standing behind the counter, he glanced up when the door opened and didn't appear happy to see me, which caused a spasm in my heart. "Hey, Phil," I said timidly, holding out the pie as a peace offering.

"What do you want, Annabelle?" he asked coldly.

"I don't want anything, Phil, except to apologize about last night."

He took a quick glance around the hardware store. "For God's sake, keep your voice down! I don't want the whole world to know we were out after midnight last night. Not that they don't already, probably," he added bitterly. "Thanks to you, everybody in town will think we were up to no good." With a hot glare at me, he said, "And they'd be right, but for the wrong reason."

"I'm sorry." I swallowed hard, hoping I wouldn't cry. "Here." I thrust the pie closer to him. "Ma made this for you and Pete and the family. She made a pie for the Calhouns, too, and I have to deliver that one next."

"Please thank your mother for all of us."

I noticed he didn't thank me for bringing it. He was really mad at me. So. I couldn't ask him to stand guard at the Calhoun house again. He'd blow his stack. Therefore, the guard would have to be Betty Lou. Betty Lou or nobody. That was a frightening thought, although I was still convinced I might find something in that wretched house that the police had overlooked.

Was that silly of me? Perhaps. But I'd read tons of books in which folks found stuff overlooked by the legitimate police departments of the world. Heck, Hercule Poirot even found incriminating evidence in twists of paper that had been stuck in a jar on a mantelpiece in *The Mysterious Affair at Styles*. I guess we Americans didn't go in so much for writing notes on twists of paper, but perhaps Mr. Calhoun had done so. And what about *The Purloined Letter*? In that story, the evidence had been left in plain sight and missed by everyone!

Mind you, I don't think either Agatha Christie or Edgar Allan Poe ever committed murder except on paper. Perhaps they didn't know the ins and outs of the real, honest-to-goodness murder game. Not that it was a game. Yet the two authors had propounded some great ideas about searching for stuff, and I aimed to put their teachings to the test, provided I could ever get into the Calhoun house when all its inhabitants were sound asleep—except, with luck, Betty Lou.

"I'll be sure to thank Ma for you, Phil." Then, in a burst of self-pity and regret, I pleaded, something I seldom do. "Please don't be mad at me, Phil. I'm only trying to clear Richard's good name."

"That's a job for the police, and you know it, Annabelle. If you keep on doing what you're doing, you're going to land us both in the muck, and I for one don't like to be gossiped about."

"I don't, either. And we wouldn't have been if somebody—not Richard—hadn't murdered Herschel Calhoun."

"It was your idiotic idea to go through their house after midnight that caused us to be caught together, damn it."

Oh, boy. Phil was swearing again. And it was all my fault. If I hadn't begged him to stand guard at the Calhoun place, he wouldn't have become a topic of gossip and wouldn't be swearing now. I heaved a sigh.

"You're right," I said at last, feeling about as low as dirt. "I'm sorry I got you caught up in the Calhoun problem. I won't do it again."

His eyebrows soared. "You mean it? You're really going to give up this harebrained notion of outwitting the cops and solving the crime yourself?"

"It's not harebrained! And I don't expect to outwit the cops. But, by gum, I'm sure going to do my best to clear Richard of any hint of suspicion. Why, there are all sorts of people who might have done it. Why, what about Mr. Tindall and Mr. Contreras!"

Another frenzied glance around the hardware store preceded Phil's next whispered statement. "Dammit, will you quit hollering? We're already in enough trouble. Bandying people's names around as murder suspects won't win you any friends, you know!"

He was right. Darn it. I hated when that happened. I glanced around the store, too, and breathed more easily when I saw the place was empty except for the two of us. "Sorry."

"Sorry, my hind leg." He eyed me keenly. Then he gave me a hideous glower. It took a lot to make Phil look hideous, because he was a very handsome guy, but he managed it that time. "You're not giving up, are you? You're going to keep poking and nosing around, aren't you?"

"I . . . darn it, Phil, I have to. Chief Vickers is still interested in Richard as a suspect in Mr. Calhoun's murder." I sniffed. "He couldn't think of a good reason for him to kill Herschel, however."

"I'm sure he couldn't. There is no good reason. At least none we know about." He maintained his scowl, and I instantly took umbrage.

"Richard MacDougall is no murderer, Phil Gunderson! He had differences with Mr. Calhoun at the bank because Mr. Calhoun was a rotten, sneaky skunk!"

"Calm down, Annabelle. I'm not saying you're wrong about that. But, dammit, you *are* wrong to go butting into things that don't concern you. And don't tell me that Richard concerns you, because I know he does. And I'm sure the police will find the real culprit soon."

"You do, do you? I wish I could be as certain as you are. But I'm not."

He rolled his eyes, and that was it for me. I turned around, huffing, and stomped to the door.

Phil hollered after me. "You're not going to go over there

again in the middle of the night, are you? Because if you are—"

I whirled around and hollered back at him. "What I do or don't do is none of your business, Phil Gunderson. You've as much as told me so, besides calling me stupid and careless and I don't know what else."

"Annabelle, if you try to do that again, at least tell me so I can—"

"Darned if I will! You've made your position crystal clear."

And before he could yell anything else, I stormed out of the place. Good thing, too, because a clump of chattering men were about to open the door and enter the hardware store. They stopped in their tracks, and one of them—I think it was Mr. Lovelady, but I'm not sure—held the door open for me. My face burned, and I'm sure they stared at me as I stepped down to the street and got into the Ford.

Life could be awfully darned embarrassing sometimes. I didn't approve.

CHAPTER FOURTEEN

Too bad life didn't care if it embarrassed me or not. I felt the stares of folks as I drove the Model T down Second Street. Huh. You'd think people would have better things to do than gossip about their neighbors. Perhaps I was being the teensiest bit sensitive that day, but I don't think so. I swear I could hear people tittering behind their hands when I passed them by in the Ford.

I saw Mae Shenkel and Ruby Bond walking out of Pruitt's Drug Store. Mae waved and then instantly turned to Ruby and whispered something in her ear. Ruby, who was a very nice person, didn't laugh, although Mae giggled like mad. Stupid girl—although she sure dressed well. That day she wore a brown suit with a fur collar and a brown cloche hat and she looked like a million bucks. Ruby, who wasn't as fashion-conscious as her friend, was clad in a sensible frock covered with a heavy coat, and her hat was just your run-of-the-mill head covering. I don't think the weather got out of the low forties all day long, and I was glad for my heavy coat and scarf.

My next duty was to visit the shoe store. I didn't want to stop and go inside. What I wanted was to keep driving clear out of town and maybe spend the day hiding out at the Bottomless Lakes. They weren't really bottomless, but they were awfully deep. There were eleven of them, and they'd got their name back in the 'eighties, when some of John Chisum's cowboys dropped ropes into them to try to discover their depths. They never did, so they thought the water went down forever. It didn't. What happened was that underground streams and rivers led into the lakes, causing currents underwater that moved the ropes so they couldn't hit the bottoms of the lakes. Scientists have since discovered all sorts of stuff like that about them. We liked to go out there in the summertime and fish or have picnics.

That day, I just wanted to go somewhere and hide. How embarrassing to have people snicker about Phil and me! And all we'd been doing was walking together on a couple of streets after dark. Shoot. If it hadn't been for the rat who'd killed Herschel Calhoun, nobody else would ever have known about our excursion, and Herschel's murder would be the juiciest topic of the day. But was it? No. It was so much more exciting to gossip about a young couple who'd been found out of doors after midnight. It wouldn't surprise me if Minnie and Miss Libby made a trip to town just so Miss Libby could berate me for bringing shame on my family. Can you blame me for wanting to run away?

But I didn't. I pulled the Ford to a stop in front of Chewling's Shoes, grabbed the package destined to be delivered there, and climbed the steps to the boardwalk. I still felt like two cents or less when I opened the door to the store and walked in.

Wouldn't you know it? There, having her feet stuffed into a pair of shoes by Mr. Meeks, sat Josephine Contreras. Blast! Of course, she might not have heard the news about Phil and me yet. Herschel's murder was of much greater import than the supposed love life of two young people.

I should have known better.

"Annabelle Blue!" she cried in great delight. "I hear you and your gentleman friend were out canoodling when you found another body."

"We weren't canoodling," I muttered, furious. Maybe I should ask the chief to look harder at Armando Contreras when it came to the murders. Not that the chief would do anything I asked of him. "We were out for a walk because I couldn't sleep. I almost fell on top of the body." I shuddered, remembering.

Firman Meeks glanced up at me. "How unpleasant for you, Miss Blue."

"It was. Very unpleasant."

"I swear, Annabelle, I've never known anyone who finds bodies the way you do," said Josephine with a laugh.

"I've only found two of them. And I didn't want to find either one of them."

"I thought you found a body last summer," said Josephine. She would.

"Yes, and that was horrid too," I snapped. "Here's Mr. Chewling's order, Mr. Meeks. I'm making deliveries today because Pa's out of town."

The man rose to his feet and took the bundle I held. "Thank you, Miss Blue." He turned to Josephine. "Will you excuse me for a moment, Mrs. Contreras? Why don't you walk a little in those shoes and see how they feel while I take these to the back room."

"All right," said Josephine. She eagerly rose from the chair and showed me a foot wearing the exact same patent-leather pump I'd seen and liked not a week ago in this very store. "What do you think, Annabelle? Do you think they'll look good at the church's Christmas dance?"

Josephine and Armando belonged to the Roman Catholic Church in town, and their church was always holding dances and stuff. We Methodists had covered-dish suppers. I wondered if Phil would ask me to go to the Catholics' dance in December or if he'd still be mad at me by then. "I like them a lot, Josephine. In fact, I was looking at that pair last week."

"Ah, yes. I recall your interest in those shoes, Miss Blue."

I swear I jumped a foot. I hadn't heard Mr. Meeks enter the

room. He sneaked around like a slithery snake.

"I beg your pardon," he said with a ferrety smile. "I didn't mean to startle you."

"That's all right," I said, although it wasn't. I turned back to Josephine "Yes. I do like those shoes. If you get them, I guess I'll have to get something else. We can't be seen in the same pair of shoes, can we?"

"I don't know why not," she said, although she wasn't really paying attention. She was occupied in looking at her feet in the little mirror Mr. Chewling had placed on the floor. The shoes were very pretty, and they looked good on her feet. As for me, I'd just wear my Sunday shoes to the Christmas dance. We Blues didn't buy a new pair of shoes for every occasion. We were thrifty that way.

"Did your mother decide about the slippers, Miss Blue?" asked Mr. Meeks.

"Not yet. She's still thinking about them. I think she thinks they might be too expensive."

"Well, for what you'd be getting, that's not a bad price."

"You're probably right. Ma's just not used to spending a lot of money on slippers."

Josephine came back over to the row of seats and plunked herself down, focusing the attention of Mr. Meeks on her. "Well, I think I'm going to buy these. Mando will be furious, but that's just too bad. I haven't had a new pair of shoes in forever."

"They're awfully pretty, Josephine. But I have to go now. Deliveries to make, you know."

"Take care, Annabelle. Don't find any more bodies, all right?"

"I'll try not to," I muttered, heading for the door.

Well. That had been an embarrassing experience. The whole blasted town was probably talking about Phil and me. But I still had to go to the Calhouns' house and the butcher's shop. Perhaps I'd be able to corner Betty Lou at the Calhoun place and ask her to leave the window open for me again that night. All these late nights were going to wear me out pretty darned quickly, so the sooner I got the onerous task of searching Mr. Calhoun's office over with, the better.

On the other hand, maybe I should leave the investigation in the hands of the police. After all, Rosedale at night was kind of a frightening place, being so dark and all. Tonight would be another moonless one, and since I'd irritated Phil beyond all patience, there'd be only one flashlight to light my way. I remembered all those lumpy shadows everywhere and shuddered.

But no. Annabelle Blue was no coward, whatever else she might be. Too bad, that, but if I left everything up to Chief Vickers and his crew, I wasn't sure what might happen. So I'd just have to go it alone. The thought held absolutely no appeal whatsoever. It was a glum Annabelle Blue who drove our Model T up Lee Avenue that crisp autumn day.

There were cars, buggies and wagons parked all around the Calhouns' house, and ladies were entering with dishes and leaving empty-handed. It was always the women of the house who made these sympathy calls. Men weren't required—or desired, would be my guess—although friends of the deceased's children were acceptable, as witnessed during the last time I'd been here. In the daytime, I mean. At least I didn't have to row to the place today.

Another day for condolence calls on the same grieving family—and it had been my own personal screech of horror that had told them the reason for today's calls. Bah. I didn't want to go in there.

This time I expected the family, what was left of it, was actually sorry to have lost another of its members. Herschel wasn't my kind of guy, from everything I'd heard about him, but his mother must have loved him, and maybe even his sister. I had to park way down the block and walk quite a ways, but that was all right. I lifted the pie from the seat and joined a couple of ladies walking toward the Calhoun place, all of us carrying foodstuffs of various kinds. I knew them both, of course, and braced myself. I didn't have to wait long.

"Annabelle Blue, I don't know why you keep finding dead bodies," said Mrs. O'Dell. She's the one who'd been looking for her chickens the day after the storm. "I'm sure your family is terribly upset."

"Yes. We all are. Finding another body was no fun, I can tell you."

"You do make a habit of that sort of thing," her companion, Mrs. Lovelady, said.

"Not on purpose," I said, miffed.

Mrs. O'Dell tutted and shook her finger at me in a playful way. "You oughtn't be out at night with Phil Gunderson, either, dear. You know how people talk."

I sure did, and she was one of the worst gossips in town. Lucky me for running into her right off the bat. "We weren't doing anything untoward, Mrs. O'Dell. I was upset about everything that's been going on lately, and Phil was kind enough to walk with me."

"Oh, *I* believe you, dear, and I'm sure Mrs. Lovelady does, too"—Mrs. Lovelady confirmed this assumption by nodding her head—"but you never know about other folks in town." She giggled, and I decided then and there that giggles didn't sound right coming from middle-aged ladies.

"Well, anyone who'd believe Phil Gunderson would do anything improper doesn't know him. And anyone who'd think *I'd* do anything improper doesn't know me." And I stomped up the steps of the Calhoun place and knocked on the door for all three of us. Curse it, why couldn't people mind their own business?

A rattled-looking Betty Lou Jarvis opened the door. She brightened some when she saw me. "Oh, Annabelle! I'm so glad you came today." Completely ignoring Mrs. O'Dell and Mrs. Lovelady, who had to carry their covered dishes into the house themselves, Betty Lou grabbed my arm and yanked me along to the kitchen. "Annabelle, tell me. Exactly what happened last night? I had the window unlocked and was expecting you to show up maybe about twelve-thirty or one, when all of a sudden I heard somebody screaming fit to kill, and then all heck broke loose. I could hardly believe it when they told me Herschel had been killed."

I set Ma's squash pie down on a table that was already nearly covered from end to end with covered dishes, cakes, pies, biscuits, jars of pickles and preserves, and just about every other edible you could imagine. After taking a glance around and finding we were alone in the kitchen, I whispered, "Lordy, Betty Lou, it was terrible. Phil came with me to stand guard. You know, in case anybody showed up or anything, but the instant I turned to go to the back of the house, I tripped over Herschel's body." Covering my face with my hands, I whimpered. "It was just awful. I never want to find another body again as long as I live. Why, I almost fell on top of him, and if I'd done that, I'd have . . . oh, mercy."

"You'd have what?" Betty Lou's tone was avid.

My heart squished and started aching as I recalled the events of the prior night. Or this morning. Whenever it was. "My very own body would have shoved the knife even farther into his back, is what. I got his blood on my hands." Not to mention having scraped said hands on the dirt and rubble scattered around the body.

"Oh, Annabelle, how horrid for you."

To my utter humiliation, my eyes filled with tears. "Yes, it was horrid. And now everyone in town thinks Phil and I were doing something dirty, and we weren't, but I can't tell anyone but you the truth. I even lied to the police chief." I hauled a handkerchief out of my skirt pocket and wiped my eyes. "And I still don't know what Mr. Calhoun was hiding in his office. If he was hiding anything."

"I bet he was," said Betty Lou fiercely. "The whole family stinks. That rat Herschel was every bit as bad as his old man."

Merciful heavens. While I'd known for a week or more that Betty Lou wasn't fond of her employers, I hadn't expected such condemnation from her. Generally even people who had disliked a person didn't say bad things about him or her after he or she was dead. Tradition and all that. "Really?"

"Really. Ever since the will was read and the family discovered Mr. Calhoun hadn't left them as much money as they expected, Herschel's been a bear around the house. Stomping and throwing fits and swearing to beat the band. And Gladys has been crying into her lace-edged hankies until you'd think she'd dry up. If Mrs. Calhoun's lip prunes up any more, she's going to have more wrinkles than a raisin."

"Oh, dear."

Mrs. O'Dell and Mrs. Lovelady entered the kitchen then and we had to shut up. They both frowned at Betty Lou, and Mrs. O'Dell said, "Miss Jarvis, here's the covered dish I brought for the family. I expect you're saving the dishes in here."

Clearly she didn't believe she should have had to bring her dish into the kitchen herself, such a menial task being beneath her. But Betty Lou only said, "Thank you, Mrs. O'Dell. I'll take it. I was just offering Annabelle some comfort. She had a terrible time last night, you know."

Mrs. Lovelady tutted in sympathy, but not Mrs. O'Dell. Eyeing the both of us with disfavor, Mrs. O'Dell said, "I suppose so, although I should say Herschel Calhoun suffered a bit more than she did."

"Of course," I said, hating her in that moment.

She sniffed and left. Mrs. Lovelady offered us a sympathetic glance and then she left, too. Betty Lou and I waited a moment, to make sure nobody else was going to interrupt us. Then Betty Lou said, "But that's not the strange part."

I perked up slightly. "There's a strange part?"

"Yes." Betty Lou took another quick gander around the kitchen. "Just yesterday, Herschel perked up. I don't know why, and I don't know what caused the change in his attitude, but he was as sassy as sassy could be and kept saying things like, 'I'll take care of everything, Ma,' and 'It's going to be all right now,' and stuff like that. He always did think he was God's gift to the world, but he got totally too big for his britches then."

"And you say this happened only yesterday?" This was indeed a puzzling circumstance, and one I didn't understand the least little bit.

"Yes. All of a sudden. I don't think he told his mother or sister what changed his attitude, either, because they were still down in the dumps, and Gladys got exasperated with him and told him to shut up. But he didn't. He only laughed and rubbed his hands together as if he knew something she didn't know."

"Hmm. How odd."

"Very odd. And it wouldn't surprise me to learn that whatever he thought he'd discovered that would change his fortune is what got him killed."

"Makes sense to me," I said after thinking about it for a second. "But, darn it, what was it?"

Betty Lou shrugged. "I have no idea." She cast a glance at the kitchen door. "But listen, Annabelle, I have to get back to work. I don't want their majesties to come in here and accuse me of shirking my duties." She rolled her eyes. "Do you want to try the office again tonight?"

Did I? Without Phil? In the dark and the cold? Well . . .

"Would you mind staying up late to stand guard? I don't dare ask Phil to help again. He's furious with me. He doesn't like being talked about."

"I don't blame him."

"No," I said, feeling truly lousy, "I don't, either."

Betty Lou thought about my question for a moment. "Yeah. I suppose I can do that. It means I'll be exhausted tomorrow but with any luck, Mrs. Calhoun and Gladys will have to go to the funeral parlor and arrange for another funeral and I'll get to rest up some."

"Golly. Another funeral."

"Yeah. At least the people who were murdered were both stinkers. It would be a real shame if they'd been nice."

"That's true."

Later when I recalled that conversation, I felt a little callous about our dismissing the lives of two men so casually. On the other hand, Betty Lou was right. They'd both been stinkers, and better stinkers die than folks people actually liked and who were kind to others.

Knowing I'd have to face Mrs. Calhoun and Gladys, I left the kitchen with Betty Lou, only she went to the front door to do her duty as maid of all works, and I went to the parlor. Reluctantly. I wasn't sure how I'd be greeted, as it had been I who'd discovered both Mr. Calhoun's and Herschel's bodies. Not that it was my fault I'd done so, but you never know how people will react. In some irrational fit of something-or-other, maybe the Calhoun ladies would blame me for the demise of their menfolk.

I paused next to the kitchen door for a moment, sucked in a big breath for courage, whispered a brief prayer to a God who, if He had any sense, had stopped listening to me whine a long time ago, and marched to the parlor. As soon as I set foot over the threshold, all conversation ceased and darned if every single person in the room didn't turn and stare at me. I felt myself get hot and wished I'd removed my heavy coat. Oh, well, too late for that now.

Holding my chin up, I approached Gladys. I didn't see Mrs. Calhoun anywhere. "Good morning, Gladys. I just came to bring one of my mother's delicious pies for the family and to say how very sorry I am about your brother."

My words seemed to break the spell of silence that had settled over the room, because people began buzzing again. It looked to me as though her brother's death had honestly rattled Gladys, and I felt sorry for her.

"Thank you, Annabelle," she said in a shaky voice. "It was very kind of your mother to bake a pie for us."

"She'd have come herself, but she had to watch the store. My father had to go to Dexter, and my brother's at school." Not that she cared about that. I'd started babbling, which is my usual reaction when I'm nervous.

"Well, it was very kind of her. And you, too. It . . . it must have been awful for you to find . . ." Her words drifted off into her handkerchief, which she held to her drippy eyes.

"I'm so very sorry," I repeated. "How's your mother? She must be terribly upset."

"Devastated," Gladys said. "She couldn't even come down to thank people, so I have to do it all. She's upstairs lying down, with Mrs. Jenkins attending to her."

Good Lord. She must be in a bad way. Mrs. Jenkins was a nurse people hired when they'd had an operation or an illness and needed somebody with nursing skills to attend to them.

"Well . . ." I didn't know what to say, so I said that. "I don't even know what to say to you except that I'm so very, very sorry. What a terrible blow to your family, and coming so quickly after your father's passing makes it even worse."

"Oh, nobody cared about Daddy," said Gladys in an

unguarded moment of truth. I heard a couple of gasps from the crowded room. "But Herschel . . . well, Herschel was an idiot sometimes, but I loved him. He was my brother. And somebody stabbed him in the back!" And she broke down in tears.

Gee, I wondered if I'd miss my obnoxious brother Jack if somebody stabbed him in the back. Somehow, I don't think I'd be as broken up about Jack's passing as Gladys was about Herschel's, but I might be wrong. Family was family, after all. Anyhow, it sounded to me as if the worst part of everything in Gladys's mind was the way Herschel had met his end.

"I'm so sorry," I repeated wretchedly, wishing I could do something for her.

"And I don't know what we're going to do," Gladys went on after recovering herself. "We have no money. I don't know what Daddy did with it, but it's gone. I might have to get a *job*! Oh, Lord!" And off she went, crying again.

Boy, I *really* didn't know what to say to that. I'd been working in our family's store ever since I was a kid, but that was merely a part of my life and an enjoyable part, too. The store also included the whole family, which I imagine made a difference. I guess suddenly having to get a job might be rough on someone who'd never been employed and who'd always considered herself above such mundane things as working in order to pay the bills. Therefore, I said, "I'm so sorry," yet once more and got the heck out of there.

What a harrowing experience *that* had been. Fortunately for the state of my mood, Mr. Deutsch, the butcher, was a jolly Swiss fellow. Some folks in town thought he might be a German masquerading as a Swiss—people didn't like Germans much in those days because of the late Great War—but I took him at his word. Anyhow, he was a nice man, and I liked him.

I was very glad when he wrapped up our family's pound of round steak and I finally got back home again.

Unfortunately for me, Pa and Jack had both returned from their various occupations while I'd been gone. Oh, joy. Another scolding. And in front of my idiot brother. I wasn't sure I could stand it.

CHAPTER FIFTEEN

Later I could only thank my lucky stars that Pa had decided to take me aside and query me about my overnight adventures out of the company of my brother.

It still wasn't easy, mainly because I had to maintain the lie about having telephoned Phil to walk with me.

"We weren't doing anything wrong, Pa," I said in a pleading tone. "Honest, we weren't."

"I hope to God you weren't, Annabelle. Your mother and I would be mighty disappointed in you if you were. We're disappointed enough already. You know people are talking about the two of you, don't you?"

I hung my head. "Yes."

"Your mother and I didn't rear our children to be talked about like that, Annabelle, and none of our children has ever given us any grief before. Well," he amended honestly, "except for Jack, but he's young. You're old enough to know better."

"But we were only walking," I said in a feeble attempt to defend the indefensible.

Pa sighed. "Just don't let it happen again."

"I won't. I promise."

It was a promise I'd be able to keep, since Phil didn't want anything to do with me after the previous night's debacle. What a depressing thought.

The rest of the day wasn't too bad, however. I manned the store and folks came and went, and some of them asked me about finding Herschel's body, but nobody mentioned my involvement with Phil. Poor Phil. I didn't deserve him. I had the sinking feeling he was beginning to think the same thing all by himself, which made me feel even lower than I already did.

Myrtle Howell came over to chat during an afternoon break. Naturally, she'd heard all about my discovery of Herschel Calhoun's body.

"Annabelle, how do you do it?" she asked, leaning over the counter in a conspiratorial manner.

After heaving a huge sigh and doing some leaning of my own, I said, "Beats me. It's a gift, I guess."

"Boy, it's not a gift I'd want."

"I don't want it either. Maybe it's more like a curse."

"And Phil was with you? You do know that's mainly what people are talking about, don't you? Whatever were you doing out in the middle of the night with Phil?"

So, since I trusted Myrtle, who was my very best friend in the whole world except maybe Phil when he wasn't mad at me, I told her.

"Oh, dear. I'm so sorry, Annabelle. Nobody wants to believe you two weren't up to mischief."

"I know they don't," I said bitterly. "People thrive on thinking the worst of each other. But there isn't a thing I can do about it. I even had to lie to Chief Vickers. I couldn't very well tell him I was aiming to enter somebody else's house and plow through an office, could I?"

She shook her head. "Can you take a little break, Annabelle? Maybe get an ice-cream cone or something?"

"It's about thirty-five degrees out there, Myrtle," I pointed out. "It's not exactly ice-cream weather."

"True, but—"

"Anyhow, I don't think my parents would be amenable to me taking a break any time soon."

"They're mad at you?"

"What do you think?"

She covered my hand with hers. "I'm so sorry, Annabelle."

And she left the store, feeling almost as sorry for me as I felt for myself.

Lucky for me, the subject of my midnight jaunt didn't come up at dinner that night. Jack, brat that he was, tried to bring it into the conversation but Pa gave him the *look*, and he shut up pronto. No one ever defies that look from my father. Dinner was good. Ma cooked up the Swiss steak as she'd promised, and we ate it with fried okra and mashed potatoes. Yum.

Then I had to stay awake until midnight. I was exhausted after that morning's antics, even though my mother had allowed me to sleep in, so sitting up late wasn't any fun. I read for quite a while, some Dr. Thorndyke stories by R. Austin Freeman. I generally loved Dr. Thorndyke, and the stories kept me interested, but that night my eyes kept sneaking shut in spite of the quality and intrigue of the stories. Therefore, I got up and walked around my room several times, thinking exercise might be the ticket. It wasn't.

The weather outside had dropped down to nearly freezing, and my room was almost as icy as the outdoors. I'd put on trousers—I didn't plan on anyone seeing me but Betty Lou—and a flannel shirt, donned heavy woolen socks and my sturdy shoes, and wrapped a quilt around my shoulders. The quilt was a pretty one my mother had made a couple of years prior, and it contained lots of my old clothes. I could look at a particular patch and it brought back happy memories of school outings, family holidays and stuff like that. But it wasn't awfully warm. Therefore, I went to my closet and got out the cardigan sweater Aunt Minnie had knitted for me a couple of Christmases back and buttoned it up. I set aside a pair of woolen gloves to put on before I went out and a woolen scarf I aimed to muffle myself in.

Still cold. Darn it. When I glanced at the clock on my bedside table, it told me the time was only ten-thirty. Another hour and a half of freezing to death and trying to stay awake. I didn't dare get into the bed for fear I'd fall smack asleep and not wake up until morning. I also didn't dare set the alarm for midnight, because it would indubitably wake up everyone else in the house when it went off. Nuts.

I grabbed my heavy coat and put it on. Then I sat on a hard chair in my room and stuffed my hands into its pockets. Something crunched.

What was this?

Frowning, I pulled several leaves and dried twigs from the right pocket. I didn't recall stuffing leaves and junk in my pocket last night, but evidently I had. I threw the leaves into my wastebasket, then noticed a crumpled piece of paper among them. I lifted it out of the basket, uncrumpled it and read, my eyes opening wide as I did so.

If you expect to maintain your charade, you'd better cough up the dough you paid my father to keep your secret. If you don't, I'll go straight to the coppers and expose you as the murdering mobster you are. H. Calhoun

What on earth?

I reread the note. It still said the same thing. But however did it get into my pocket?

Then I remembered that when I'd stumbled over Herschel Calhoun's body, I'd braced myself on the ground around him in order to keep from landing on him. Had I picked up those leaves and this note by accident and shoved them in my pocket when Phil helped me to my feet? Heck, I must have.

Golly, was this note connected with whatever had caused Herschel Calhoun to jolly up during his last day of life on this earth? Was he blackmailing somebody? Somebody his father had been blackmailing? And had that somebody killed both father and son? That's what it sounded like to me, although I admit to having had my attitude influenced by the detective novels I read.

But . . . shoot. I'd have to show this to the police chief. He'd not be happy with me for keeping it from him this long, but it wasn't my fault I didn't know it was in my pocket, was it? No, it was not, and I'd tell him so, too. I'd been in serious shock after almost falling flat on top of a dead body.

It turned out that finding the note jolted me into wakefulness, for which I was grateful, even though the note puzzled me a good deal. I prowled my room, thinking, thinking, thinking, wondering who in the tiny town of Rosedale, New Mexico, could have a past black enough to engender blackmail. And a mobster? We didn't get a whole lot of mobsters in Rosedale. They mostly hung out in New York City and Chicago.

Chicago . . .

But that was nonsensical. Firman Meeks looked about as much like a mobster as I did. Or Phil. Or poor Richard. Still and all, he'd come to us from Chicago. On the other hand, he was small and skinny and looked kind of like a pencil, and I couldn't, even when I squinted into the dark night and tried my best, feature him being a bloody murderer. I didn't much care for him, but he evidently possessed enough good qualities for Betty Lou to have become fond of him. Betty Lou was a sensible girl who wouldn't fall for an evil person. Wasn't she? Mind you, Firman Meeks seemed a little oily to me . . . but more in the vein of a Uriah Heep than a vicious murderer. Picturing him as a killer was far-fetched, especially in light of the fact that both Edgar and Herschel Calhoun had been big, hearty men, either one of whom could have sat on Firman Meeks and squashed him flat.

So who did that leave? Bother. It left darned near everyone else in town. Edgar Calhoun had taken business trips to Chicago and New York City, and he wasn't the only man in town to do so. Lots of the ranchers went to Chicago, because that's where the big slaughterhouses were. Any one of them might have got himself into trouble in the big city. Young men were said to do that sort of thing all the time, although in the case of the younger generation their trouble generally came in the way of wine, women and song. Well, maybe not song, but you know what I mean. However, older men managed to get themselves into trouble too, particularly of a financial nature. Witness those whom Edgar Calhoun had cheated. I knew about a few of them, but I'd bet there were more.

It was the "mobster" part of the note that baffled me the most.

I couldn't imagine Micah Tindall being any kind of mobster. Or Mr. Feather, either. And definitely not Armando Contreras.

On the other hand, Phil and I had accidently busted up a murdering bootlegging operation during that terrible summer I'd spent with Aunt Minnie, so I guess such a thing wasn't necessarily impossible. I looked at the note again. Still said the same thing.

Darn it! I wished it was daylight so I could take the blasted note to the police chief and let him deal with it. Maybe he could make something of it, although I'd begun to doubt his competence ever since he'd first questioned Richard about the murder. If anything, this note should go a long way toward removing Richard from the suspect list. There was no way on God's green earth that anybody could mistake him for a mobster. Not only was he a stuffy banker, but he hadn't been out of town for eons, if ever, except maybe to El Paso or Santa Fe on banking business. I couldn't imagine a mobster hiding himself in Rosedale and keeping his occupation a secret.

Of course, perhaps the note referred to a retired mobster. Were there such things? Most of the mobsters I'd read about in the newspapers were dead, which is one way of retiring, but not the way that could get you blackmailed since you can't very well blackmail a corpse.

Which made me think that maybe I had the whole situation backwards. Maybe someone was blackmailing Herschel.

Use your brain, Annabelle Blue! Herschel was the one who wrote the note, according to the signature. Anyhow, he wouldn't have been acting happy and smug for his last day or so if he was being blackmailed. I guess tiredness was making me loopy.

Blast it, why hadn't Herschel written the name of the person to whom he'd addressed the note on the note itself? People could make life so difficult for others without half trying, couldn't they?

However, it was time for me to set out for the Calhoun house, so I put the note under my mattress. Then I tried to table thoughts of it as I grabbed my flashlight, pulled on my woolen scarf so that it covered my head, ears and nose—no sense risking frostbite if the weather got any colder—put on my gloves, and skedaddled out of the house.

I don't recommend walking in a place with no streetlights in the pitchy darkness of a moonless, freezing November night when clouds obscured even the stars while you're on an unlawful errand without a companion. Even with my flashlight, I couldn't see much of anything, and I felt alone and vulnerable and scared to death. It occurred to me that perhaps I ought to have begged Phil for help, even knowing how angry he was with me. Too late now. Shadows hovered everywhere, and it seemed to me that every one of them concealed a murderer.

Of course, I thought about mobsters and monsters as I walked, although I'd known since my early childhood that the latter didn't exist. The first did. Mind you, as I said before, I hadn't noticed any mobsters cluttering up Rosedale recently. None that I'd recognized as such, anyway. Evidently there was at least one mobster or ex-mobster here in town. But not even mobsters walked the streets on a bleak fall night alone, did they?

Then it occurred to me that, while I was alone, perhaps the mobster to whom Herschel Calhoun had written his note wasn't. Maybe he had cohorts.

But, heck, I knew about them or him—sort of—but they didn't know about me. Yet. I hoped. Egad.

What a miserable walk that was. It didn't help that my heavy shoes clumped along the boardwalk and sounded like thunder. In fact, I got so scared someone might hear me that I climbed down from the boardwalk and walked in the street, which made things quieter but not any better, since the bulk of the boardwalk made my walk even darker than it had been before—and it had been dark as, well, onyx, even when I was on the boardwalk. I was still alone and scared and cold and unable to see anything and wishing I hadn't set out on this errand, which was beginning to seem brainless to me. What was I, Annabelle Blue, nineteen-year-old child of a grocer and his wife, doing, trying to solve two brutal murders?

Oh, yeah. I remembered now. Richard. The chief still thought Richard might have done at least one of the deeds.

Maybe Chief Vickers didn't really think Richard was a viable culprit. Maybe he'd only questioned Richard again in order to throw his real suspect off the mark and cause him to make a mistake that would nail him. I frowned when that thought entered my fuzzy head, the chief never having struck me as a particularly subtle thinker.

Bother. All this cogitating was only confusing me more, so I attempted to stop it. That was, of course, akin to attempting to stop a herd of rampaging hippopotami. My brain continued to whirl as I turned up Lee and made for the Calhoun place, stumbling and tripping over objects my flashlight didn't il-luminate.

You can be sure I flashed my light all around the front yard of the place once I got there. I tried to be subtle about it, but I had absolutely no desire to stumble over the body of, say, Gladys Calhoun, as I made my way to the back of the house.

No bodies. I silently offered up a brief prayer of thanks.

I was as quiet as I could be while walking to the back window. At least people hadn't planted a bunch of decorative trees and so forth in Rosedale, and nobody had a green lawn like those my brother George wrote about from Alhambra. Dirt was it in November in Rosedale. Even those folks who planted grass— and there weren't many of them—didn't bother to try to keep anything alive and green past the first frost in October or thereabouts. The town was downright ugly during the fall and through our dry and blustery spring. Every now and then some green things appeared during the summer months when the rains came. Most of us living in Rosedale had a thirst for all things green and growing because we so seldom saw any in real life.

After I made my way to the back of the Calhoun house, I looked at all the windows. They stared back blackly. Was one of them open? How could I tell without flashing my light on them, thereby taking a chance of waking the members of the house-hold? This was a problem I hadn't contemplated, and I stood there, mulling, until I heard a soft "Psst."

The whisper made me jump about six inches in the air and have a heart spasm that I'm surprised didn't kill me right then and there. However, it was then I noticed a head, which looked like a roundish something only a little blacker than its sur-roundings, sticking out of a window. Betty Lou. Thank God. I made my more-or-less-soundless way to the window out of which Betty Lou's head poked.

I'm five feet, four inches tall, and I'm pretty spry, being nineteen and all, but crumb. How the heck was I going to get myself up to the sill and through that window?

"Can you get in?" asked Betty Lou in a whisper so soft I almost couldn't hear it.

Darn Phil Gunderson! If he'd been with me, he could have boosted me up. But no. He wasn't there to help because, at the moment, he was sulking because he was mad at me. "Um . . . I don't think so. I should have thought of this before." Stupid, stupid, stupid, Annabelle.

"I thought of it," said Betty Lou, surprising me, although I don't know why. I'm sure she was as enterprising as anyone else in town. Clearly she was more enterprising than I. "Here's a stool."

She poked a three-legged stool out the window, and I grabbed it and set it on the dirt beneath, making sure it was steady on the uneven earth. Then I climbed on the stool and, although it was a struggle, managed to pull myself through the open window. Betty Lou helped by yanking on my arms. Boy, was I going to be sore in the morning.

That, however, was of no consequence. "Thanks, Betty Lou."

"I'll stand by the door and warn you if I hear anyone coming."

"Thanks."

I glanced around, using my flashlight. So this was old man Calhoun's home office, was it? And it had been searched by the police, who were experienced in things like searching for stuff. Well, we'd just see. I tried to recall every mystery novel I'd ever read. Some I remembered were more useful than others. For instance, in *The Circular Staircase*, Mary Roberts Rinehart had her elderly heroine discover a hidden room, but I didn't think I'd have any luck if Mr. Calhoun had built himself a secret room. However, lots of other books mentioned hidden desk drawers and things shoved under carpeting and floorboards or stashed away in secret ceiling recesses and so forth.

Looking up, I decided that if Mr. Calhoun had hidden his incriminating papers in the ceiling, there was no way I'd be able to discover same. I wasn't tall enough, and Betty Lou hadn't provided a ladder. I'm not much of a one for ladders anyway. I again regretted Phil's absence.

Therefore, greatly hoping, I began lifting all the little rugs scattered around the room. Nothing. I prodded every piece of furniture in the room, sticking my hands between chair covers and under cushions and opening the long casement clock in the corner, praying it wouldn't start chiming. Nothing. Rats.

"Hurry up," whispered Betty Lou.

"I'm trying to hurry," I whispered back. That made me think of my father's usual response to one of his children who said he or she was trying: "You surely are." Not exactly a confidence builder under the circumstances. But that didn't negate the fact that I was there and I'd never get another chance to do this. At least, if another chance were offered, I wouldn't take it. This was too nerve-racking.

So I went on to the desk. As quietly as a shadow, and holding the flashlight in my teeth, which was terribly uncomfortable, I went through every drawer in the darned desk. Nothing. Then I pulled out each drawer and felt around in the recesses made thereby. Nothing. Double drat.

Then I decided to look at the drawers themselves. I carefully dumped all the papers out of each one and felt around, hoping my fingers would encounter a secret hiding place. Nothing.

Discouraged, I put all the drawers back in their proper places and stared at the desk—I'd taken the flashlight out of my mouth, by the way. There were lots of little cubby holes in the thing, so I poked around in them, too.

It was an accident that made me shine my light on the ceiling above the desk. I almost dropped the flashlight and caught it before it could hit the floor.

"Careful!" Betty Lou warned in a hissing whisper.

"Sorry."

But I'd seen something up there. It wasn't much: just a square of plaster that didn't quite meld with the rest. It was almost as if that square were . . . well, removable.

Good Lord, had I really found something important? If so, how the heck was I going to find out what it was? Even if I stood on the desk, I couldn't reach the ceiling.

It was then that I suffered my second heart attack of the night.

"Annabelle!" came a whisper from the window.

"Who's that?" whispered a frightened Betty Lou.

"It's me," came the whisper from the window.

And darned if Phil Gunderson didn't climb into the room. Being six feet tall, he probably didn't even have to use the stool to gain entry. I'd never been so happy to see a person in my entire life.

"Phil!" I wanted to holler and hug him, but I could only do one of those things without waking the Calhoun family, so I did.

He still wasn't happy with me. After giving me a brief hug and then thrusting me away from him, he whispered, "I knew you were going to do this, dammit."

"But I found something," I told him, praying he'd be willing to climb onto the desk and see if the space behind that square of ceiling plaster held anything of import.

"What?"

I pointed at the ceiling. "See that square of plaster? It looks suspicious to me."

"Criminy, Annabelle, everything looks suspicious to you," Phil grumbled.

Bless his heart, though, he actually climbed on top of the desk, pushed that odd square of plaster aside, and when his hand came out again, it was holding one of those banker's folders with a string tied around it.

Be still my overworked heart! Had we actually found something?

"I hear somebody coming!" Betty Lou whispered suddenly, sounding panicky.

"Let's get the hell out of here," said Phil, holding the folder in one hand and shoving the plaster square back into place with the other. He climbed down from the desk with the agility of a cat, and it suddenly dawned on me where the expression "cat burglar" came from. How could I think about anything so irrelevant at a time like that?

Anyhow, Phil grabbed my arm with the hand not holding the folder, and we both dashed as quietly as possible to the open window. He pushed me out first, and I almost broke my ankle when I missed the stool and plopped to the ground. Fortunately, I didn't make much noise, the ground being dirt and softish. Then Phil was there beside me. He shoved the stool into Betty Lou's hands and she hauled it inside and closed the window with a noiseless swish.

I wanted to run for it, but Phil slammed an arm against my body, and my back hit the wall of the house. "Stay still," he commanded.

Golly, he was quite forceful when he wanted to be. I stayed still, flattened against the Calhoun house.

I don't know what Betty Lou did to hide herself. Maybe she hid under the desk. All I know is that we heard the door to the office open and somebody walk in.

Then we heard Gladys Calhoun's voice. "Is someone in here?"

Silence. Except for our breathing and our beating hearts, which sounded loud as thunder to me but probably weren't.

We heard Gladys walk into the room, and I saw the light of a lantern being held up. I believe I've mentioned that the Rosedale Electric Company turns everything off at midnight. I was glad of it just then. *Please, God, don't let her be a discerning individual,* I prayed. Had I left anything out of place? I couldn't remember. Blast it! Why'd Gladys have to wake up, anyhow? We'd been quiet as mice in that dratted room. I prayed hard that Betty Lou had found a good hiding place.

After what felt like approximately sixteen hours of pure terror, the lantern light got dimmer, and we heard the door close again. Once more, I was ready to scram out of there, but Phil continued to hold me smack against the wall of the house with his arm, which, I noticed, was quite heavily muscled. Hmm. Nice.

What a time to think about Phil's masculine qualities! I forced my mind back to the problem at hand, which was perilous. From the corner of my eye, I saw lantern light travel from room to room as Gladys made her way through the house. It's a good thing Phil had decided to show up, or I'd have been caught for sure. No impulse control. That's me all over.

At long last, we saw the last of the lantern light and heard Gladys head back up the stairs, thank God. It was only then that Phil removed his arm. Before I could move, he said, "Walk very slowly and quietly. For God's sake, don't run or anything. With luck, nobody will see us. Let's cut across back yards until we get to Second."

We did better than that. We made our way to the alley behind the Calhouns' place and walked down the very middle of it to Second Street, Phil leading the way and only flicking on his flashlight every now and then so we could see obstacles in our way. Smart guy, Phil. I don't know why he puts up with me.

CHAPTER SIXTEEN

Naturally, as soon as he figured we were safe, Phil began lecturing me. I almost didn't mind.

"Curse it, Annabelle Blue, you don't give up, do you?"

"Not when my family's in trouble." I tried to sound noble, but by that time I was suffering from the effects of too much excitement and fright and felt like folding up like a fan and crying. I wouldn't do that in front of Phil, though. I had my pride, after all. Tonight my gratitude overwhelmed my pride long enough for me to say, "I was scared to death. Thank you *so* much for coming to my rescue."

"Hell," he muttered.

As I believe I've said before, Phil wasn't much of a one for swearing, but I'd driven him to do a lot of it recently. I was ashamed of myself, but I was also happy to have escaped unscathed—and with something to show for my night of terror.

"Do you want to go through that folder with me?" I asked timidly.

"No, I don't want to go through that folder with you," he said, thrusting said folder at me. "For God's sake, Annabelle, I don't want anything to do with your crazy antics. But I couldn't very well let you go to the Calhoun place all by yourself. God knows what trouble you'd have got into on your own. I'm only glad we didn't get caught."

"Me, too. But, Phil, you found something the police missed!" I thought that was pretty exciting.

Phil plainly didn't. "Damn it, they're probably old racing forms or something Calhoun didn't want the family to know about."

"What's a racing form?" I asked, never having encountered the term before.

"Criminy." I think Phil bowed his head, although it was really too dark to tell for sure. "What I mean is that the man might have been betting on the horses and didn't want his family to know about it."

"Do we have a racetrack in town?" If we did, I sure hadn't heard about it, and a racetrack sounded too large a thing to hide in so flat a place as Rosedale. I mean, it wasn't as if we had hills and dales. All we had was flat land, scrub brush, poisonous snakes, prickly plants and insects and heat. Except when the weather got cold, as it was that night. Morning. Whatever it was by that time.

"No, but there's one in Juarez, and I know guys who bet on the ponies there."

"You do?"

"Yes."

"How do they bet on horses in Mexico if they live in Rosedale?"

"Have you ever heard of a telephone or a cable, Annabelle Blue? Christ, I can't believe you sometimes! You're going to get the both of us killed one day with your blasted investigations."

It was my turn to bow my head, only in shame. "I'm sorry, Phil. I honestly don't like to make you go out of your way to help me."

"Yeah. Right."

Very well, he didn't believe me. Can't say as I blamed him. It did seem as though I was forever finagling him into doing things he didn't want to do.

"I'm sorry," I whispered, meaning it. "I don't *want* to get mixed up in stuff like this, you know. But Phil, if we don't do something to clear Richard's name—"

"I *know*," he said harshly. "You don't want your brother-in-law arrested for murder. *Everyone* knows you don't want your brother-in-law arrested for murder. But most people are willing to allow the coppers to do their jobs and don't think they know more than the police, for crumb's sake. It's not as if Chief Vickers has pointed his finger at your brother-in-law and said he's the only suspect around. He's looking at other people too, you know."

"Well . . ."

"Well, my aunt Fanny! You know it's true."

Oh, my. "But you found something they missed," I pointed out.

"You don't know that. For all you know, they found that very same folder, looked inside it, and decided its contents weren't worth their time."

"I don't believe that for a second."

"Christ."

We didn't talk again until we got to my place. Then Phil left me to make my own way from the store to the house while he stomped off to his brother's house. Although he wouldn't have believed me if I'd told him, I loved him very much in that instant.

My luck, if luck it was, held, and none of my family members heard me sneak back into the house. When I got to my bedroom, I heaved a sigh of relief, glanced at my bedside clock, noticed that it was one-thirty in the morning, and decided to look at the contents of the folder at work the next day. Or that day, I mean. I shoved it under my mattress where I'd shoved the note earlier, took off my clothes in the freezing-cold room, flung my flannel nightgown on, kept on my woolen socks, and snuggled under several quilts. I thought I'd be too wound up to sleep, but I think I was asleep in maybe a minute and a half.

When Ma tapped on my door at six-thirty that morning, I groaned. I wanted to sleep for another day or so. But I couldn't. Therefore, I got myself up and dressed and out to the kitchen, where I ate the nice breakfast Ma had prepared for us all.

Jack, as usual, was obnoxious. "Gee, Annabelle, you look tired. Did you and Phil go out again last night?"

Darn him anyhow! Both of my parents squinted at me narrowly, and I knew they too were wondering the same thing. And I had, but I wasn't about to let them know it.

Scowling at my horror of a brother, I said, "Thanks, Jack. I had trouble sleeping, so I read and stayed up too late. No, I wasn't out with Phil, thank you very much. You don't look so great yourself."

"That's enough, you two."

Ma was totally impartial when dishing out discipline. Most of the time I didn't mind. That morning, I wanted somebody to slap Jack out of his chair and tell him it wasn't nice to tell ladies they looked less than perfect. Not that I was a lady, as you've undoubtedly already figured out.

Jack stuck his tongue out at me, but I ignored him and took a bite of scrambled eggs. Jack piled his eggs on a piece of buttered toast, slapped another piece of toast on top of the eggs, and ate his breakfast as a sandwich, with bacon on the side. Stupid child.

"Annabelle, you'll have to mind the store again today," said Ma. "I have more preserving to do. I'll be so glad when it's all done."

"That's fine, Ma. I'll just take a couple of books with me for the dull moments."

"Wish I could read instead of going to school," muttered Jack with his mouth full.

Pa slapped him gently on the head. I'd been hoping for

something of the sort, only harder. Oh, well. "Annabelle went through the twelfth grade, Jack Blue, and graduated from high school. She got better grades than you're getting, too. She had good enough grades to get into college, in fact. She deserves to read when she doesn't have work to do. You need to pick up your grades, young man."

Wow, that was a surprise. Pa had actually praised my scholastic achievement. Of course, he'd only done so in order to teach Jack a lesson, but I appreciated him for it. I had done well in school, so that was no lie. I kind of wished he'd left out the college part, since that was still a sore spot on my ego, but still . . . I wanted to stick my tongue out at my brother as he'd done to me, but naturally, being a semi-mature adult, I didn't. I only made a face at him.

"And don't talk with your mouth full, Jack," said Ma severely.

Ha. Both parents were on my side—that morning, anyway.

It was an exhausted Annabelle Blue who grabbed *The Green Mummy*, by Fergus Hume, and *The House of the Whispering Pines*, by Anna Katharine Green, and then lifted the mattress off her bed and slid a banker's folder out from under it. I left the note from Herschel where it was, stuck the folder between the two books and headed for the store, calling out to Ma as I passed the kitchen. "Good luck with the preserving. What is it today?"

Wiping her perspiring brow—although the weather remained cold out of doors, the kitchen had already steamed up from boiling water—she said, "More squash. I swear, I don't think it will ever end."

"How are the pumpkins?" I asked, aiming for a casual note and feeling guilty about keeping my activities from my parents. That folder seemed mighty heavy to me that morning.

"I think they're going to be all right. The hail damaged a couple of them too badly to sell in the store for Thanksgiving, but the rest of them look good."

"Good. Well, see you."

I made my way to the store while poor Ma continued to steam in the kitchen. Boy, it was cold outside! I do believe the weather had dipped into the twenties overnight. November is an iffy month in Rosedale. Every now and then we'd get snow, but more often than not it was only windy, cold and bare, bare, bare. And then it would warm up and we'd bake for a few days before it got cold again. The only living green could be found some seventy miles west of us in the Sacramento Mountains, up near Lincoln, where Billy the Kid had made his name. Some name. Heck, speaking of Billy the Kid, Rosedale had once actually sported a hero of sorts. Pat Garrett had lived here a couple of decades after he'd rid the world of Billy, but then he'd been shot to death, too. Come to think of it, Rosedale and vicinity carried a reputation as iffy as the weather.

But that doesn't matter now, and it didn't matter then. What mattered was that I had the folder somebody, probably Edgar Calhoun himself, had secreted in his home office, and I could hardly wait to find out what was inside it. Unfortunately for my wishes and wants, the store was busy that morning. It was getting on towards Thanksgiving, and folks came in for cans of cranberries so they could make cranberry sauce for their holiday meals. We had stacks of canned cranberries and even carried canned pumpkin, although most folks either grew their own pumpkins and squash or bought either or both in order to make their pies. We had a whole pile of pumpkins outside on the boardwalk that morning. I presumed Ma and Pa had forced Jack to carry them out there and arrange them artistically before he went to school. They were pretty and colorful, making a nice contrast to the general beige color of the town and its buildings.

The wind blew hard that day. I watched swirls and eddies of dirt from the windows as I walked back and forth, helping first one customer and then another with various demands. Lots of ladies came in for fabrics, including Mrs. Wilson. Ma always gave her a discount and told her not to pass it along to her customers, but Mrs. Wilson was such an upright, honest lady, I doubted that she took Ma's advice.

I felt sorry for Mrs. Wilson. At that time, she was probably about forty-five years old, but she looked a hundred and ten. That's what a hard life will do for you, and if there's a harder life than that of a widowed woman rearing a whole passel of children in a three-room house with the money she made as seamstress in Rosedale, New Mexico, I don't know what it could be. She had a soft French accent, which was quite lovely. According to what her kids had told me, she'd come from Switzerland sometime in the 1880s. With a sigh, I measured some lovely light-blue georgette for her. It was one of the most expensive fabrics in the store, and Ma only stocked it because the wealthier ladies in town liked people to know what they were worth. Money-wise. Character-wise, they varied.

"Who's this going to be for?" I asked in order to make some kind of conversation.

"Mrs. Shenkel. It's for her daughter's wedding."

"Oh, yes. I ran into Mae the other day, and she told me she was marrying."

"Yes, indeed. A happy time for the family come spring."

Yeah, maybe. However, Mae was different from me. She was so . . . well, not bright, that marriage was probably the best she could hope for out of life.

Speaking of which, Mrs. Wilson's oldest daughter, Marie, was attending college at that very moment. I guess she got a scholarship, because the good Lord knows Mrs. Wilson couldn't afford to pay tuition at Missouri University. Probably Marie also had a job up there in Missouri. She'd always worked hard. Most of the Wilson children did. They had to. Perhaps I should have applied for a scholarship, but I hadn't thought about it when it would have done me any good.

"Here you go. Do you need any notions to go along with the fabric?"

"I'll take some mercerized thread in the same color, please, and some white bias tape."

Ma's fabrics corner was very well organized, and we found Mrs. Wilson's sewing notions in no time flat. Ma was a wonder with the ordering and stocking of merchandise for the store. For instance, she never bought a bolt of cloth without also thinking of the notions that might go with it.

Mrs. Wilson paid her bill, from which I deducted the twenty-percent discount Ma always gave her, and I found myself saying the same thing Ma always said. "Don't pass this discount along to Mrs. Shenkel, Mrs. Wilson. She can afford to pay full price." Then I added on impulse, "And please help yourself to a pumpkin for your Thanksgiving dinner from the display on your way out." What the heck. Ma wouldn't mind, and a free pumpkin was a free pumpkin.

To my utter astonishment, Mrs. Wilson smiled and patted my cheek. "You're a good girl, Annabelle."

I was? Tell my folks that. Or Phil. I only said, "Thank you, Mrs. Wilson. Coming from you, the words mean a lot."

She hobbled out of the store—I think she had corns on her toes—and I wandered back to the counter, thinking to myself that if ever there was a good reason never to marry and have children, Mrs. Wilson's story was it. I'd hoped to be able to glance inside the folder then, but Mrs. O'Dell and Mrs. Lovelady entered, and I had to wait on them. Before they left, more people walked into the store. Why the heck was everyone so eager to shop for groceries and dry goods that day, of all days?

It was beginning to look as though I'd never have a chance to go through that wretched folder when a lull finally hit about eleven o'clock. I grabbed a pickle from the barrel and munched on it as I took the folder from where I'd stuffed it under the

213

counter, along with the two books in case I had to plop them on top of the folder to hide what I was doing if a customer arrived. Then I sat myself on the high stool behind the counter, untied the tidy bow, unwound the string and opened the folder. Papers lay within, and I took them out in a clump.

The first thing that struck me as I gazed at the top-most paper was that Mr. Calhoun was a meticulous record keeper. Columns of numbers, my least favorite things, met my eyes, and each column was as straight as a soldier standing at attention. My own personal columns generally head to the right or left of a paper unless the paper has lines to help me. Not Mr. Calhoun's. They were as straight as straight could be. The headings at the beginning of the columns at first appeared extremely esoteric to yours truly: MT, GF, FM, RB, DC. Underneath the headings were what looked to be dollar amounts: 125.00, 2,500.00, 500.00, 75.00, 800.00.

Whew! What did it all mean? Well, I imagined it meant that Mr. Calhoun had received certain sums of money from certain people, but who were the people and why were they giving Mr. Calhoun all that dough? I'd especially like to know who GF was and how he'd got his hands on twenty-five hundred dollars, a sum that boggled my mind. Also, where had Mr. C. stashed all the moola? It hadn't been found at the bank or at his home—although, thanks to Gladys Calhoun, Phil hadn't had the opportunity to grab more than the one folder. Maybe there was money concealed behind that ceiling plaster too. Or did Sadie Dobbs have some of the loot? All of it? Any of it?

Could Mr. Calhoun have been blackmailing all those people? Good Lord, what a thought! Or . . . wait a minute. Perhaps these were private loans Mr. C. had made outside the bank. That made more sense. Kind of. Bother. I wished I knew more about financial matters.

Placing that first paper under the stack, I looked at the second piece of paper and blinked. It was a handwritten note: "Damn you, Calhoun, if you don't stop demanding money, I'll tell the police what you're doing. I don't care what it costs me or my family." Underneath the profane note, Mr. Calhoun had written in his precise script: "Bluff."

Shoot. Maybe he *had* been blackmailing folks in town. I didn't know so many of Rosedale's citizens had dark secrets they'd pay to keep covered up, but I was relatively innocent in the ways of the world. I didn't like admitting it, even to myself.

I slid that note underneath the rest of the pile and glanced at the third piece of paper. It contained more columns of figures, only with different initials heading the columns. Boring. Well, they were boring to me, but that's only because I didn't know what purpose the columns served or why the money had been paid or from whom it had come. Darn it, the only reason I'd gone through that awful man's office, nearly being discovered in the process and scaring myself to death, was to find answers, not more questions!

I looked at another piece of paper. This one was more interesting. In a different script from the first note I'd found, I read: "You don't want to do this, Mr. Calhoun. Trust me. You don't know with whom you're dealing." I stared at the writing, which was even more precise than Mr. Calhoun's, straight up and down, tiny and spiky. Unusual, at least to my eyes.

Beneath that note, Mr. Calhoun had written a snide "Sez you."

Hmm. I thought that particular note might be of real interest when viewed in light of Herschel Calhoun's own note about mobsters. Could both Calhoun men have made the mistake of trying to blackmail a real, honest-to-goodness bad guy and managed to get themselves killed for their efforts? Plausible. Maybe even probable.

It occurred to me, briefly, to wonder why Mr. Calhoun had

kept the nasty notes. Then again, what could he have done with them? I suppose he could have burned them. Or torn them into shreds and tossed them into a wastepaper basket. But either of those options were iffy. A member of his family, or Betty Lou Jarvis, might have wondered at him burning papers. And remember what happened in *The Hound of the Baskervilles*? The butler had been able to read a note even after it had been burned. Same went for tearing up stuff you didn't want people to read. If something could be torn apart, it could be pasted back together again. If Mr. Calhoun was truly the crook I believed him to be, he probably figured it was safer to keep all his unwanted papers in one place until he could safely rid himself of them. Maybe he'd planned on taking the incriminating paperwork with him on his next trip out of town and burning everything in a convenient hotel fireplace.

Why ever he'd kept the notes, I'd have to show all this stuff to Chief Vickers. He'd be mad as fire that I'd managed to find the folder and its contents, and I'd have to think of another lie to tell him about how I'd come to possess them. I sighed, thinking what a tangled web one wove when . . . well, you know the rest of it.

Myrtle came in about then, and I plopped *The Green Mummy* on top of the Calhoun papers.

"Hey, Annabelle. Whatcha doing?"

"Hey, Myrtle. It's been a busy morning. The store's finally empty for a few minutes, so I thought I'd read until the next mob comes in."

"The drug store has been busy, too. I guess people are buying things for Thanksgiving."

"What would they be buying for Thanksgiving in a drug store?"

She shrugged. "Perfume and powder from me. I don't know about the rest of the store. So have you heard anything else about the Calhoun case?" She settled her elbows on the counter and leaned toward me. I slid the book aside, making sure the papers went with it, and leaned toward her. "Not a thing. I want to visit the chief again today and see if I can't find out more about the case. He can't still be thinking of Richard as a murderer. Shoot, the same person must have killed both Calhoun men, and why would Richard have killed Herschel?"

"I'm sure Richard didn't kill anybody, and I hope you're right about it being one murderer. I don't like to think there are two murderers cluttering up the town."

I vaguely recalled the two of us voicing similar sentiments the prior month when a couple of murders had taken place. Then again, Rosedale had been violent since its inception. "Face it, Myrtle, we might live in a backwater, but it's got a bloody history."

She drew herself up a bit. "Well, I wouldn't put it like *that*."

"Why not? It's the truth. Heck, even Mr. Chaves, after whom our county is named, was murdered while he was dining with friends. And don't forget Pat Garrett. We're still kind of the Wild West in some ways."

Myrtle sagged back into her slouch. "I guess so, but I don't like to think about it. Anyhow, we're more civilized now than we were then. That was back in the last century, for heaven's sake."

"If you say so. Anyhow, Pat Garrett was killed in nineteen-oh-eight." I really wanted to go back to those papers, but I couldn't very well tell Myrtle about them. She'd have been shocked and appalled that I'd sneaked into someone's house and gone through their private belongings. Heck, my actions appalled me, too, but they'd been initiated out of frustration and righteous thinking, so I believed them to be justified. More or less. I know Phil wouldn't agree.

"Can you take a break?" asked Myrtle. "Or do you have to stay in the store."

"Ma's in the kitchen preserving squash right now, and I don't know where Pa is. Jack's at school, thank God, but I guess I have to stay here for a while yet. Probably Ma will come out and relieve me for lunch unless Pa comes back before then. Want a pickle?" I waved my half-eaten dill at her.

"No, thanks." She sighed. "Well, I wish you had more time. I'd like to walk to the library or take a picnic lunch to the river or something, but I guess you're too busy."

"I'm sorry, Myrtle. I'd like to do that, too. Especially the picnic lunch thing." I glanced out the window. "Well, maybe not today. It's cold and windy out there."

She sighed again. "I guess so. I'm just sick of the weather and the . . . I don't know. All the brown, I guess."

"Maybe we should take a trip to Lincoln one of these days."

"It'll have to be come springtime. Pretty soon you won't be able to ford the rivers for the ice, and the roads will be covered in snow."

I added a sigh of my own to the atmosphere. "You're right, of course. I'd really like to visit George in Alhambra one day. I hear California is green all year long."

"Yes. That's what it says in all the magazines."

We stood there together, hunched over the counter, both of us thinking about how nice it would be to visit California, when another customer walked in. I released yet another sigh. "Gotta go back to work, Myrtle. Thanks for stopping by for a chat."

"We didn't chat much," said she as she headed for the door. "Maybe we can go to the flickers one of these days."

"Good idea. Phil and I saw that Harold Lloyd picture last week. It was fun. If Sonny comes to town, maybe we can all go together."

She seemed a little brighter after I brought up Sonny Clyde's name. She even blushed a bit when she said, "He's coming to our house for Thanksgiving dinner."

"That should be fun."

And then I pasted on a smile and greeted the newcomer. "Good morning, Mrs. Jenner. What can we help you with today?"

Darned if the store didn't remain busy until lunchtime, when Ma, looking flushed and drippy, came in to relieve me of my duties. Poor Ma. She worked so hard.

"I made a sandwich for you, Annabelle. It's in the kitchen with an apple, and there's some pie for dessert."

"Thanks, Ma. I appreciate you making my lunch. You shouldn't have. You work too hard."

"If the garden didn't produce so well, I wouldn't have to," she said, and laughed. "Maybe I shouldn't feed it so much chicken pooh."

I laughed too, grabbed my books and the papers, and walked back to the house. As I ate my sandwich, I looked through the rest of the papers. I discovered that a whole lot of people had grievances against Mr. Calhoun. I was again surprised that he'd kept all the notes condemning him as, and I quote here, a bastard, a villain, a crook, a scoundrel, the devil, a rat and a fool. The note calling him a fool had been written in the same itsy-bitsy, tidy script as the note telling him he didn't want to do what he was doing.

The only thing I could think of he might have done that might label him as a fool was blackmail someone who was dangerous. Who the heck in this hick town of ours was dangerous? I suppose anyone *might* be, if push came to shove, but it was difficult for me to imagine, say, Micah Tindall having the nerve to shoot one Calhoun man and stab the other one.

So who did that leave? The rest of the initials on the lists, I supposed. I wracked my brain—which was feeling rather feeble that day, due to lack of sleep—and thought I'd come up with names to go with most of the initials. MT was probably Micah

Tindall. AC was probably Armando Contreras—although I wasn't sure why his name was on the list if the story he told me was correct. FM was . . . Firman Meeks? Maybe. RB might be Ronald Burton, a farmer who was known to have had financial troubles in recent years. Farming was an unreliable business at best, especially in Rosedale, where you couldn't depend on decent rainfall. DC? Who was DC? Donald Colbert? Possible. I'd heard stories about his money problems, too. He'd dropped a bundle trying to get a canal built from the Hondo River to his farm, and the canal idea hadn't panned out because of our clay-like soil. It was possible Mr. Calhoun had lent him money under the table. And who was the either wealthy or poor GF? For the life of me, I couldn't think of anyone in town with the initials GF, probably because I was too tired to think clearly.

Anyhow, those columns probably documented loans and payments. According to Pa, sometimes people like Mr. Calhoun would make personal loans to people whom the banks wouldn't lend to and then charge them extortionate interest. I wouldn't put it past the late Edgar Calhoun to have attempted to squeeze money out of his fellow citizens, evil person that he'd been.

Piffle. I still wasn't sure about anything at all, which was moderately frustrating. However, I did know that I had to deliver to Chief Vickers these papers and the note I'd discovered among the leaves in my pocket, and the sooner I did that, the sooner all the scolding I'd get from him would be over.

Therefore, after I finished my lunch and washed my dishes and put them away—darned if I'd make more work for my mother than I had to—I went to the store, which was empty of customers. Ma sat behind the counter, her head resting in her palms, her elbows on the counter, and her eyes shut. My heart suffered a little spasm because she looked so very tired. But I still needed to see the chief.

"Do you mind if I run a quick errand, Ma? I found something

in my coat pocket that I think Chief Vickers needs to see."

She blinked a couple of times, making me think that she might have dozed off for a second, and I felt guilty for waking her up.

"What did you find in your pocket, Annabelle?"

So I showed her the note, which seemed to wake her up instantly. "Good heavens. Whatever does that mean?"

"I don't know. I must have picked it up when Phil and I found Herschel Calhoun's body, although I don't remember doing so. But I was pretty upset and scared, and there were leaves and debris all over the place, so I must have stuffed everything in my pocket when Phil helped me up. I darned near fell on top of Herschel, after all, and what happened afterwards is kind of blurry in my mind."

Shaking her head, Ma said, "I swear, Annabelle Blue, you can get into more trouble just going for a walk with your gentleman friend than anyone else I know."

I hung my head. "I know."

But she told me to go to the police station. "Don't be gone long," she said as I headed for the door, wearing the same coat in which I'd found the note.

"I won't," said I.

And I wasn't.

CHAPTER SEVENTEEN

"What do you mean, you can't tell me where you got this folder and these papers, young lady?"

Chief Vickers was very unhappy with me, but there wasn't much I could do about it. Darned if I'd tell him I'd been rummaging around in the Calhoun house, who'd let me in, or that Phil had rescued me. Again.

I did tell him which men in town I thought went with which initials, but that was it.

My heart hammered like a maddened woodpecker in my chest, but I stood my ground. Both Betty Lou Jarvis and Phil Gunderson had assisted me the night before, and there was no way I'd give them away. "I just can't, Chief. I found the note"—I pointed at said note—"in my coat pocket along with a bunch of leaves and twigs. I guess I picked them up after I tripped over Herschel's body, although I don't remember doing it."

"What about the folder containing all these papers?"

I hung my head. "I'm sorry, Chief, but I can't tell you."

He chuffed out an irritated breath. "You don't want to incriminate someone else, is that it?"

I kept my mouth shut, something I seldom do, but I felt a mighty obligation to Betty Lou and Phil, so I did it that day.

"Criminy, Miss Annabelle, you're putting me on the spot here, you know."

My head lifted at that news. "What do you mean?"

He shook the papers at me. "How the devil do you expect

me to use these if it comes to a trial for murder if I don't know where they came from? For all I know, a competent defense attorney will accuse you of forging them all."

I felt my eyes go round. "He couldn't! I didn't!"

"I'm sure you didn't, but the law's the law, young lady, and you're obstructing it by refusing to tell me where you got this stuff. Do you understand that?"

Did I? Oh, brother, how'd I get myself into this mess? I said, "Yes. I think so. But I still can't tell you."

"You're tying my hands, Annabelle. You understand that, don't you?"

"I guess so," I said miserably. Then it occurred to me that if someone *were* actually arrested for murder based on the information contained in those papers, both Betty Lou and Phil would undoubtedly speak up for me, so I said, "If it comes to a trial, I'll be able to tell you exactly how I came by that folder."

The chief squinted at me. He was so annoyed, his face was brick red. "Well . . ."

"Listen, Chief Vickers. I just can't tell you *now* where or how I got it, but . . . well, I'm sure I'll be able to if the matter goes to trial. I'm . . . well, I'm *really* sure of it." Heck, even if Betty Lou refused to 'fess up, Phil certainly would. He always helped me out, even when he didn't want to. Witness the prior night's adventure. If you could call it an adventure. It wasn't the kind I was thinking of when I'd said I wanted an adventure or two before I got married, that's for sure.

"Go on home, Miss Annabelle. I'll go through these papers and think about 'em."

"Thank you, Chief. And . . . well, I'm sorry I didn't get the note to you sooner, but I didn't find it in my pocket until last night."

He nodded, a grim set to his jaw. "And then you conveniently found the folder containing the rest of the papers. I see."

223

Deciding it would be better to keep mum about the folder from then on, I merely nodded. "Thanks, Chief. I'll be at the store if you need me." And I scrammed out of there as fast as I could.

Hurrying back to Blue's, I passed Chewling's Shoes and glanced in at the window to see Firman Meeks putting a shoe on Mrs. Lovelady's foot. Hmm. Maybe after work, I'd just pop into the shoe store and ask Firman Meeks flat out if Mr. Calhoun had tried to blackmail him. He probably wouldn't tell me, but there was no harm in asking, was there?

Ma had dozed off again by the time I reached the store, and I felt guilty about being such an awful daughter to two such wonderful people. My parents deserved better than to have a daughter who sneaked out of the house at night to do illegal things.

I stiffened my spine. They might not mind if my midnight escapades cleared their son-in-law of a charge of murder. I held that thought close to my heart as I pushed the door to the store open. Years earlier we had hung a couple of bells on the door so we could hear whenever anyone entered the store. When she heard the bells, Ma jumped a little on the stool and lifted her head. The little potbellied stove on one side of the store was giving out enough heat to keep the outside chill from freezing those of us who worked in the store, although Ma had her sweater on.

"I think you ought to go back home and take a nap, Ma. You look exhausted."

She yawned, covering her mouth with her hand. "I am exhausted. It's from working in all that heat in the kitchen. But I got the squash put up at last."

"I'm glad. You work too hard."

"It's probably silly to preserve all that food, but I still think it might help out some family during the winter months. These past couple of years have been quite hard on a lot of folks."

I thought about the initials heading those columns Mr. Calhoun had written down, and a surge of hatred toward the dead man flared in my chest. Unchristian, I know, but there you go. I'm no saint, unlike my mother. I decided to tell her so. "You're a saint, Ma."

She laughed as she slid off the stool. "Thanks, Annabelle. You only wish your mother was a saint."

"But you are."

She gave me a quick peck on the cheek. "If you say so, dear. I hope you don't mind if I leave you in the store again. I'm going to fix a pork roast for dinner and have to get it started."

"I love pork roast."

"Me, too. And so does your father."

I noticed she didn't mention whether or not Jack liked pork roast, leading me to believe she didn't much care what her youngest liked or didn't like. Jack was in such disfavor with our parents, it made me glad. And yes, I know that was small-minded, but you don't know Jack. Anyhow, she left me alone in the store and went back home to work some more. I don't know how she did everything she did and remained on her feet at the end of the day.

The rest of the afternoon was almost as busy as the beginning of the day had been. I was surprised when, along about three-thirty, Phil walked through the front door, tinkling the bell, his boots sounding hard clunks on our old wooden floor.

A little nervously, I said, "Hey, Phil."

"Hey, Annabelle." He walked over to the counter, and I braced myself.

With an edginess to my voice, I asked, "Did you come here to scold me some more?"

He frowned. "No. But I did come to see if you did the right thing. Did you take that folder to the chief?"

"Yes," said I, relieved to be telling the truth. "But I didn't say a single thing about you or Betty Lou."

"No? Did you tell him how you got the folder?"

"Good Lord, no! Jeez, Phil, I'm not crazy."

"No? You could have fooled me."

"That's not very nice."

"It's not very nice to rummage around in other people's houses, either."

"But I found what I went there for. Well . . . you did, anyway."

"Huh. You're only lucky we didn't get caught."

I wanted to argue with him, but I couldn't do it. "You're right. I'm so glad to be rid of that folder." Then I decided to tell him another truth, as hard as it was to do so. "The chief told me that unless I can prove where I got the folder, a competent defense attorney would get it kicked out of court."

"Of course."

I stared at him. "Of course? What do you mean 'of course'?"

He shrugged. "I think it's called the chain of evidence or something like that. You can't just spring a bunch of papers or whatever on a courtroom and expect everyone to take your word that they're what you say they are. If anyone's arrested for the murders, you're going to have to confess to where and how you got that folder, Annabelle, and then pray like fire that a judge will believe you."

I stared at him some more. "You're kidding."

He rolled his eyes. "Cripes, Annabelle, do you *ever* think through some of the nutty things you do?"

Burying my head in my hands, I moaned a little. "Evidently not. Oh, Lordy, Phil, I was so hoping those papers would clear Richard once and for all." Lifting my head, I told him what the papers contained in the folder had said, including the threats against Mr. Calhoun's person. "Surely there are samples of the man's handwriting at the bank or at his house or something, aren't there? Nobody can accuse me of forging them if they can prove the handwriting is his, can they? And maybe the people whose initials appear on the lists, too."

"I have no idea. But if you're right, a whole lot of people in town won't thank you for exposing their dealings with Calhoun."

"Oh, shoot." Talk about depressing. All that work and fear and walking after dark in the pitch-black night, and all my efforts—and Betty Lou's and Phil's—might come to naught. I couldn't stand thinking about it.

"I just stopped in to see if you were all right," said Phil then.

Floored, I said, "You mean you still care what happens to me?"

His gaze paid a visit to the ceiling. "For crumb's sake, Annabelle, you're my girl. Yes, I care what happens to you. I don't like it that you're always getting yourself into trouble—"

"I am not! I saved your life last month, if you'll recall!" I had, too, but that's another story.

"I know it, and I appreciate it. But you still take terrible risks."

"They weren't all that terrible." Feeble, Annabelle Blue. Extremely feeble.

He gave me a look that told me exactly what he thought of my comment, which was approximately the same thing I thought of it. "You could have been arrested for breaking and entering," he said, his voice flat. "If that's not a risk, I don't know a risk when I see it."

"But . . . but I didn't break anything. Betty Lou opened the window for me."

"Doesn't matter." He shook his head. "For that matter, I could have been arrested, too."

"Oh, Phil, no!"

"Oh, Annabelle, yes," he said, giving a weak imitation of my cry of dismay. "And I won't do it again, so you'd better not be

227

planning any more midnight antics."

"No. I found what I was after. Or you did, I mean."

"Papers the law can't use. Is that what you were after?"

Once more, I buried my face in my hands. "Lord, now I don't know what to do."

"Let the police do their job, would be my suggestion."

"You're probably right." It galled me to think about Chief Vickers attempting to put anything together from the papers in the folder I'd given him. Maybe I wasn't giving the chief enough credit. I hoped he was more competent than I feared he was. Heck, my whole family's future might depend on him being smarter than I believed he was.

Talk about a melancholy afternoon; after Phil left—and he didn't lighten up on me one little bit—I had to serve customers and worry. And worry. And then my obnoxious brother came home from school, and Ma set him to work dusting the shelves and tidying up our displays of cranberries and canned pumpkin and making sure the pumpkins on the boardwalk were still artistically arranged. The whole time he did it, he whined about having to work. I wanted to beat him with a stick just to make him shut up, he was trying my already-frazzled nerves so much.

A little before five o'clock, Pa came home from wherever he'd spent the day and told me I could go on about my business.

"What about me?" whined Jack.

"You finish your work, young man, and then you can go do your homework until your mother calls us in for supper."

"Gee whiz, Pa. I've already—"

"Shut your mouth, Jack Blue, and do what you're told."

To my amazement, Jack did what Pa told him and shut his mouth. On the other hand, Pa didn't take much guff from anyone, a lesson he'd taught Jack by hand several times.

And then an astonishing thing happened. Myrtle Howell barreled into the store, her eyes wide, and her face a becoming pink. Since I was pretty sure Sonny Clyde wasn't going to appear in town until Thanksgiving, I cried, "Myrtle! What's going on?"

"Annabelle! You'll never believe this!" Then she saw my father. "Oh, Mr. Blue, please forgive me, but I just had to come in and tell Annabelle—and the rest of you, too, of course—the news! Mr. Pruitt just got a telephone call from somebody, and whoever it was says the chief just arrested Micah Tindall for the murder of both the Calhoun men!"

If there had been a chair handy, I'd have sunk into it in shock. Since there wasn't, I clutched the counter and stared at Myrtle. "You're kidding!"

"Am not!" She shook her head violently to add credence to her denial. "It's the truth. Well, that's what Mr. Pruitt told me, anyhow, and I expect it's the truth. Apparently the chief found papers in Mr. Calhoun's house that proved he was blackmailing Mr. Tindall or something, and when the chief went to Mr. Tindall's brother-in-law's house, Mr. Tindall kind of collapsed, and they arrested him."

"Good heavens. I know Mr. Tindall told me Mr. Calhoun had cheated him out of his ranch, but . . . my goodness." Somehow, it was very hard for me to picture the admittedly bitter and angry Mr. Tindall as a murderer. Then again, if all crooks looked like crooks, they'd never succeed at their professions, would they?

"Micah Tindall?" said Pa, sounding as incredulous as I felt. "But that poor man has a wife and four children. Why would he jeopardize his whole family . . . ?" His words trickled out, and he ended by just shaking his head.

"It's hard to believe, isn't it?" said Myrtle. "Mr. Pruitt even said he didn't believe it to whoever called, but it's the truth, I guess. The police arrested Mr. Tindall, so I guess they think he did it."

And they used papers I'd given them as their proof. Oh, boy, that made me feel lower than the scum under a pond rock. But what about the gun that had been found in Richard's house? Had Micah Tindall planted it there? Hard to imagine. Yet I'd seen his initials on that piece of paper, too, and I'd read all those notes people had written to Mr. Calhoun. I wished I could ask all the men whose initials had appeared on that list to write a few words on a sheet of paper for me and then compare the handwriting to see if any of them matched the notes berating Mr. Calhoun.

"But I have to get back to work now. I'll telephone you later, Annabelle," Myrtle promised, leaving the store almost as quickly as she'd entered it.

Pa and I looked at each other. Pa shook his head. Jack, oddly enough, didn't say a word. Having a person you know and like arrested for murder will do that to a person, I reckon, even if he is an obnoxious twelve-year-old.

As for me, I was feeling glum and useless and as if all I'd done was mess things up for Micah Tindall.

Pa turned me loose. I took my books back to the house, and then I decided to go for a walk. The house already smelled like roasting pork, which is one of the most delicious smells in the world. I breathed in deeply and wished I'd taken another pickle before I left the store.

Ma called out to me as I passed the kitchen on my way to the front door. "Annabelle, will you stop by the shoe store and get those slippers for your father? Let me get the money for you. Three dollars, you said?"

"Yes."

So I waited while she climbed on the step stool and got down the sugar bowl in which she kept her little stash of disposable cash. Even though we ran a successful grocery and dry-goods business, neither she nor Pa threw money around.

Holding on to the money, she hesitated for a second and then asked, "I haven't seen the slippers. Do you really think your father will like them?"

"They're very nice. Fine soft leather lined with sheepskin and everything. They ought to keep his tootsies warm even when it snows outside. I know they're expensive."

"Yes, they are. But your father deserves a luxury or two."

"Yes, he does. So do you."

"If I didn't know better, I'd think you were trying to butter me up, Annabelle Blue."

"Am not."

She shook her head, probably thinking, as I did, that three bucks was a pretty steep price for slippers, lined with sheepskin or not. She gave me the money, and I took off for Chewling's, glad to have an excuse to exercise my blues away. Walking through town in broad daylight was a heck of a lot more fun than walking through town in the black of night.

Nobody was in the shoe store when I arrived. Mr. Meeks was nowhere to be seen, so I went over to the display of slippers to see if they still had the ones I wanted for Pa. They did. They'd also added some new slippers to the ladies' shelf, and some of them didn't hardly look like slippers at all. There was a pair of fluffy pink things with heels that looked to me as though they'd be far from comfortable. If I wanted to wear slippers, I'd prefer flat-heeled ones that were warm and cozy, not high-heeled toe-crushers. Clearly I wasn't conversant with modern-day fashions. When it came to slippers, that was all right with me.

"May I help you?" came a voice from behind my back. By that time, I was almost used to Firman Meeks creeping up on me. Maybe he couldn't help it because the floor had a thick carpet on it. I acquitted him of attempting to frighten me, anyhow.

I turned around and smiled at him. "Yes, please. My mother

wants to buy those slippers for my father. Size eleven, please." I pointed to the slippers in question.

"Very well. Let me fetch the proper size from the back room."

So I sat in one of the seats provided for customers and rested my feet on the little stool the shoe-store clerks sat on when they were helping people on with their new shoes. When Firman Meeks came back, I decided I might as well ask him a blunt question. Heck, why not? Micah Tindall was in jail, Phil and the chief were both mad at me; why not irritate him, too?

"Mr. Meeks, was Mr. Calhoun blackmailing you?" Then I felt my face flame. I wasn't a deep thinker, especially when it came to butting into other people's business, but I wasn't generally *that* blunt.

He stood in front of me, a shoe box in his hands, gazing down upon me with an expression as blank as one of Mae Shenkel's on his face. "My dear young woman, whatever are you talking about?"

I felt at a disadvantage being seated while he stood, so I stood too. "I found your name on a list of people who were giving Mr. Calhoun money. I . . . well, he was an awful man and cheated people all the time. I figured he'd either given you a loan at an exorbitant interest rate or he was blackmailing you, and I wondered if I was right." Suddenly feeling very alone in the store, I added, "The police will probably come by to question you about it, too."

"They will, will they?"

"Well . . . maybe they won't. They arrested Mr. Micah Tindall for the murders of both the Calhoun men."

"I see. Well, then, no matter what my answer might have been, I consider it quite impolite of you to have asked that question of me, Miss Blue, but I forgive you."

Gee, thanks, I thought. However, I'd been terribly boorish to the man, so I just said, "Thanks. Sorry to have asked such an . . . ugly question."

"That's quite all right. Miss Jarvis has told me you're an inquisitive young lady."

"Yeah," I said, feeling stupid and sad. "I am. Sometimes that's not a very good quality."

He only smiled as he set the box of slippers on the counter. "Would you like me to wrap these in brown paper?"

I thought about it. Unless I wanted to walk around our grocery store, I'd have to walk through it to get the slippers to the house, and I didn't want Pa to see the box. On the other hand, a shoe box looked like a shoe box even when wrapped in brown paper. On the *other* other hand, if it was wrapped in brown paper, Pa wouldn't know the box contained slippers in his size, would he? Therefore, I said, "Yes, please."

"Certainly. Just let me write out a receipt for you."

So I handed him the money, he put it in the cash register—a newer model than ours and not nearly so pretty or with such a lovely chinking sound—and wrote out a receipt. As I watched him write, a sick feeling crept into my tummy. I'd seen that handwriting before. Neat. Precise. Tiny. Spiky. Up-and-down. Not slanted one way or the other. Just like the handwriting on that note threatening Mr. Calhoun's life if he didn't stop doing what he was doing.

"Um . . . ," I said, and stopped talking.

Mr. Meeks glanced up at me, tilted his head to one side, and then walked around the counter.

"Um, what are you doing?"

He didn't answer me as he thoughtfully made his way to the front door. My heart jumped into my throat when I saw him lock it. Then he pulled the blinds on the window, and I got *really* scared. "Wait! What are you doing? My mother knows I'm here!"

"I'm afraid it doesn't matter, Miss Blue," said he, coming back to me. "I saw the dawn of recognition in your eyes, my dear, and we can't have that, can we?"

"What? What recognition? I didn't recognize anything! What are you talking about?"

"I think you know. I didn't get this far in life without being a discerning individual. You, Miss Blue, are clever, but you have yet to learn discernment. I fear now you never will."

"What? What do you mean? I don't know what you're talking about!" I tried to slide away from him, but his hand shot out like an angry rattlesnake and grabbed my wrist. When I lifted my arm with the intention of clocking him on the head with my fist, he grabbed that hand, too. Shoot, for such a scrawny guy, he was sure strong.

I struggled like a fiend, but he held on tight, dragging me toward the door to the back room. I thought I might have a chance to race away from him when he let go of me to open the door, but I was wrong. Darned if he didn't put both of my wrists together with one of his hands, which were clearly larger than I'd bargained on, and then grab a man's belt from a nearby display. He belted my hands together so tightly behind my back, I feared for my circulation.

If you think I was quiet as a lamb while all this was going on, you'd be wrong. I shouted and hollered like a crazy woman. After he got my wrists under control, he smacked me across the face so hard, my ears rang.

"Please, Miss Blue. That noise is uncalled for. No one can hear you." His voice was calm as a stagnant puddle.

My senses reeling, I was unable to rebut this assertion, but I resisted when he attempted to drag me into the back room. "No!" I said, not very loudly due the aforementioned reeling-senses thing. "No!"

"I fear you're wrong about that. It's unfortunate. I know you're one of Miss Jarvis's friends, and I truly regret taking a friend away from her, as I'd intended to marry her and settle down here. However, if you've discovered as much as you have in your unofficial capacity as an ordinary citizen, it looks as if I'll have to be on my way again. This is very annoying, young woman." The frown he gave me might have been bestowed by a frustrated first-grade teacher on a naughty child. "Not that I expect the police will ever find me. Not as stupid as they are. They aren't as clever as you, are they, my dear?" His smile almost made me throw up. "But then, as we discussed before, you have yet to learn discernment."

I swallowed my nausea. "But why?" I asked. "I still don't understand. What are you going to do with me?" I hadn't liked that comment about depriving Betty Lou of a friend the least little bit.

"I'll have to leave you in the back room until I close the shop. Then, I fear, I shall have to take you out onto the desert and shoot you."

"Sh-shoot me?" I think I whimpered. "But why? It's no matter to me if Mr. Calhoun gave you a loan or was blackmailing you. I don't care. Anyhow, I told you they've arrested Mr. Tindall."

His smile gave me the creeps and the willies. "Ah, but you see, I *do* care. I had hoped to erase my Chicago past by coming to this backwater. God knows, men have run away from their pasts in the Wild West from time out of mind. But if you've uncovered evidence of my dealings with Mr. Calhoun, I fear the police, however dull, won't be too far behind you. They'll probably discover Mr. Tindall has an alibi or something and do some more digging. Especially with you having gone around goading them, as I've been told you've done."

As he spoke, he was tying my feet together with another belt. Then he stuffed me into a crevice between two rows of shelves jammed with shoe boxes.

"You mean, *you're* the mobster?"

He gave me a funny look. "However did you come up with that word?"

Oh, Lord. Me and my big mouth. But what the heck. He had me, and I really wanted to know the answers to some questions, so I decided to tell him. "I—I picked up a bunch of leaves when I stumbled over Herschel Calhoun's body. When I emptied my pockets, I found a note among the leaves. In it he told somebody to keep paying him money or he'd expose him for the mobster he was. That was you, wasn't it?"

"Curse that idiot boy. And curse me, too, for not thinking to find that note and do away with it."

"You mean you actually *were* a mobster."

"More of an enforcer, actually. I'd get an order of execution and carry it out." He shrugged. "It was a job."

"You? You were a hired assassin?" There went my mind, reeling again.

"I suppose you could call my former occupation that of a hired assassin. It certainly paid well."

Something else occurred to me. "Are you the one who planted the gun in my brother-in-law's house?"

"Indeed, yes. The police at that time considered him a likely suspect." He shook his head. "That wretched Calhoun boy. If he hadn't butted in, this never would have happened."

"You'd have let Richard—and now Mr. Tindall—take the blame for a murder you committed?" I know it sounds idiotic, but I couldn't conceive of a person doing that to another person. Yet I was talking to a self-confessed murderer even as I spoke the sentence.

"Yes."

And he grabbed a rag from somewhere or other and tied it over my mouth. Guess that was it as far as questions went, at least for now. Probably forever, if I couldn't figure how to get myself out of this mess.

CHAPTER EIGHTEEN

I struggled like the very devil, but those belts were buckled really, really tightly. There were also no lights on in the back room, which smelled like shoes. That made sense, but I didn't think I'd ever be able to enjoy a pair of new shoes again in my lifetime. Provided my lifetime lasted longer than the closing hour at Chewling's. I also decided I'd been in the dark entirely too much lately. So to speak.

Good Lord, what to do? What to do?

Well, not a whole lot, actually. However, not for Annabelle Blue to go to her doom without fighting as hard as she could for her freedom first. I might be stupid about blurting out the wrong things at the wrong time to the wrong people, but my instinct for survival was as alive and well as I was, and I hoped to keep both of us around a good deal longer than Firman Meeks wanted.

Therefore, although I couldn't see a blessed thing, I gently lowered myself to the floor and scooted on my butt to where I thought a back door to the shoe store might be, then stood up. I was wrong the first three or four times, but managed to find a doorknob at long last. But what door did it belong to? Bother. If it was the door to the shoe-store innards, I'd be okay if I opened it and flopped out like a landed trout as long as someone was in the store with Mr. Meeks. If not, he'd just shove me back into the shoe-storage room and tie me up even tighter.

I stood there in blind panic—blind because there was no

light in the room—and cogitated for a second. Then it occurred to me that probably the door to the salesroom wasn't locked, as opposed to the door to the alleyway outside in back. This might prove to be a blessing and a curse both. If the doorknob twisted without any trouble, I just wouldn't open the door. However, if I ever did find the door to the alley, how the heck was I supposed to get it unlocked if it was locked, and why wouldn't it be? Heck, even in Rosedale, we merchants took precautions.

Bother. However, nothing ventured, nothing gained, as my mother was fond of saying whenever she tried a new recipe. This was much more ominous than a new recipe, but still . . .

With my back to the door, I found the doorknob and twisted it. It turned and I let go of it instantly. I wasn't going to chance Firman Meeks discovering me up and about. So, my back still pressed against the wall, I slithered along it until I bumped into a shelf. I kept my back to the shelf, which felt as though it was loaded with shoe boxes, and slid along some more until I got to a wall. More slithering until, wonder of wonders, I came to another door. Now what?

Without much hope, I twisted the knob. No luck. Locked. Praying like mad that it wasn't getting close to closing time, I felt all around the door, wishing to heaven that Firman Meeks had belted my hands in front of me and not in back. No key hung on a handy hook near the door; at least none that I could reach. Blast!

So I slithered some more, this time for only a couple of feet before I nearly fell on top of what might well have been a desk. A desk? Of course! Mr. Chewling had to reckon his accounts somewhere, didn't he? What better place than a desk in the back room?

Again I prayed, this time that Mr. Chewling kept the key to his back door in the top drawer of his desk, and that I could find it with my back turned to it and in the dark. I discovered right off that he was a tidy man. Pens. Pencils. Account book. Well, I only guessed at that, since I couldn't see it. A ruler. A revolver.

A revolver? Good Lord. Well, we did live in Rosedale. I expect every man in town had a revolver or a shotgun in his store or his house. Pa kept a shotgun under the counter, just in case. He'd even taught Jack and me how to shoot it, although I prayed neither of us would ever have to. For only a split second, I thought about picking up the revolver, refinding the door leading into the store and shooting my way out.

But that was an incredibly stupid idea, and it didn't last long. Heck, if anyone was in the store besides Mr. Meeks, I might shoot him or her. Besides, I was no Annie Oakley. No way could I peer over my shoulder and shoot anything with a revolver held in hands belted together behind me.

I continued feeling around in the drawer as best I could until—could it be?—by gum, it could be! A key! I fumbled it up in fingers that were just about numb by that time after having been belted so tightly for so long. Then I slithered my way back to the door.

Boy, if you want to set yourself a difficult task, have someone tie your hands behind your back and try to find a keyhole in a doorknob in a dark room someday. I was practically crying with frustration by the time I finally got key and keyhole together. Then I darned near dropped the key in my joy. But I held firm and twisted.

The key worked! And the door opened! And I hopped out into the alley behind Chewling's Shoes as fast as I could, considering my ankles were belted as tightly as my hands, and my balance wasn't the greatest. I did take time to push the gag down from my mouth, using the outside wall of the store and scraping my cheek pretty badly in the process. But I wanted at least one advantage, darn it, and it looked as if my mouth and lungs were it as far as advantages went.

I hopped like a bunny—or perhaps a drunken toad—to Second Street, and then I hopped right out into the middle of the street, hollering for all I was worth, and to heck with any automobiles, buggies, horses or wagons in my way. I must say, I did stop traffic that day.

Mr. O'Dell was the first person on the scene. His big old Hudson screeched to a stop, sending up a comet's tail of dust behind it, within perhaps a foot of my own personal body. It then occurred to me that perhaps I'd been a trifle precipitate in rushing out onto Second, the busiest street in town. But I'd been so darned happy to get out of that storeroom I guess I wasn't thinking properly.

"Annabelle Blue, what the devil are you doing? Why are you tied up like that? Your cheek's bleeding!" Mr. O'Dell hurried over to me, and it looked to me as if he didn't know whether to scold me or hug me.

"Curse my cheek! It's Firman Meeks! He's the one who murdered Mr. Calhoun and Herschel! He was going to kill me!" And then I burst into tears, thereby humiliating myself in front of not merely Mr. O'Dell, but half of the rest of the residents in Rosedale, all of whom came running to see what the kerfuffle was about. Sniffling miserably, I said, "Please take me to the police department."

Mr. O'Dell's mouth had dropped open. "Firman Meeks?"

"Yes. Oh, please, don't waste time!"

"Right. Right."

He began hurrying back to his machine, but I hollered after him. "Wait! Unbuckle me first!"

Whirling around, agog—as well he might be—he said, "Oh. Certainly. Sorry, Miss Annabelle."

A dozen or so other people had gathered around me by that time, all babbling. I heard queries and exclamations and lots of curse words. The only thing I could think of to say was, "Be sure Mr. Meeks can't get out of the shoe store. He's a killer, and he's aiming to run away. Somebody watch the alley, and somebody else watch the front of the store."

They all stood there, gawping at me, and I got mad. I mean, I got really, really mad. I guess my rage was due to pent-up anxiety coming to a boil. "*Damn* it! Do as I say, you fools, or he'll get away!"

"Better do what she says, folks," said Mr. O'Dell, unbuckling my ankles and then my wrists. "It sure does look like something weird happened here."

Weird. That was one word for it.

I whispered, "Thank you, Mr. O'Dell." To everyone else— those who remained; the rest of them had rushed to do my bidding—I said, "Sorry I swore at you."

Murmurs and coos followed me to Mr. O'Dell's automobile, into which I climbed, feeling as though I'd just been rescued from certain death. Which was the truth.

Chief Vickers wasn't a happy man, but after I told him my tale, he couldn't very well not act upon it. As I waited in the police station, shaking from leftover terror, Firman Meeks was arrested very shortly after my escape. He tried to shoot his way out of the shoe store, but either Deputy Parker or one of the other men in town shot him in the thigh, and I guess he went down like a gored ox. Deputy Parker took the credit, but nobody knows for sure whose bullet felled him.

Neither Ma nor Pa was happy with me, either. Jeez, you'd think they'd be proud of their daughter for discovering a vicious murderer, but no. They were angry that I'd managed to get myself into another pickle.

"It wasn't my fault!" I cried in indignation.

"I don't know, Annabelle," said Pa, handing me a damp cloth to hold against my cheek. "You're the only person I know who gets into messes like this."

241

"That's not fair, Pa." I regret to say the words came out on a sob.

"And where, pray, are the—" Ma glanced at Pa and decided not to say the word *slippers*, I reckon. "Where's the thing I sent you out after?"

Aw, shoot. "Um, I guess they're still on the counter. But I paid for them, so I'm sure Mr.—um, I'm sure we'll be able to get them back. Mr. Meeks wrote a receipt for them. In fact . . ." I gulped. "In fact, it was his writing on the receipt that clued me in that he was the one."

"Oh? And why is that, young woman? What exactly have you been up to these past few days, Annabelle Blue?" asked Ma.

Curse my too-ready tongue! "I mean . . . aw, nuts." And I gave up and told on myself.

Ma and Pa stared at me with patent incredulity mixed with anger. Jack was jealous; I could tell.

But it turned out all right in the end. Firman Meeks was bandaged by one of the many doctors in town, and then locked in one of the two jail cells the town boasted. Chief Vickers sent telegraph wires to Chicago, and in return received I don't know how many return wires, claiming police interest in Mr. Meeks. Turned out Meeks was wanted for murder not merely in Chicago, but in Cincinnati and New York City, as well. Firman Meeks, a fellow who looked like a little gray mouse. You figure it out; it's beyond me.

Word got around the town fast. Phil Gunderson ran all the way—well, it wasn't really very far—from his brother's hardware store to Blue's. Ma and Pa had sent Jack out to man the counter. Naturally, Jack griped about that, but he went, while Ma tended to my scraped cheek and Pa talked to Chief Vickers, who came to our house as soon as he'd locked up Mr. Meeks. I guess Deputy Parker had been left to guard him. I figured even Deputy Parker wouldn't have too much trouble with the weasely Firman Meeks, since he had a gunshot leg. I wouldn't necessarily have left Parker to guard a whole man, even one who was locked up behind bars. Not that the deputy isn't a nice guy, but . . . well, never mind that.

"Come in, Phil," Ma said when she answered his knock at the door.

Ripping his hat from his head like the gent he was, Phil said, "Thank you, Mrs. Blue," but he was looking at me as he said it. "Criminy, Annabelle. Is it true, then? You captured Firman Meeks, and he's the killer?"

After giving the chief a quick gander, I told Phil, "I didn't capture anyone. Firman Meeks captured me, but I managed to escape. Poor Mr. O'Dell almost ran me down, but that wasn't his fault. He unbelted me and drove me to the police station while everybody else who was there at the time kept Meeks holed up in the shoe store."

Phil goggled at me. "He unbelted you? What the . . . I mean, what do you mean, Mr. O'Dell unbelted you?"

So I told my story again. In a way, it was good that Phil was there, because he could back up my story about how we both got into the Calhoun house. Neither the chief nor my parents were happy with either of us.

"It wasn't Phil's fault," I said stoutly, both because it was true and because I hated to see the hangdog look on Phil's face. "In fact, the last time I went over there, I went alone but Phil second-guessed me and came to rescue me. He's a hero."

Phil rolled his eyes, which I think was pretty poor payment for so grand a commendation.

"It would have been nice if either of you had thought to inform the police department," grumbled the chief.

"I *did* inform you!" I said. "Only I left out the part about how I came by the papers. And you can't blame me for that," I said because it looked as if the chief wanted to argue about the matter. "I couldn't very well implicate Phil or Betty Lou in my crazy scheme, could I? That wouldn't have been fair to them."

"I suppose I should admire your loyalty to your friends," the chief said as if he didn't mean it.

"And you'd probably better look more closely at that hole in the ceiling. There may be more stuff up there. Maybe even some money Mr. Calhoun hid there. I think he was saving so he could run away with Sadie Dobbs."

"We'll be sure to do that, Miss Annabelle." Still, the chief looked sour. But it wasn't my fault his men didn't properly search the Calhoun home office, was it?

Pa shut his eyes and shook his head. Ma grabbed his hand, and they stood there, gazing at me as if they'd only now realized they'd loosed a monster into the world. Their joint expression of disapproval and disappointment made me want to cry. I was really glad Jack wasn't there.

Pushing himself to his feet with a grunt—Chief Vickers's tummy seemed to grow bigger daily—the chief said, "Well, I don't approve of how you did it, young woman. But if you hadn't done it, we wouldn't have Firman Meeks in custody, so I guess everything worked out in the end."

Everyone in the room who wasn't me said something that sounded like "Huh."

I said, "Thank you," in an extremely small voice.

"I hope to God Micah Tindall doesn't hate us all now," muttered Pa. "He's a good man and doesn't deserve what Calhoun or you, Annabelle Blue, did to him."

"*I* didn't arrest him!" I said indignantly, which was only moderately better than feeling two inches tall. "By the way, Chief, Mr. Meeks said he planted the gun in Richard's house, since it looked as if you were going to arrest Richard for Mr. Calhoun's murder that first day or two."

The chief sighed.

Pa's face set hard, like it did when he smacked Jack upside the head, and I decided it would be better if I stopped defending myself. It was my fault, in a way, that the coppers had gone after Mr. Tindall, and I felt bad about that. But I'd only been trying to clear Richard. Was that such a bad thing? I had the good sense, for once, not to ask the question aloud.

But the police eventually found a huge stash of money in the ceiling hideaway Mr. Calhoun had kept, along with enough information to show that he'd been blackmailing men in town for everything from running around on their wives to making illegal liquor. So everything worked out all right eventually.

Well, except that Betty Lou Jarvis wasn't awfully happy with me when she stormed into the store the next morning. I'd just got to the most exciting part of *The Green Mummy*, and wasn't pleased to hear the bells on the door chime. When I glanced up to see who'd entered Blue's, I became even less happy.

Betty Lou stormed over to the counter. "Annabelle Blue, what in the name of God possessed you to go after my special gentleman friend? They have him in *jail!*"

My mouth hung open for a second or two before I found wit enough to say, "But he murdered two men."

"Huh! Neither of the two men he killed was worth spitting on!"

Good heavens. And that made murdering them all right? "Well, he also killed people in Chicago and Cincinnati and New York City."

"They probably weren't worth spitting on, either."

I stared at Betty Lou, who stood in front of the counter, her fists on her hips, her cheeks blazing with fury, and I didn't know what to say. If you used Betty Lou's criterion, I expect you could find all sorts of people to kill. Heck, Miss Libby would have been an ogre of the past years earlier, if everyone thought like Betty Lou did.

"He was going to kill me, too," I reminded her.

She said, "Huh."

I guess she didn't think I was worth spitting on, either. Melancholy thought.

"But . . . but, Betty Lou, you can't just take the law into your hands the way Mr. Meeks did. It's not right."

She gave me one of the hottest glares I've ever received. "*You* took the law into your hands that night you sneaked into the Calhoun house." She sniffed. "And I even helped you. Lord."

"Um, speaking of the Calhouns, don't you still work there?" I hoped and prayed news of my idiotic acts hadn't got my friend fired from her job.

"I quit," Betty Lou said. "I hate those people. Anyhow, I'm going to work at the shoe store. Mr. Chewling says he needs another sales person now, so he gave me the job."

There went my jaw again, dropping until it darned near hit my chest. "You're going to take Firman Meeks's place?" I stammered when I could manage to get tongue and teeth to cooperate.

"Don't mention that man's name to me," growled Betty Lou. "Killing people, of all things!" She gave me another good glower. "Do you know that Mr. Chewling is going to have to replace that carpet? He said blood never comes clean out of carpets. That's your fault, Annabelle, and I hope you know it."

"But . . . but . . ."

"Oh, very well. I suppose it was Firman's fault for being a murderer, but still."

She spun on her heel and stormed out of the store very much as she'd stormed into it. Sometimes I think I'll never understand people for as long as I live.

We Rosedale-ites never did get to see Firman Meeks tried and convicted of the Calhoun murders, because Chicago, Cincinnati and New York City got first dibs on him. That was all right, because he signed a full confession before the coppers from the other three cities took him, handcuffed and looking smaller than ever, onto the train that would take him eastwards.

If he hadn't done what he'd done to me in the back room of Chewling's Shoes, I never would have guessed such a weedy, insignificant fellow could be a real, honest-to-God cold-blooded killer. Then again, I suppose his appearance had helped him in his craft, because he sure as anything didn't look like a thug.

I told Phil that very thing the night Myrtle, Sonny Clyde, Phil and I all went to the flickers together. We were sipping sodas at Joyce Pruitt's at the time.

"Annabelle Blue, I swear, something's wrong with you," said Phil, frowning at me.

"Why?" I asked, honestly surprised by his reaction. "It's the truth. If he'd looked like a criminal, he'd never be able to get close enough to another criminal to shoot him dead, now would he?"

Sonny and Myrtle started laughing. I didn't understand that, either.

Phil only heaved a huge sigh. Then he took my hand under the table and cradled it in his, so I guess he didn't hold against me what he considered to be my odd opinion.

All in all, I suppose the Calhoun murders and my involvement in solving them might be considered an adventure, but, as I mentioned earlier, it's not the kind I was thinking about when I said I wanted to experience an adventure or two before I married Phil and settled down. I was thinking more along the lines of an African safari or a trip to England or something. Heck, even a trip to Alhambra, California, would be an adventure to me.

Still, I reckon it's true what Pa said to me when he gave me extra chores to do: beggars can't be choosers.

Being the obedient daughter that I am—most of the time—I didn't call him a spoilsport to his face.

By the way, it rained again a couple of days after my misadventure in the shoe store. Only, this time, the rain came softly, in the afternoon, and we got to see a lovely double rainbow in the sky through the front windows of Blue's. No floods followed. Sometimes rain is a good thing.

ABOUT THE AUTHOR

Award-winning author **Alice Duncan** lives with a herd of wild dachshunds (enriched from time to time with fosterees from New Mexico Dachshund Rescue) in Roswell, New Mexico. She's not a UFO enthusiast; she's in Roswell because her mother's family settled there fifty years before the aliens crashed. Alice no longer longs to return to California, although she still misses the food, not to mention her children, one of whom is there and the other of whom is in North Dakota. Alice would love to hear from you at alice@aliceduncan.net. And be sure to visit her Web site at http://www.aliceduncan.net.